Praise for *T*

"Betancourt, the victim of a well-
kidnapping in Colombia, can cer......y be taken seriously as a
chronicler of South American brutality and repression, and she
does not turn away from the ugly truth in her fiction debut. . . .
The novel generally propels the reader along with its conviction and moral force." —*Library Journal*

"Betancourt writes unflinchingly. . . . [She] tells an anguished
story of passion, sacrifice, imprisonment, torture, and exile
with often gruesome detail, historical accuracy, and rising
suspense. . . . Betancourt orchestrates an intimate conflict and
shocking denouement that fuse the personal and the political in
a twenty-first-century variation on Greek tragedy." —*Booklist*

"The perfect summer read, à la Isabel Allende." —*Libération*

"A wonderful first novel . . . It's got what it takes to become this
summer's bestseller." —*RTL*

"[Ingrid Betancourt] has written her first adventure novel and
it's a great success. . . . The writing is vivid and strong."
—*Le Figaro*

"Striking the perfect balance, *The Blue Line* is serious and enter-
taining at once. . . . Thoughtfully constructed between the past
and present . . . [it] gets to the heart of the matter: how hard it
can be to love, but also the horror of not loving and the pain
of no longer loving. It is as dense and beautiful as a fall in slow-
motion." —*Le Point*

"An intense, moving, and gripping book."   —*Version Fémina*

"An adventure novel reminiscent of Isabel Allende or Oriana Fallaci's *A Man*. The torture scenes are Dantean. The novel's structure allows Ingrid to come back to many of the themes that made *Even Silence Has an End* so powerful. They reappear in the hearts of new characters, yet are no less believable."
                                                             —*Paris Match*

"A successful and enthralling first novel."   —*Europe 1*

"In *The Blue Line*, Betancourt tells a love story—that of Julia and Theo—which also underscores the horror of political persecution and torture during the Argentinian dictatorship. She does so with great narrative strength and a touch of magical realism."
                                                             —*El País*

"Bewitching."   —*Point de Vue*

PENGUIN BOOKS

THE BLUE LINE

Born on December 25, 1961, in Bogotá, Colombia, Ingrid Betancourt was a politician and presidential candidate celebrated for her determination to combat widespread corruption. In 2002 she was taken hostage by FARC, a burtal terrorist guerrilla organization, and held for more than six and a half years in the Colombian jungle. She was rescued in 2008. She is the author of the *New York Times* bestselling memoir *Even Silence Has an End*.

ALSO BY INGRID BETANCOURT

Even Silence Has an End:
My Six Years of Captivity in the Colombian Jungle

Until Death Do Us Part:
My Struggle to Reclaim Colombia

Letter to My Mother

THE
BLUE
LINE

Ingrid Betancourt

PENGUIN BOOKS

PENGUIN BOOKS
An imprint of Penguin Random House LLC
375 Hudson Street
New York, New York 10014
penguin.com

Originally published in French as *La Ligne Bleue* by Editions Gallimard, Paris, 2014
First published in the United States of America by Penguin Press
an imprint of Penguin Random House LLC, 2016
Published in Penguin Books 2017

Translated by Lakshmi Ramakrishnan Iyer, in collaboration with Rebekah Wilson

THE LIBRARY OF CONGRESS HAS CATALOGED THE HARDCOVER EDITION AS FOLLOWS:
Names: Betancourt, Ingrid, 1961– author. | Ramakrishnan Iyer, Lakshmi,
translator. | Wilson, Rebekah (Translator), translator.
Title: The blue line : a novel / Ingrid Betancourt.
Other titles: Ligne bleue. English
Identifiers: LCCN 2015043410 (print) | LCCN 2015047221 (ebook) | ISBN
9781594206580 (hc.) | ISBN 9780698196537 (ebook) | ISBN 9780143109969 (pbk.)
Subjects: LCSH: Young women—Fiction. | Visionaries—Fiction. | Perón, Juan
Domingo, 1895–1974—Fiction. | Organización Montoneros
(Argentina) —Fiction. | Political fiction. | BISAC: FICTION / Political. |
FICTION / Political. | GSAFD: Bildungsromans.
Classification: LCC PQ2702.E87 L5413 2016 (print) | LCC PQ2702.E87 (ebook) |
DDC 843/.92—dc23

Printed in the United States of America
1   3   5   7   9   10   8   6   4   2

Designed by Gretchen Achilles

To my father,

Gabriel,

Always present.

1.

THE YOUNG WOMAN IN BLACK

End of Boreal Summer
2006

S he looks into the distance.

She sees the mauve line between the sea and the flawless blue sky.

She sees the wind moving across the water. She can see it coming. Then she's not quite sure.

But the wind sweeps over the path of trembling grass. It slithers, climbs up the bank, and chafes the hedge that ends at the beach in a cross shape. Then it falls silent, crouching like a wild animal, watching the street. Gathering momentum, it swoops down onto the asphalt, skips over the manicured hydrangeas, and picks up strength.

She watches, intrigued, as it advances. It's coming closer now, brushing against the painted wooden houses, very close. It glides up the old maple tree that fills her window and coils itself snakelike around the trunk, transforming the branches into long, twitching fingers.

It taps at her window. It presses up against the glass. It whistles and calls to her as the rattling branches beat against the panes.

Julia is happy. She tugs impatiently at the lock on the frame and forces the window open. Leaning out, she allows the vagabond wind to sweep in and fill her entire being, breathes in deep lungfuls of its sharp air. She closes her eyes. She recognizes that salty, tarry smell. This Connecticut wind is strangely similar to the wind of her Buenos Aires childhood. It's not as intense, perhaps; lighter, more delicate. Or perhaps not. She knows from experience that memory can't be relied on to capture the true essence of things. The present often seems less vibrant than our recollections of the past.

Even so, Julia couldn't be happier.

She smiles. She likes the restraint of her surroundings: the neatly clipped shrubs in the gardens across the way, the carefully aligned elms along the avenue that runs perpendicular to the beach, the hedge and the grass that frame the fine sand like a rampart stretching parallel to the waves, and the horizon like a straight line drawn from one end to the other.

It suits her, this symmetry. She has finished putting her life in order. She is in her rightful place, living the destiny she has chosen for herself, with the man she has always loved. Julia feels fulfilled.

She looks up at the azure sky above her maple tree. Happiness is blue. Blue horizon, blue water.

A Mark Rothko painting, she thinks, forming a picture frame in the air with her fingers.

She'd like to hang that painting just in front of her face to remind herself that happiness is right there, within arm's reach.

Funny. This idea that happiness is blue: it's as if she's had this thought before.

All of a sudden the wind sets up a high-pitched whistling and rushes in through the window. Maple twigs catch at Julia's dress and scratch her skin. The sky has gone dark. Julia shivers. The air smells humid. The next moment a flash of lightning rips her painting from top to bottom. The light is blinding. It hurts, as if a razor had slit her retina.

A sharp cracking sound shatters the silence. The tree across the road has been split in two. Its heart is blown open, scorched, but the tree has not caught fire. One of the severed branches dangles dangerously close to the power lines along the avenue.

Julia ducks her head back in, pulls the window shut, and turns around, trembling. She scans the room, ready to face whatever might be coming. But everything is in order, each item sitting silently in its assigned place. Still, her eyes continue flicking back and forth, lingering on dark corners, decoding shadows.

Seized by an irrational feeling of panic, she gathers up the dirty clothes piled in the hamper and hurries downstairs to the basement laundry room. She arrives panting. *Such a fright, for no reason!* She shrugs her shoulders.

And then she feels the tremors begin. They always start the same way: a tingling in her heels, getting sharper as it travels up her calves, intensifying as it reaches her knees.

Julia knows she has only a few minutes before she passes out. She climbs the laundry room steps on all fours and crawls across the kitchen and into the living room. She needs to get into a corner of the room and prop herself up before it's too late. She wedges herself into the corner, sits up straight, legs stretched out in front of her for balance. One brief moment to congratulate herself for reacting in time, and then her world turns upside down. Her inner eye has taken over.

She feels herself slipping away. Her gaze clouds over; her eyes are choked with a thick white mist, and her mind shifts to another place. Julia floats into nothingness, beyond time and space. She has lost control of her body. She has abandoned it, like a lost glove, between two walls of her living room.

She is familiar with this journey, though she can never predict how long it will last or where it will take her.

Julia's not scared anymore. She knows she won't die; she knows she won't suffocate in the white substance enveloping her. She has the gift; she has received instruction; she is part of a lineage. All of her energy is being channeled into the connection that is about to take place. Her inner eye will graft itself onto someone else's vision—someone completely unknown to her.

Suddenly Julia finds herself in a dimly lit room, looking through a half-open door. She can see a young woman with her back turned illuminated in the glare of a neon light. The woman is wearing a skin-tight black dress down to her ankles. Her black hair is pulled back into a perfect chignon, as round and shiny as a pebble. She is carefully applying her makeup, her graceful neck bent forward to bring her face closer to the mirror covering the wall.

The eyes through which Julia is looking trace the young woman's slim figure from the nape of her neck to her heels, lingering on the hollow of her back. Aware she is being watched, the woman turns around. She has Oriental eyes and full red lips. They part in a distant smile, revealing perfect teeth.

Julia's source is sitting on the edge of a bed. A man. She glimpses his strong knees, realizes he is naked. Her peripheral vision takes in the drawn curtains, the mussed sheets, a chest of drawers behind the half-open door, articles of clothing thrown carelessly over a chair.

The man gets up and walks toward the young woman. Julia sees a small, impersonal bathroom. She recognizes the logo of a large American hotel chain on the damp towels lying on the floor.

The young woman holds out a hand in a gesture of affection and finds herself being swept up into a passionate embrace from which she hastily disengages herself, laughing. She spins around, throwing one last look at herself in the mirror, picks up her handbag from beside the washbasin, and walks quickly out of the room, perched confidently on her high heels. The door clicks shut behind her.

Julia searches in the shadows for a long moment, then her field of vision shifts to the left. It travels up the bed and comes to rest on a mobile phone that is buzzing insistently, like a fly on its back. The man ignores it. He lies down and closes his eyes. Julia remains trapped in the dark for some time, helpless, unable to enter the thoughts or dreams of the person she's been twinned with.

And then the connection breaks. Julia feels herself being propelled to the surface. She breaks free from the darkness and travels through the milky white haze. Light restores the shapes of objects, signaling the gradual return of her sight. Slowly things come into focus. Her hands are still on her knees; her body is still wedged into the corner. Only her head has moved. It hangs heavily in front of her. The nape of her neck is sore, the way it always is after one of her journeys.

She rubs the back of her neck hard. Then she begins the set of stretches she learned from her grandmother. She circles her head slowly, from left to right and back again, until the stiffness eases. The inside of her neck crunches like crumpled paper. This journey was particularly long. She folds her legs into a lotus position and stretches her back, sticking her neck out like a turtle. Julia breathes slowly, centers herself. She regains control of her body by repeating the movements that have been part of her return ritual since childhood.

Little by little she becomes aware of the noises coming from the street. Looking out the window, she sees a team of uniformed men busy clearing away the remains of the dead tree. All signs of the storm have vanished and the sky has cleared. Only then does it occur to her to glance at her watch. It's noon. She hasn't had breakfast yet. She hasn't even started work. Luckily Theo's gotten into the habit of coming home late from the office. This gives her a few extra hours to finish her translations and get them to the client on time.

Ever self-disciplined, she prepares a large bowl of yogurt, almonds, and dried fruit so she can eat while reading through the pages. The text is beautiful. She has no problem finding the right words to transpose thoughts from one language to another. But she finds it harder to capture the harmony of sounds, their rhythm, their cadence. The task of re-creating the music of one language in another is more like art than anything else. It is what she finds most challenging. She plunges into her work with enthusiasm.

Julia jumps when she hears the front door open and realizes it's already 7:30 P.M. She hastily closes her laptop and smooths out the creases in her red dress. She glances in the mirror on the landing before going downstairs, relieved to find she looks nice. No traces of her journey, no need for explanations.

Theo is in the kitchen sorting through the mail. He has emptied his pockets and placed his keys on the countertop. He pauses when he sees Julia. Smiling, he takes her in his arms and spins her around. Then he kisses her on the forehead, as if to indicate that playtime is over.

"I'm starving, my love," he says. "I'm exhausted."

Julia's face clouds over. She pulls away, disappointed. She stares at Theo's shirt, at his hands. Lost in thought, she slowly opens the refrigerator.

"Tomorrow's Friday," she says in a level tone. "Maybe you could take the day off."

"Didn't I tell you? They've changed the rules. No more working longer during the week and taking Fridays off."

"But you're still getting up really early. Earlier and earlier, in fact. Wait, let me do the math. . . ."

"It doesn't work that way anymore, sweetheart. Anyway, I'm putting in overtime because it looks like I might be getting a promotion."

Julia gives him a blank look.

Theo slips in front of her and pushes the refrigerator door shut. "You still haven't learned to close doors, Julia my love," he says with a hint of irritation.

He walks out of the kitchen and goes upstairs. Julia follows mechanically. She wants to tell him about the lightning and the tree. But before she can catch up with him, he's gone into the bathroom and double-locked the door.

2.

THE FIRST JOURNEY

Austral Summer
1962

S he must have been five years old the first time it happened. She was living in Colonia del Sacramento, in Uruguay, in an old house behind the port, overlooking the
estuary. She was playing in a dusty courtyard, away from the
older children, who had devised a game of jumping off a low
wall into the garden next door and terrorizing the neighbor's
old dog.

Julia knew she was poor. Not because she lacked anything
but because her mother complained about it. The word "poor"
meant nothing to Julia. Oddly enough, she associated it with
her carefree existence, far removed from adult preoccupations.
But she also understood that it was the reason why her father
had gone away and left them. And she missed him. Her mother

would point to the Río de la Plata* and explain that he had gone to look for work over there in Argentina, on the other side of the water.

"The river of silver, the river of silver . . ." Julia would say to herself over and over, like the words of a magic spell. She would stand at the railing for hours on end, staring down at the port of Colonia and the expanse of gray water flecked with silver that stretched as far as she could see. What more could there possibly be on the other side? She didn't understand.

"Mom," she would ask, "why has Dad gone away?"

"To get money for us, of course!"

Julia would stare with fascination at the platinum glint of the water below her. Turning to her mother, she would insist: "But, Mom, what about all the silver in the river? We don't need any more!"

Her exasperated mother would roll her eyes and reply: "¡Nena! ¡El Río de la Plata no es ni un río, ni es de plata!"†

Her twin brothers were only too delighted to hear their mother scolding Julia. They were nearly two years older and liked to treat her as a punching bag. They taunted her mercilessly, shoved her around, and tripped her up. Anna, her older sister, would rush to her rescue, gathering her up and chasing the twins away with a slap. "Daddy will be home soon, Julia. Don't worry," she would whisper in her ear.

---

* In Spanish the word "plata" is used interchangeably to mean either "silver" or "money."

† "Girl! The Río de la Plata isn't a river, and it's not made of silver or money!"

Anna was the only one who could console Julia, because she too was desperately impatient for their father to return. For that reason, and because her mother was so distant and so strict with her, Julia showered all the love she was storing up for her father on her older sister. She would have liked to be included in the twins' games but she was too scared of them; they were such daredevils. Besides, they had taught themselves to swim and spent most of their time in the river, where Julia couldn't follow them.

On the afternoon of her first mysterious journey, Julia was in the backyard, sitting on the kitchen steps. She was playing by herself, drawing shapes in the dirt with her finger and filling an old oil canister with pebbles. At that time of day, the children had usually finished their lunch. It was Anna's job to reheat the meal their mother had made at dawn before leaving for work. But on that particular day she had told Anna to wait: she would bring some groceries back from town.

The sun was beating down. Wearing a cotton dress that was too short for her—one of her sister's castoffs—Julia was getting bored as she sat uncomfortably on the uneven stone steps. She started to feel unwell, almost feverish, but kept quiet as usual for fear of being scolded. Then she began to feel a prickling sensation up and down her legs. Thinking she was being bitten by insects, she swatted at her legs in annoyance.

The tremors spread very quickly, rising up through her body and stiffening each limb in turn until she was completely immobilized. Panic-stricken, she called to Anna as loudly as she could, but the twins' high-pitched shrieks and the barking of the old dog drowned out her thin little voice.

All at once she couldn't see. She thought she had fallen into the River of Silver. She was suffocating, trapped inside a thick white substance with no taste or smell. Disconnected from her body, petrified and blinded, she floated in a state of nothingness. She would remember that moment for the rest of her life. Emptied of her being, she understood what it meant to die.

She didn't start breathing again until her eyes pierced the milky haze around her and she could once again make out the shapes of things and people.

That was when Julia became convinced that her sense of sight was not her own. The wide-angle images were moving, as if she were walking, but she knew she was totally paralyzed, unable even to control the direction of her gaze. She might almost have thought she had nodded off and was dreaming, except that this was different: it felt like she'd been cut in half and was seeing through someone else's eyes, like an intruder catapulted into a strange world.

Julia, with her child's mind, couldn't comprehend why it was already night. She could make out a full moon hidden behind a flurry of clouds overhead. She saw the prow of a boat pitch upward on a nasty swell, as if she were on board. Violent gusts of wind whipped up the waves and sent them sweeping over the deck. Fascinated by the majestic scene unfolding in front of her yet feeling strangely protected from it, she forgot to be afraid.

Suddenly Anna crossed into Julia's field of vision. She was walking toward the prow, every muscle in her body straining as she clung to the rail. She was trying to reach the twins, who were huddled on the deck in a pool of vomit, dangerously close to the edge. Julia couldn't see her mother, but out of the corner of her eye she spotted her father standing next to the tiller, directly to her left.

Just then a huge wave crashed onto the deck, and the prow disappeared behind a curtain of spray. The next moment Anna had vanished. Julia's field of vision panned around and she found herself looking in the opposite direction. She tried to will the vision to search for Anna, but what she saw instead was her father's distorted face, screaming. In the foreground she recognized her mother's white, veined hands clutching at him. She was her mother. Terrified, she realized she was seeing through her mother's eyes.

The next few seconds changed Julia's life forever. Her father's face was as hollow as a dead man's. She saw her mother's hands lash out and scratch him as she tried to grasp control of the tiller and turn the boat around. He was staring, transfixed, at a dot in the water, a dot that was getting farther and farther away, that was being lost in the furious agitation of the waves. Unable to move, he looked on as his world was being swallowed up. Julia wanted to throw herself at him too and force him to jump into the water after Anna. Why wasn't he doing anything?

All at once her view shifted again. For a fraction of a second she saw herself, as if in a mirror. She was clinging to her mother's skirts, her body rigid, panic in her eyes, screaming as loudly as her father.

The shock of seeing herself as another person was so brutal that it broke the connection. Shaking uncontrollably, she tumbled into empty space and plummeted down, sucked into a vortex. She wanted to cry out, to shout for help, to shake off this unfamiliar body. A second later she found herself entering the viscous white substance, coming up for air, ready to implode.

She landed with an abrupt thud and opened her mouth as wide as she could, gulping for air. Her lungs began to reinflate slowly and painfully. She recognized Anna by her smell of salt and guava alone: Julia's eyes had dried out in the white-hot December sun during her trance and she couldn't see. Anna was calling out her name in desperation and shaking her like a rag doll.

Julia let out an inhuman scream and burst into tears of fear, rage, and powerlessness. She didn't yet have the proper words to express her emotions, so she clung to Anna's neck and howled.

The next thing she knew she was lying on her bed, covered in blood. Anna told her she had toppled headfirst down the kitchen steps and cracked her forehead. Then Julia noticed the twins: just standing there, same hollow cheeks, same dazed expression. Struggling free from her sister's arms, she flung herself at them, scratching and biting them with her tiny teeth, her small fists, spluttering that it was all their fault, that Anna was dead and they hadn't done anything to rescue her.

Hearing her cries, her mother rushed into the room. It took all her strength to separate Julia from her brothers. She spent hours trying to calm her daughter down, offering cuddles, sweets, and rewards. But even Anna's appeals couldn't convince Julia to let go of the crazy idea she'd gotten into her head. Clinging to her big sister's neck, she kept screaming that Anna was dead and that no one had tried to save her.

She remained in the same state for the next few days. She refused to have anything to do with the twins and insisted on being allowed to go down to the sea on her own. She had decided she wanted to learn to swim. Her mother watched her from a distance, overcome with a feeling she hadn't felt for any of her children, more akin to resignation than to affection.

She let Julia have her way and sent Anna to keep an eye on her. Anna had an instinctive aversion to the brackish water the twins swam in. Out of love for her little sister and in the hope of curing Julia's madness, she overcame her disgust. She agreed to accompany her sister into the enigmatic waters of the river, but there was no getting Julia out. For hours on end Anna would hold her up in the water as she tried to do the breaststroke like the twins. Julia finally learned to swim and soon became as bold as her brothers. Through sheer persistence she managed to get Anna to swim too, though her sister went

along with it more out of devotion to Julia than from any natural inclination.

Christmas Day came. And as one good thing often leads to
another, their father returned from Argentina laden with food.
He had gotten himself a decent job in Buenos Aires and found
a house for the whole family. His wife was overwhelmed with
a joy that quickly spread to everyone else—everyone except
Julia, who kept fiercely to herself.

One night she heard her parents talking at the kitchen
table for hours after her older siblings had gone to sleep. So
they really were going to leave Uruguay. Though Julia wasn't
quite sure what that meant, the tone of their voices was enough
to set her heart beating faster. Julia didn't want to leave Colonia. She liked her little world: the cobbled streets that wound
upward as if searching for the sky; her own sloping, rickety
house with its roof of crooked pink tiles—the exclusive do-
main of the neighborhood cats that Julia fed in secret. She felt
she was the mistress of this small, safe world where she could
do as she pleased with her days; where Anna alone was allowed to enter; and where everyone except her mother re-
spected her desire for childhood solitude.

For some time there was no further talk of moving, and
Julia thought they had given up the idea. Gradually her distress began to fade. Maybe it had just been a dream after all.

Like everyone else in the family, her father had been trying to coax her out of her shell. Walking to the market with him one day, her hand in his, Julia looked him straight in the eye and said with a grown-up air, "Alone at last!" Her father gave a shout of laughter. He lifted her up and twirled her in the air. Julia thought she would fly off into the blue sky that sucked her upward, taking her breath away, and was glad of her father's strong arms around her.

The departure took them all by surprise. A man in a sailor's cap arrived one morning and gruffly announced that the boat was ready and that they would have to set sail that evening. The household was thrown into utter upheaval. Everything was taken apart, stacked, folded, rolled, trussed, and piled up outside the house. They all found it hard to believe that their entire life could be reduced to such a small number of possessions.

Julia gathered up the things the others were throwing away. She found a long piece of string and threaded it through all the empty containers she found in the house and the garden. She dragged her train of dented receptacles behind her like some precious treasure. Amid the chaos her family greeted her eccentric behavior with relief. They had been worried she would have a nervous fit in the middle of their preparations to leave.

They set off toward the pier in a little procession at dusk. The captain was waiting for them. Julia instantly recognized the boat. The dread she had felt during her vision returned, and she began screaming in terror. The captain, all black beetle brows and bulging eyes, thought the child was throwing a

tantrum and lost his patience. He even threatened to punish
her, having decided that her parents lacked authority.

Julia became hysterical. Clutching her string of bottles
and cans, she took refuge between her father's legs, but nothing could calm her. Despairing, he took her in his arms,
climbed into the boat, and instructed the elder children to
join him in the stern. Meanwhile, the captain was loading the
boat and balancing the cargo in the hold under their mother's
watchful eye.

There was a full moon, and the night sky was clear and
starless. Large black clouds were building up in the distance,
but the crossing wouldn't take long—two hours at most.
However, the wind began to pick up as soon as they sailed out
of the port, and the rising swells slowed the boat's progress.

Just as in her trance, it all happened very quickly. The
twins began to feel seasick, and the captain sent them to the
prow. Anna wanted to help them and began to make her way
to the front, gripping the rail. The boat pitched dangerously,
and the captain left the tiller to secure the front hold. Their
father took his place.

It was at that precise moment that a giant wave surged up
and crashed with the sound of thunder across the deck. The
captain had just enough time to snap on his safety harness,
grab hold of the twins, and pull them to him. Anna went overboard. The roar of the wave drowned out Julia's screams. She
was still gripping her string of bottles and cans. Left alone at
the controls, her father yelled with fear, unable to steer the

boat and thrown into a further panic by his wife's hysterical shrieks as Anna disappeared into the hollow of the wave. The boat had filled with water and the captain was frantically attempting to bail it out in order to escape disaster, all the while bellowing instructions to Julia's father, who seemed incapable of understanding him.

The twins hesitated for no more than a second. They exchanged a meaningful glance, launched themselves at Julia, grabbed her string of bottles, and jumped overboard. The last thing Julia saw before she passed out was Anna's head bobbing like a cork in the trough between two waves.

3.

MAMA FINA

Julia remembers every moment of her life from her first "journey" onward. She knows she hadn't yet turned six, because they celebrated her sixth birthday at her grandmother's house sometime after. Looking back, she thinks it was probably then that she became an adult.

Her grandmother had a lot to do with it. Hers was the first face Julia saw when she came to after the boat incident. She had never met this grandmother from Buenos Aires her father talked about so often. She remembers immediately feeling safe with her.

"Anna and the twins are alive," her grandmother told her. Julia stared at the unfamiliar face and then instantly fell asleep again, but this time into a child's deep sleep. She spent her convalescence in a bright room that opened onto an inner courtyard with an endlessly cooing stone fountain at its center. She could hear her mother's voice and the shouts of the twins from outside, like an echo. But it was her grandmother who was always there, all the time, right beside her.

Mama Fina had clear gray eyes so gentle you could lose yourself in them. Her voice, in contrast, was deep, rasping, even, almost masculine. She sat patiently by Julia's bedside for hours on end. From time to time she would lean forward to stroke her face and Julia would feel the touch of her hands, the skin as rough as a cat's tongue.

Julia thought Mama Fina was beautiful, with her hair in a heavy braid across her shoulder and her large, full-lipped Neapolitan mouth. Julia's father had inherited her transparent eyes, but the rest of her features had skipped a generation. In adulthood Julia would be pleased to see a younger version of Mama Fina looking back at her in the mirror. She was the image of her, except for the large, dark eyes she had inherited from her own mother.

Julia didn't speak during her convalescence. As the days passed, she became increasingly fascinated by Mama Fina. Her words were enchanting. They transported Julia to another country and another time. Mama Fina told her how she had left Italy when she was not much older than Julia, about the ship, her family, the starry sea under the heavens, the forbidden races on the first-class deck, and the games of hide-and-seek in the engine room. And the arrival in Argentina: different smells, a different language that she could understand but not speak. Mama Fina described her trials with all the words she needed that kept eluding her and playing tricks on her. Identical words that meant one thing in Italian and another in Spanish. She was told to watch out for the *burro*, and she'd be looking around for the butter when they were talking about the donkey. And Julia laughed. For the first time ever, she laughed a real child's laugh. Finally she understood her own mistake with the Río de la Plata.

Mama Fina's stories penetrated deep into her like balm. She explained to Julia what had actually happened on the night of the storm. Thanks to her bottles and cans, the twins had been able to save Anna. Julia sensed that, oddly enough, it was she Mama Fina was most proud of.

Mama Fina's description of what happened was better than if she'd seen it with her own eyes. The twins had jumped into the sea in order to disprove Julia's prophecy that blamed them for the death of their big sister. The swell prevented them from seeing where Anna was, but she had managed to stay afloat, certain the twins would come after her because she too realized that Julia had prepared them. Hanging on to their containers, the twins had spotted Anna's head above the water several times, only to see her disappear the next moment, getting farther away each time. They were half-dead from their exertions when suddenly she appeared, like a vision, suspended on the crest of a wave just above them. Crying out, they fought through the swell and managed to catch hold of Anna as she came down. She grabbed onto the floats; only then did she nearly pass out. But the boys had no intention of letting go of her. Adrift in a raging sea in the middle of the night, the three children hung on.

At last the wind let up and the captain managed to turn the boat around. Instinctively calculating a possible drift, he tried to track them down. All of a sudden, their mother thought she heard cries. The captain shut down the engine. She hadn't been mistaken.

Once Julia had recovered, everyone noticed she wasn't quite the same. There was something precocious in her eyes, almost painful, like a scar.

One day, when the family was gathered for lunch, Julia's father made an announcement: their house was finally ready and they could move in over the next few days. He told them it was in an attractive neighborhood in the western suburbs of Buenos Aires, with parks, flower-decked balconies, and lots of children. The twins began to race around the table in excitement, and Anna was overjoyed. Only Julia didn't look up from her plate. Her mother, noticing her silence, tried to cheer her up by pointing out that there were four bedrooms. As there was no question of separating the twins, Julia would have her own room. But there was no convincing her.

Mama Fina got up to clear the table and disappeared into the kitchen. An embarrassed silence fell. Anna stared uncomprehendingly at her little sister. Their father tried to explain that La Boca, the noisy neighborhood where Mama Fina lived, with its old port and nightlife, wasn't really suitable for children. Julia held her older sister's gaze for a long moment, as if to give herself courage. Then, in a clear and final voice, she said, "I'm staying here."

It was the first adult decision of her life.

Anna sided with her little sister. In a way, she understood better than anyone just how much Julia needed her own space. She also sensed intuitively that Julia would blossom at Mama Fina's.

The family moved into their house. By way of marking the beginning of their new life together, Mama Fina enrolled Julia in the parish school and took her to the cinema for the first time to see a Cantinflas film. The movie theater seemed enormous to Julia, with its white pillars flanking the entrance and its heavy red velvet curtain with gold tassels. The film posters showed a funny little man with a ridiculous mustache and baggy pants who seemed to be inviting her in. Mama Fina had made her wear a sailor dress for the occasion and a white coat. Julia was worried she would get it dirty. She also had on a round hat with a trailing dark blue ribbon that tickled her neck. A gaggle of similarly dressed children were racing around the lobby and jumping from the grand staircase as they waited for their parents to finish buying candy.

A man wearing a small flat hat and a red uniform decorated with a long row of gold buttons went past, ringing a bell. The gaggle of children dispersed, and Mama Fina led Julia into the darkness of the huge air-conditioned theater. She handed her a little paper bag filled with popcorn, which Julia didn't want because she was thirsty more than anything. The beam of a flashlight directed them to two seats in the center of the theater. They slipped into their places, apologizing. The giant screen lit up and Julia felt overwhelmed by its presence. Hypnotized, she followed the movements of the little man with the silly mustache, unable to understand why the other children were laughing when she felt like crying.

"Did you like it?" Mama Fina asked as they walked out of the theater.

Julia thought for a moment, then turned to her and asked solemnly, "Was it real, Mama Fina?"

"No, it's a movie."

"But when I see movies . . . they become real afterward."

"We'll have to have a proper talk about this!"

One evening, when Julia had finished her homework, Mama Fina took her by the hand. "Come with me. I want to have a word with you."

She led Julia through the narrow streets of La Boca, along a familiar route that led to the church. They sat down on the low wall at the entrance. Intimidated by the solemnity of the occasion, Julia didn't dare open her mouth. After several long minutes of reflection, Mama Fina turned to Julia, looked her straight in the eye, and began, weighing her words: "This is a very important moment, in your life as well as mine. I'm going to tell you a big secret—the one my father's mother told me sixty years ago, before we left Italy. I was exactly the same age as you, because you'll be six in a few days' time.

"You told me that before the boat accident, when you were playing on the steps, you fell into the 'silver water.' You were very scared because you couldn't breathe, and then you saw things in your head that scared you even more. You were very angry because nobody seemed to understand.

"What happened to you, my grandmother used to call it the 'inner eye.' It's a gift. Like a special present. Only a few girls in our family receive it. . . . I did, and so have you, but nobody else. We don't know who gives us this gift; we only know it's always a bit difficult to pass it on.

"If you want to give your gift to someone else, for example, first you have to become a mommy and have a boy. Sometimes mommies have little girls and sometimes they have little boys. But in your case, to pass the gift on, you have to have a boy.

"So you see, Julia, it's not all that easy, because we don't choose. Do you understand?"

"So the mommies don't say what they want when the baby is in their tummy?"

"No, not the mommies or the daddies. It's a surprise."

Julia began to swing her legs, hitting her heels against the wall. "And I'll give my inner eye to my son? Like you gave your eyes to Daddy?"

"Yes, but the gift skips a generation. That means your

daddy has the gift, but he can't use it. The daddy has to have little girls, and then one of his little girls will receive the gift and can use it."

"Like me. It's your gift that you gave to Daddy, and now it's mine."

"Exactly."

"But why did Daddy give it to me?"

"You know, that's a big secret. Your daddy doesn't know the inner eye exists."

"Why not?"

"Because it's a secret."

"But why is it me who has the inner eye and not Anna?"

"Because usually it's not the eldest girl who inherits the gift."

"Why not?"

"Because nobody should be able to guess who will have it. That way it's a real secret."

"So nobody knows I have the inner eye?"

"Nobody except me. Because I have it too, so I can recognize it. You didn't know either, Julia, even though you have the gift. Now that you're a big girl, I can tell you about it and you can keep it a secret."

Julia drank in her words, enchanted. She wasn't sad anymore; she wasn't angry. Mama Fina had put into words the thing she hadn't been able to understand. She felt herself coming out of chaos.

Her grandmother paused, searching Julia's face, then

carried on, fixing her with her translucent eyes: "Do you understand what the inner eye is?"

"It's a present nobody knows about."

"Yes, but the main thing is that it's a gift. It means you have a talent for something. Everybody has a gift of some kind. Some people are better at singing, other people at drawing, some at talking, others at listening. Sometimes it's a tiny gift, like being good at organizing a closet. Sometimes it's a very big gift, like being able to understand the stars. This gift can be wasted. Or it can be used to make other people happy. If I die before I've had the time to teach you everything, remember this above all else: we were given our gift so we can help others."

Mama Fina broke off and said in a schoolmistress voice, "Julia, repeat what I just said."

Julia took a deep breath and recited carefully: "We were given our gift so we can help others."

Mama Fina smiled, patted Julia on the cheek, and carried on. "Our gift is different. It's secret because it's unique. Other people don't understand, and they might be scared. The way our inner eye works is a bit like looking through a keyhole: we can see things, but nobody knows we can see them. It's like when we went to the movies to see Cantinflas, remember? We sat in our seats and we watched the story, but we weren't in the story."

"That was why the children were laughing, wasn't it, Mama Fina? Because they weren't in it."

"The difficult thing for us is to figure out who it is who's lending us their eyes. . . . Remember, when you saw Anna falling out of the boat, you guessed it was your mommy."

"Yes, because I was scrrrrratching Daddy with Mommy's hands," Julia said, screwing up her face in an effort to mimic the gesture.

"You weren't scratching Daddy. You were using Mommy's eyes to see, and you recognized the hands that went with the eyes. They were Mommy's hands."

Julia looked puzzled. Her grandmother paused, then whispered in a sympathetic tone: "I know, *mi amor*, it's difficult for us to imagine. Your mother asked you for help without knowing it, and you saw what was going to happen through her eyes."

"Mommy never asks me to help her," Julia said sulkily.

"She did on the boat."

"But Mommy didn't call out to me on the boat!" Julia protested.

"Your mother doesn't know she called you because it comes from the heart, not the head. She didn't think, *I'll ask Julia to help me*, but when she was on the boat . . ."

"She was screaming and she was scratching Dad," Julia interrupted, screwing her face up again, her little fingers outstretched.

"Yes, because she was very scared, and without thinking about it, her fear called out to you. Like when the telephone rings. And you answered."

"You mean my inner eye answered?"

"Exactly. We can respond to other people's feelings with our inner eye, you and me. That's how it works. And most of the time, what we see hasn't happened yet. It'll happen the next day, or the day after, or even later."

"So the telephone rings backward?"

"Something like that. The person who is calling us—our source—is experiencing what they see in the future."

"Why?"

"That's just the way it is. When our inner eye answers, we set off on a journey through time. Our gift lets us go forward or backward while everyone else is caught in the present."

"Is that why it's a gift?"

"Yes."

"Why is it a good thing to travel through time?"

"Because we can help other people. Like you helped Anna."

"But it was the twins who . . ."

"We've already talked about this, Julia. You're the one who wanted Anna to learn to swim. You're the one who took those containers on the boat. If you hadn't done that, *mi amor*, I wouldn't be able to tell you our secret, and your inner eye would wither by itself."

"I would have lost my gift?"

"Yes."

"I don't want to lose it, Mama Fina."

4.

DECRYPTION

Boreal Autumn
2006

She stands at the top of the stairs, dumbfounded. *Come on, it's perfectly natural to want to be alone in the bathroom.* All the same. He has never felt the need to lock himself in before.

She lingers there for a moment, then retraces her steps slowly, needing to clear her thoughts, to put some distance between the two of them. Get too close and love suffocates. The other person's presence becomes oppressive. So you learn to live without seeing each other, the way you stop noticing the pedestal table in the hallway.

Julia comes back downstairs and sits in the living room. She has already laid the table and tossed a salad. Distracted, sitting on the sofa in the dark, she stares through the window at the corridor of shadows formed by the elms and maples.

It is the same ritual after each journey. She has to be sitting

down, alone. When she was younger, she would wait for the
dead of night and the privacy of silence. She needed to go
back over her journey while the world was extinguished so she
wouldn't have to worry about being caught unawares. She is
practiced enough now not to have to wait until midnight.
She can blank out the world with her eyes wide open. Only
the sequence of images already etched in her mind flashes
before her eyes. The images come back to her, not like the
blurred recollections of memory but with a clarity and precision that sight alone can produce. It's like a store of pictures
compressed between her eyes and her brain. Her pupils are
contracted even though she's in the dark because she is staring
at a light source inside her head. The film of her latest journey
plays in a continuous loop: the hotel room, the young Asian
woman, the man. She repeats the same sequence once, twice,
a hundred times.

Julia has been rigorously trained to gather the information
and sift through it. Nothing can be dismissed out of hand. She
knows from experience that the most obvious details, the ones
most likely to be overlooked, are often the most useful.

She needs to establish whom the images captured by her
inner eye come from. She has to understand the connection,
the reason why she has been linked to this particular person
at this particular moment. Sometimes her source is a family
member or friend, but very often it's someone she can't identify because she hasn't met them yet. After a journey, she
knows for sure that the person will one day pass through the

meridian of her life. It is a rule. But Julia has to understand her role, the reason she has been called on to intervene.

This evening she feels a bit lost. The most surprising thing about the scene she's watching is precisely that there is nothing surprising about it. That's why she was able to sit down at her desk and finish her translation in one go. She'd nearly forgotten about the young woman with Oriental eyes, her cold smile, and the man with her. Nothing disturbing, nothing urgent about any of it.

What's more, she's not exhausted, the way she generally is when she returns. Because it's usually difficult, traumatic moments that take place in the antechamber of death: accidents, terrible suffering, crimes of passion, and murders. She intercepts a pivotal moment in the lives of people who, for one reason or another, are between life and death, faced with a crucial choice.

She goes back to the starting point, to the beginning of the sequence, in the room bathed in shadow. She is with her source in the hotel room. She hears Mama Fina's voice, her words directing her still. She has to look for details that will enable her to identify the source. Because this person wants to communicate something. Their subconscious is calling for help; they are leaving traces so they can be recognized.

She saw his knees, a shirt. She is sure it is a man. She is rarely mistaken: men have a particular way of seeing the world. Their vision is selective; they use different criteria from women to choose what information to store in their brains. They are more interested in things that move, that change, that make contact. Women, on the other hand, dwell more on what remains hidden, on details and structures, on what is intangible. Julia wants to examine the room. She sees the clothes on the chair again; they look thrown rather than placed there. Is he in a hurry? Impatient? Young, perhaps? His standpoint is out of sight of the bathroom mirror. She can't see his face.

Are they a married couple? Maybe not. The young woman's hasty departure, her final gesture . . . There's a lack of intimacy, and not enough indifference for them to be an established couple. It could be a secret meeting, a passing fling. Julia sees the young woman's face again and focuses on it, trying to decipher her smile. Could she be an escort? Difficult to say. Casual and anonymous relationships do seem to have become a sort of hobby for some people. But perhaps not. There is something restrained about this young woman, a distance. She is protecting herself, as if she needs to stay out of reach.

The stairs creak. Theo is coming back down; she must regain her composure. Her pupils are already dilated when she turns to smile at him. He kisses her with irreproachable tenderness and tells her he'll get dinner. Julia takes her time; she would like to carry on thinking. But she is drawn by the smell coming from the kitchen.

Theo is busy making himself an omelet out of egg whites, which he's recently taken to buying in bulk from the discount supermarket. Someone told him they're a great source of protein. He is obsessed with getting back into shape, and egg whites have become his passion. Julia is unable to share his enthusiasm. The very thought of that viscous substance makes her feel nauseated. But she doesn't say anything.

They sit down opposite each other. She nibbles at her salad while Theo wolfs down his omelet.

"How are you?" Julia asks in an attempt to fill the silence.

"Tired," says Theo, getting up without looking at her.

Julia sighs. Maybe it's inevitable.

Her mind hauls up a catch of old memories. Their first date. He must have been barely nineteen, she fifteen at most. She was still living with her grandmother, he with his parents.

Sitting in a cafeteria in San Telmo, not far from Julia's school, he had ventured to take her hand. His daring had met with a cold reception. Not that Julia thought it improper: far from it. But she found some codes of behavior totally meaningless. By way of explanation, she'd nodded in the direction of a couple in their thirties sitting opposite each other two tables away. They were savoring a huge bowl of ice cream that was dripping down the sides; it was decorated with a small fuchsia-colored Chinese paper umbrella. Intent on wasting nothing, without exchanging a single word, they held hands while using their free hand to eat.

Theo had given a baffled shrug. Julia found it sad, not talking, not looking at each other. They had stacked their hands one on top of the other like two dead fish. Two hands tidied away on the side of the table: that was what they had done with their love. Julia didn't want a tidy love. She hated red roses and Chinese paper umbrellas. She didn't want to end up eating ice cream in the company of a man to whom she no longer had anything to say. Theo had burst out laughing, and Julia had found him almost handsome. He had answered her in his own way. The next day, as she was running out of the house, late for school as usual, she had nearly gone flying on a carpet of red roses laid out on the doorstep.

Julia lets out another sigh. Theo has finished eating and is now absorbed in one of his electronic games. After thirty-one years and a life that has never conformed to convention, they have still managed to end up like that couple at the cafeteria in San Telmo, staring down at their plates while eating, unable to find anything to say.

They have endured too much suffering, overcome too many obstacles. Julia cannot resign herself to this. They do not have the right to settle into boredom when they have only just reached their goal.

She takes the stairs four at a time to their bedroom, opens the closet, slips on her black party dress, rummages through her shoe boxes, and pulls out the black stilettos that drive him crazy. She rolls her hair into a chignon and puts on some makeup, face inches from the mirror, drawing a black line above her lashes. She steps back and looks at herself. Yes, she looks good.

Julia turns around. Theo is standing stock-still in the doorway.

"What's got into you?" he asks.

"Come on. We're going out to have some fun."

She pulls him to her and presses herself against him.

He is about to tell her he's tired, but he peers at her for a moment, then whispers teasingly in her ear: "Are you sure you want to go out?"

The tone is almost perfect. But it doesn't ring true to Julia. He has put his mask back on.

5

THE MASK

Austral Summer
1972

They met for the first time at Anna's eighteenth-birthday party. The family had recently left the suburbs and moved into a two-story house in the Liniers neighborhood. Anna was thrilled, not only because it was a bigger house but because now she would be closer to Julia. She had always refused to let any distance come between them. It was Anna who came to Mama Fina's place in La Boca after school twice a week to see Julia, and it was she too who first told Julia what it felt like to be in love. The girls would lock themselves in the big bathroom for long confabs that could go on until dawn. Julia immediately knew when Anna was in love, because she would deny it while batting her eyelashes like butterfly wings. Julia found her sister's emotional states ridiculous and told herself she'd never be in love that way. But she did feel a prickle of envy as she watched her sister plotting to win over whichever young man she'd set her heart on.

When Anna stayed over, Mama Fina's phone never stopped ringing. It was Julia's job to pick up and pretend she didn't know whether her sister was in, to give Anna time to decide if she wanted to take the call or have the person call back later. If Anna's favorite suitor, Pablo, called, Julia had to make a huge effort not to roar with laughter. Anna would fling herself to the ground and pedal frantically in the air, unable to control her emotion, while Julia, bent double, did her best to cover the receiver. Anna would exhale in small puffs to calm herself down. When she was breathing normally again, she would take the telephone, acting perfectly naturally, and apologize to the boy for keeping him waiting. As soon as Anna hung up, Julia would find herself racing around the fountain in the courtyard with her, whooping like a Sioux, as excited by the invitation as Anna.

So Julia went to help with the preparations for the party with the feeling that she had an important mission to accomplish. She'd heard that Pablo had just confirmed his attendance. She took charge of the decorations, making bright garlands from the glossy pages of magazines her mother had collected. She blew up multicolored balloons and hung them in clusters in the corners of rooms and above doors. She fitted colored lightbulbs in the ground-floor lamps and ceiling lights and turned the living room into a dance hall by pushing all the furniture against the walls. Finally she helped her mother stir the huge pot of *spaghetti napolitana* and stack up plates on the buffet table.

The guests arrived all at once and Julia felt like an outsider. The boys strolled easily into the kitchen, kissed her mother, greeting her by her first name, and came out again holding the glasses she'd handed them. Standing next to her mother, Julia felt invisible.

When Anna, radiant in a turquoise print dress, switched on the new record player and Pablo unpacked his collection of LPs of the latest hits by Almendra, Sui Generis, and Led Zeppelin, Julia sought refuge in the small garden at the front of the house. She was too eager to dance, too afraid of not being asked, and even more afraid of being asked and not knowing what to do.

Through the wide-open door Julia watched the twins spinning all the girls around and Anna changing partners each time a new song came on, under Pablo's amused gaze. None of the boys was paying any attention to Julia. She was almost ashamed and berated herself for having dressed like a child, in a long blue paisley-print cotton dress with a smocked top that flattened her breasts.

A young man with rumpled hair and a blasé air came out, glass in hand, and sat down at her side, so clumsily that for a moment she thought he would spill his drink over her. Finally he turned around and gave her a beaming smile. Julia nearly walked away, horrified at the thought that he might be motivated by pity. But she found him so unattractive, with his pockmarked skin and huge lips, that she felt as if their roles had been reversed and allowed herself to be pleasant.

He held out the glass to her. "An improvement on what your mother's dishing out," he said.

Julia raised one eyebrow, half-offended, half-amused.

"It's Coca-Cola . . . with a dash of rum!" he went on.

"It's not really my thing," Julia retorted.

"You're mistaken. Not only does it taste good, it'll make you friendlier. It's Cuban rum, you know. If you want to dance with me you'll have to drink some, like any self-respecting young revolutionary."

"I don't want to dance with you." As if to justify her lack of humor, she added: "I don't even know who you are."

He jumped up, gave a bow, and, after ceremoniously kissing her hand, said, "My name is Theodoro d'Uccello—Theo to friends—and I am henceforth eternally at your service."

Julia couldn't help cracking up. Theo had just won the first round.

He pulled Julia into the living room and they began to dance, roaring with laughter, heedless of the other couples they kept bumping into. Julia's mother wasn't exactly pleased with her daughter's behavior. In the end she got her husband to come in and restore order. Julia's father made a conspicuous entrance into the living room. The young guests looked on apprehensively, stepping back to let him pass. Grim faced, he walked slowly toward the boy who had his younger daughter mesmerized.

"I'm going to have to put my mask on," Theo whispered, winking at Julia, as the head of the household approached.

Julia watched him, alert for the slightest faux pas. But Theo surprised her. He had morphed seamlessly into an adult: her father's equal. He apologized for his childish behavior, then proceeded to take the lead in the conversation, proving to be remarkably intelligent. He spoke about politics, happy to discuss the latest events in national life. He openly declared that he was a Peronist and was confident the general would make a triumphant return, because the military would eventually have to give in to pressure from the people. Julia's father, who made no secret of his support for the old leader, couldn't have been more pleased with Theo's politics.

Everyone knew Perón would soon be visiting Argentina for the first time since being forced into exile. But hardly anyone, not even his most loyal supporters, dared to envisage a general election that would see his definitive return to the presidency, as Theo maintained. And to tell the truth, Julia couldn't have cared less.

She went back outside and sat down, leaning against the garden railing. Being with the others had exhausted her and she needed to get away. She stared down the deserted, ill-lit street. Though the sidewalks were fairly narrow, space had been left to plant trees. Now they had to fight against the invasion of electricity poles and streetlights, half of which didn't work. The large, faded houses, the slender windows decorated with elegant wrought-iron balconies, and the crenellated roofs bore witness to a more glorious past. There was something fragile about it all that appealed to her.

The party began to wind down, and one by one the young people took their leave. The house fell silent and Theo, one of the last to leave, kept his mask on to the end. He bade Julia a polite good night and walked off. He could be so respectable! She followed him with her gaze until he had turned the corner.

She shakes her head as she does her hair, as if to chase away these memories, then combs it into place with her fingers. He brings his mask out to hide something, as a last resort when he is feeling trapped. Julia pretends she hasn't noticed. She doesn't want to put him on his guard. Yes, she wants to go out. She is set on it now. She insists, as if acting on a whim. But she's shaken.

They take the car, avoiding each other's gaze, and scour the streets in search of some action. Julia affects a cheerful, casual air. But they're driving through a ghost town: all the bars are closed. They scour the streets near the station, venture down to the marina, around the shopping mall. Nothing. They are almost secretly relieved. On the way back home, they are suddenly blinded by some roadside neon signs just behind the heliport. It's a biker bar. And it's packed. Through the fogged-up windows they can make out a dance floor and a pool table. A crooner's baritone punctures the night through a swinging door held open by a couple.

They park the car and hesitate. There are some black girls singing in front of a huge karaoke screen. Julia rouses herself and drags Theo inside. The girls' crystal-clear voices are at odds with the heavy bodies they shake at a devilish pace while the men slouching at the bar ignore them. Theo doesn't pay them any attention either, at least no more than he does Julia. He seems distracted.

He goes to the bar to order a couple of beers, shunning all contact, and returns, lost in thought. Julia makes a fresh attempt at conversation. "It would do us good to go on a motorcycle ride one weekend."

Theo's gaze returns to her for an instant.

"We could tour the Berkshires," she suggests.

It will be beautiful there now, at the tail end of summer, and Julia knows Theo likes riding on mountain roads. Labor Day is coming up; it would be the ideal time to make the most of a long weekend.

Theo puts his glass down. He takes a second too long to answer.

"Yes, we could take a couple of days and leave Friday," he admits. "But I'll have to be back Monday morning to hold down the fort."

Julia doesn't want to ask any more questions. Hold down the fort on Labor Day, what a great alibi. Like the excuse he invented this summer not to go to New Zealand to visit their son. In spite of all evidence to the contrary, Theo claimed the trip had been planned without consulting him, and there was no way he could leave the office. Julia went anyway, outraged by his dishonesty and because Ulysses had scheduled his vacation for the dates they'd planned. Besides, she wanted to meet her son's fiancée.

Her trip hasn't made things any better. Theo has been irritable since she got back and has gotten into the habit of making hurtful remarks. If he's run out of gas, it's because Julia doesn't contribute to the household expenses. If he can't find the remote for their new TV, it's because Julia isn't organized. If Julia walks into their bedroom unexpectedly, it's because she's spying on him. He's moved his office to the laundry room so Julia won't disturb him.

But that's not all. In spite of herself, Julia can't help keeping count of his new eccentricities: a sudden enthusiasm for heavy metal, a new interest in electronic games, and his latest craze, egg whites. For some reason Julia connects all of this to the story of a staff conference that Theo attended recently. He came back from it all excited. He told her about a colleague, a young Korean, whom he'd hit it off with. Then he told her he'd be back from work late sometimes because he planned on going to the gym with his new friend.

Funny, that's stuck like a fishbone.

Theo has set two beers down on the table.

"By the way, thanks for the lunch, honey. The guys at the gym were green with envy. We were all starving after the workout."

He sits down close to her and kisses her passionately on

the mouth. All of Julia's wild imaginings evaporate in an instant. *Maybe it's just a fit of jealousy, an aftereffect of my trance.* The
thought takes her by surprise. She isn't tired; why make this
connection? Mechanically she replays the images of the young
Asian woman putting on makeup in the bathroom, the bed,
the clothes on the chair. Theo puts his arm around her waist
and pulls her to him. They get up, hand in hand, and dance
between the pool tables. Julia thinks back to her Rothko painting and feels guilty for allowing doubt to creep in.

In bed later that night, Theo feels her moving and holds
her close. Julia prays they'll stay this way always, pressed close
together. A plane flies over the house. Its drone is soothing.
She wouldn't want to be anyplace else but in his arms.

She wakes at dawn. Theo is already in the shower. She
pulls on her dressing gown and goes downstairs to make him
some lunch to take to the office. She opens the bag he uses to
transport his gym clothes and lunch box. Yesterday's shorts
and T-shirt are impeccably folded, the lunch intact, untouched.

Julia's heart freezes. Yesterday Theo described his gym
workout to her in detail. He even mentioned he had heated up
his lunch in the office microwave. Julia stops dead, staring at
Theo's things. My God . . . what if there's someone else, and
he meant her to find these things so she'd guess? Has he done
it on purpose?

Julia doesn't hesitate for a second. She races up the stairs,
pulls on a gray cotton shirt and a tracksuit, knocks on the
bathroom door, and, taking quick, short breaths so her voice

won't betray her emotion, says, "I'm going for a run. I've left your breakfast on the table."

She rushes back downstairs. She goes out by the main door and skirts the house to where Theo's car is parked on the private access road. She opens the door, taking care not to set off the alarm, climbs into the backseat, lifts the lever that locks the seat back, and folds the seat forward to access the trunk. She crawls inside, pulls the seat back into place, and freezes in her hiding place, panting.

Curled up in a ball in the darkness, her heart thudding and her palms sweating, she feels like throwing up. It isn't wanting to know the truth that is making her feel sick. It's finding herself once again shut up in the trunk of a car.

6.

THE EZEIZA MASSACRE

Austral Winter
1973

Julia was fifteen. She'd been in love with him for a few months now. Her grandmother had warned her: women of the lineage were never happy in love. But Julia refused to listen. She would be the exception.

The callow youth who had approached her at her parents' home had become a man. He had enrolled in the School of Sciences at the University of Buenos Aires. He wanted to become a computer scientist. He'd been good at math in school and had developed an interest in systems programming—a new field that had managed to survive the flight into exile of Argentina's finest minds following the Noche de los Bastones Largos.*

---

* Night of the Long Sticks, July 29, 1966: the end of university autonomy and the persecution of Argentine scientists and academics by the military regime of General Juan Carlos Onganía.

Theo would have liked to work with Clementina, the pride of the faculty. It was the first computer programmed entirely in Argentina—a bulky piece of equipment occupying an entire room. Unfortunately Clementina had just been dismantled on the pretext that a new machine was going to be put into service. Theo was hoping to be part of the new team. His exam results were excellent, and his professors considered him a particularly brilliant student.

Theo was ambitious. He read almost everything he could get his hands on. He had an opinion on every subject under the sun, because even when his knowledge of something was superficial, he could support it with convincing remarks. Mama Fina said he had "presence." He wasn't handsome by any means, but he had the appeal of young people who enjoy other people's company. His gift for repartee soon made him the center of any conversation; he could be self-deprecating and make people laugh. He often said he'd learned to play the clown to keep Julia's heart, and she knew it was true.

But above all—and this was what made him irresistible to Julia—Theo made it a point of honor to nurture his inner child. He was up for any game, curious about anything new, open to any craziness. Julia felt like she'd been caught up in a whirlwind. It was her turn to keep Anna up at night with her tales of Theo.

Theo was very close to his brother, Gabriel, who was five years his elder. His admiration for Gabriel knew no bounds. They had both graduated from the Colegio Nacional de Bue-

nos Aires. It was there that Gabriel had made friends with Carlos Gustavo Ramus, a classmate who would later meet a tragic
fate. In 1964, at just seventeen, Ramus had become the leader
of the Catholic students' organization in Buenos Aires. At
twenty-three he had helped to launch a revolutionary movement opposed to the military dictatorship: the Montoneros,
named after the guerrillas who had fought against Spanish rule
in the nineteenth century. He was killed a few months later
during a confrontation with police. It was through Ramus that
Gabriel, aged barely eighteen, had become an activist within
the Catholic Student Youth, the JEC. It was also through
Ramus that Gabriel had made the acquaintance of the young
priest Carlos Mugica, the movement's spiritual adviser.

Gabriel had gotten involved in politics in 1966 while studying for his entrance exams to the faculty of medicine. Theo
assumed that his involvement in politics simply consisted of a
few meetings with friends. Gabriel's circle was made up of
young nationalists, most of them conservative and Catholic,
who were also attracted, paradoxically enough, to the ideas of
Che Guevara and Mao Zedong. They viewed Father Mugica
as a mentor because he talked about social justice and worked
on the ground in the *villas miserias* of Buenos Aires. He had
taken his young followers there several times on vaccination
campaigns and similar missions. The brush with poverty had
put some of them off but encouraged the hardier ones to get
more involved. Hence why young people from the Mataderos
neighborhood, where the d'Uccello brothers lived, read Pierre

Teilhard de Chardin, Yves Congar, and René Laurentin before they read Marx's *Capital*.

Young Theo's room reflected the influence of his older brother. Instead of the posters of Ursula Andress that held pride of place in his friends' bedrooms, his room was decked out with photographs of Che Guevara and Perón in full dress uniform. It didn't seem to bother him in the slightest that his heroes embodied contradictory ideals. At the foot of his bed lay piles of *Christianity and Revolution* salvaged after they'd been read from cover to cover by his brother's political circle. One of the shelves behind the door held a dusty copy of a book that had once been required reading in school: *La Razón de mi vida*, with a picture of Evita Perón on the cover. The book had recently been banned by the military junta.

Theo was an eager participant in the meetings Gabriel organized at their house, especially when Father Mugica was present. The young priest argued that the temptation of armed struggle was a trap and that only democratic action could break the military's stranglehold. Although he admired the success of the Cuban experience, he refused to justify revolutionary violence. He liked to remind them of the biblical reference to turning swords into plowshares, although that hadn't stopped him from clashing with Cardinal Caggiano, the archbishop of Buenos Aires and the head of the Argentine church, who openly supported the military dictatorship.

Gabriel had briefly nursed the idea of entering the seminary. He had been tempted to follow in Mugica's footsteps and become involved in the antiestablishment Movement of Priests for the Third World, an organization of young Argentine clerics that had become extremely popular because of its outspoken criticism of the abuses of the military junta.

Perhaps that was why Gabriel hadn't joined his friend Ramus when the Montoneros formed their first armed unit in the early 1970s. Gabriel believed subversion would exacerbate the country's social malaise, not remedy it. Nor did he approve of Operation Pindapoy, the kidnapping of General Pedro Eugenio Aramburu. The former head of the military junta had been hauled before a people's court. Charged with multiple crimes, particularly that of stealing Evita Perón's body, he had been killed by a bullet to the head. The Montoneros had published a statement declaring that they would give up his body only in exchange for Evita's remains.

This was when Theo, who had just turned seventeen, decided to become a Montonero, against the advice of his older brother and despite Father Mugica's warnings. His decision came just a few weeks before the news that Aramburu's body had been found by the army in a hacienda owned by Ramus's parents. Their property, La Celma, was situated in Buenos Aires district. Gabriel knew the place and had been there on a number of occasions.

Theo asked Gabriel to put him in contact with Ramus. He was convinced his brother knew where Ramus was hiding, and he wanted to join the organization right away. Gabriel refused outright. Whether it was because he condemned the Montoneros' act or because he wanted to protect Theo, Gabriel became angry with his brother and retreated into an obstinate silence. Theo was furious at him.

The discord between the d'Uccello brothers lasted until the tragic events of the spring. On September 7, 1970, Carlos Gustavo Ramus died as he was pulling the pin out of a grenade during a confrontation with police in a pizzeria in the center of Buenos Aires. The leader of the Montoneros, Fernando Luis Abal Medina, was also gunned down in the shoot-out.

The news spread like wildfire. Theo's father and mother listened to every report on the radio, consumed with anxiety. Gabriel didn't show up at dinnertime. The atmosphere around the table was fraught; their plates remained untouched, and none of them dared comment on the affair. The previous evening Gabriel had quarreled with his father, who had upbraided him for his leftist views and accused him of being a bad influence on his younger brother. Theo felt terribly guilty, knowing how strongly Gabriel opposed the violence of the Montoneros and how unfair their father's accusation was. But he had lacked the courage to stand up for his brother, both the previous day and during the long, silent wait with his parents at the dinner table.

Overtaken by remorse, Theo waited up for his brother until dawn, sitting in the kitchen glued to the radio. When Gabriel finally appeared, Theo threw himself at his brother and hugged him, putting an end to the feud that had separated them for months.

Neither of them wanted to admit it, but they each felt the other had been right. A gradual change in their feelings, coupled with the recent events, had led them to see the political situation from the other person's point of view. Gabriel began to reconsider his categorical refusal of the armed struggle, while Theo pondered the possibility of joining the Peronist Youth instead of an underground organization like the Montoneros.

Father Mugica officiated at Ramus's funeral. A huge crowd had assembled near the church of San Francisco Solano, right in the middle of the bourgeois Mataderos neighborhood. Gabriel and Theo attended the ceremony, feeling part of their country's history for the first time. Ramus's death manifested a new reality to the d'Uccello brothers: it brought supporters of the Montoneros onto the streets, revealing the importance of the movement as a political force to be reckoned with and no longer merely an urban guerrilla group.

The day General Perón returned from exile for the first time, Gabriel and Theo went to welcome him with a group of about a hundred young people. They had gathered in the rain against the orders of the police, who had forbidden them to go anywhere near Ezeiza Airport. It was November 17, 1972, a few days before Anna's eighteenth birthday. Perón was detained at the airport for hours before being released into a deserted

Buenos Aires on a tight leash by the military, which had imposed a curfew.

Seven months later, on June 20, 1973, Gabriel, Theo, and Julia found themselves among a huge crowd come to celebrate Perón's definitive return. Following the democratic election of March 1973, the Peronist Héctor José Cámpora had been named president of the republic, since Perón himself was not allowed to run. Everyone knew it was merely a transition to pave the way for the general's return to power.

When Theo stopped by to pick up Julia on his way to join the welcome rally at Ezeiza Airport, Mama Fina's desperate attempts to dissuade them were no match for their enthusiasm. After all, Julia had changed a lot too. In the space of just a few months she had become a young woman, keen to prove her independence.

They arrived at Ezeiza under the thrust of the vast sea of humanity that had come to greet the general and was now fanning out around the platform that had been set up for him to deliver a speech. Hand in hand, Theo and Julia squeezed their way through to the pillar where activists representing the political arm of the Montoneros had gathered next to youths from the Justicialist Liberation Front and Peronist Armed Forces militants. They hoped they might find Gabriel there. Their mission proved completely impossible. There were more than two million people gathered there on that winter morning.

The weather was cold with a biting wind, but the young

people, dressed in thin clothes, seemed not to notice. True, it was a sunny day. But what was really keeping the crowd warm was their newfound freedom following the military junta's departure. As the excitement grew to a fever pitch, so the temperature rose too. The Montoneros, who had recently formed a political wing, were chanting their overtly revolutionary slogans loud and clear. Despite knowing very little about politics, Julia could see that the Montoneros were the most numerous among the Peronist forces present and were in a position of strength. She could feel herself getting carried away by the collective emotion; she was part of this human mass whose heart was beating in unison with hers. There was a primitive feeling of power and victory in the air that she had never experienced before and that she found intoxicating.

Giving up on the idea of trying to find Gabriel, Theo and Julia elbowed their way toward the platform, hoping to get a closer view of the man who stirred the hearts of all Argentines. A rumor began to spread that the general's plane had been diverted to Morón Airport, and a ripple of anxiety spread through the crowd.

That was when the shooting began. Bullets sprayed in all directions. The crowd panicked and began to crush and sway, swallowing Julia. Her hand slipped out of Theo's and she lost sight of him. Summoning all her strength, she tried to fight against the tide in the direction in which he had disappeared. She was jostled and fell to the ground, narrowly escaping being trampled underfoot in the stampede. Someone collapsed at her feet, spattering her with blood. The crowd scattered, screaming, leaving Julia at the center of a wide circle next to a wounded young woman lying in a dark puddle. They immediately became a target for the snipers. Julia grabbed the young woman under her arms and began to drag her backward, trying to regain the shelter of the crowd.

She managed to pull the woman to a spot where the ground sloped down. She stayed in her improvised trench until late afternoon, when the shooting finally came to an end. The girl had sustained a bullet wound to the leg and was still losing blood. Julia laid her down as best as she could and, as a last resort, used the belt of her dress as a tourniquet, tying it above the woman's knee. She had to get her out of there right away.

She followed the shadowy figures that rose up out of hiding places like her own and fled silently into the grayness. Julia and the wounded young woman reached the road. She begged Julia not to take her to the hospital, confessing that she was an active member of the Montoneros' clandestine networks. Her name was Rosa.

A shopkeeper on his way to Buenos Aires gave them a lift in his van in the dead of night. Julia asked him to drop them off outside Theo's house. She prayed the whole way that the d'Uccello brothers had returned home and would be able to help them. Theo was already back and was keeping a close watch on the street from the window. He rushed out the minute he saw Julia, firing questions at her. He had been injured too. Gabriel, who'd been the first to come home, had quickly

set up a makeshift infirmary in the living room and was tend-
ing to half a dozen wounded.

Still in a state of shock and not yet aware of the scale of the
incident, the young people were already calling it "the Ezeiza
massacre." They knew that hundreds of people had been
wounded but still didn't know how many were dead. Over the
next few days, graffiti on the city's walls accused some government ministers of the crime, and a rumor began that right-
wing Peronists had given the order to fire on the crowd. As for
Perón, he blamed his left-wing supporters for the massacre,
calling them "beardless youth." Some people claimed that
Perón feared the revolutionary excesses of the Montoneros,
others that it was a military tactic to pit the Peronist factions
against each other.

By October 1973, when Perón was elected president for
the third time, Theo had hung the flag of the Montoneros
next to the general's photograph: a black rifle crossed with a
spear on a red background, with the letter M in the middle. In
his view, Perón was the natural leader of the Montoneros.
Gabriel, for his part, could not forgive the general for having
scorned the young Peronists by using the humiliating expression "beardless youth" when so many of them had given their
lives to enable him to return to the presidency.

Mama Fina warned Julia that hard times were ahead, but
her granddaughter was defiant: if Mama Fina had had a vision,
she only had to tell her about it. Julia was old enough now to
take care of herself. Whatever Mama Fina might think, Julia

remained optimistic. Like Theo, she maintained that Perón had had nothing to do with the massacre; now that he was actually back in power, things could only get better.

In fact, as far as Julia was concerned, things were getting better. She had grown in self-confidence and become popular at high school; she was closer to her father, and, above all, like Anna, she had found true love.

Because of Theo, Julia began to take a genuine interest in politics. She participated in several of the meetings Gabriel organized at his home. Julia was happy to see Rosa at the meetings. She had recovered from her wounds and was now a regular. Julia and she were fast becoming friends.

It was at one of these meetings that Julia met Father Mugica. She couldn't take her eyes off him all evening. At forty-three Carlos Mugica was a very attractive man, even in his cassock. With his light-colored eyes, wry smile, and lock of blond hair falling across his forehead, he was simply irresistible. He spoke plainly, exuding an undeniable charisma. Julia listened to him, trying to understand his arguments and struggling not to allow herself to be influenced by his charm.

7.

FATHER MUGICA

Austral Autumn
1974

The priest noticed Julia's embarrassment and, believing her to be shy, took it upon himself to include her in the conversation. They were talking about the Ezeiza massacre. Each of them described their experience, because all the people in the living room had been at the rally. One of the young men standing near Father Mugica confirmed that the shots had been fired by snipers positioned on the roof of the airport. Ordinarily security would have fallen to Cámpora's interior minister, Esteban Righi, himself a left-wing Peronist. But apparently Perón had insisted that security during his speech at Ezeiza be entrusted to a colonel with connections to José López Rega, who represented the Peronist far right and had become close to El Conductor.*

---

* "El Conductor" means "The Guide" or "The Leader." Honorific title given to Perón by his followers.

Father Mugica explained that if Perón was elected, the government would have to make some painful choices. Peronism could unite the far right and the far left for as long as it was a case of confronting the dictatorship, but once they were in power, the internal divisions would become unmanageable.

Theo insisted, as if trying to convince himself, that if Perón had to make a choice, he would come out in favor of the Montoneros. "Perón knows he owes us everything. He said so publicly when he was in exile. It was the Montoneros who destabilized the dictatorship. Perón even praised the 'wonderful youth' after the execution of General Aramburu!"

"Yes, but that same 'wonderful youth' is now 'beardless.' Make no mistake, Theo, the general has already made his choice," shot back Augusto, one of Gabriel's friends.

Julia had been listening attentively to the discussion from the start. She hesitated for a moment, then ventured: "Maybe Perón has changed since he remarried. If Evita were still alive . . ."

"What are you talking about?" Theo interrupted, annoyed at being contradicted twice.

His reaction threw Julia, who fell silent like a scolded child. Father Mugica intervened to encourage Julia and calm things down. It was true, he said, that Evita's absence was a factor that had to be taken into account. Even though she had been dead for twenty years, her name continued to have genuine political significance.

"Perón's marriage to Isabel hasn't simplified matters,"

Augusto added. "You can't really say he made a good choice! She can try all she likes to look like her and copy her hairstyle; she's not fooling anyone. Evita was the idol of the *descamisados*, but Isabel's sympathies lie with the right."

"Funny, I get the impression that in Argentina we talk more about the wives than the presidents themselves!" came a voice from the back of the room. Everyone laughed.

"Maybe so, but it's strange, to say the least, that Perón didn't make any attempt to have Evita's body brought home. . . ." Augusto continued.

Theo returned to the fray. Given that Aramburu's body had been found before the junta returned Evita's remains, Perón could surely not be held accountable in this respect, he argued.

Rosa, who was also at the meeting, asked to speak, cleared her throat, and said, "Didn't General Lanusse return Evita's body to Perón and Isabel two years ago, when they were in Madrid? Or if not, he at least told them how to get it back. I've heard the Vatican secretly helped bury her somewhere in Italy. . . ."

Everyone turned to Mugica.

"I don't know, to be honest," he said. "But it's highly likely that was the case, or at any rate that the Vatican made sure Evita had a Christian burial." Choosing his words carefully, he went on: "I too have wondered whether the general's obvious shift to the right would have been possible if Evita were still alive. But, general speculation aside, it's clear that the success of the Montoneros and the demonstrations of power by the youth since the Cordobazo* have unsettled Perón. . . ."

He scratched his head, preoccupied. "Obviously, while Perón was in exile it was easy for him to encourage unrest. He knew it would weaken the putschists. But now that he's back as head of state, it's more alarming than anything else. Now, none of us knows who is really influencing the general. Has he made secret deals—with the USA, for example?"

Gabriel interrupted him. "If, as you say, Perón's government has shifted to the right, it's possible that what we're witnessing is the start of a civil war."

Everyone leaned forward to listen more closely.

"Like you, Father Carlos, I've always been opposed to violence," Gabriel continued. "But I'm convinced it takes a great deal of courage to give up swords for plowshares, as you've always told us. Aramburu's assassination wasn't just a despicable crime; it was a strategic mistake on the part of the Montoneros. Now people who don't share our views think we're monsters and that we have to be gunned down.

"In my opinion, the Ezeiza massacre was the first step in an extermination plan. There were all kinds of innocent people in the crowd—lots of young people, but also pregnant women, children, elderly people. Where are the murderers? Where is the justice? My dear father, the question we should be asking

* "El Cordobazo" refers to a civil uprising against the military junta in the city of Córdoba that took place on May 29, 1969.

ourselves is whether, in these circumstances, we should now turn the other cheek. To be honest, what's worrying me most is this Triple A business."

"What's Triple A?" asked Julia.

Father Mugica bit his lip, then said slowly, "It's little more than a rumor. At least for now. Apparently a group of men with close ties to Perón have set up death squadrons under the leadership of El Brujo,* They call themselves the Triple A: Argentine Anticommunist Alliance."

"And who is El Brujo?"

"The minister for social welfare, José López Rega. It's his nickname because he dabbles in the occult, that kind of thing. I'm sorry to say I'm well acquainted with him. I worked with him at the ministry when the Cámpora government was in power. I resigned because of him. He used to be a police corporal several years ago. He's very close to Isabel. Maybe that's why he's one of the few people to have survived from one government to the next."

Then, as if holding back from saying more, he added with a frown: "You'd have to have a pretty dark sense of humor to appoint a man who's supposed to be the head of a gang of killers minister for social welfare, don't you think?"

The conversation took a new turn. The minister for social welfare was doing absolutely nothing to improve the situation in the *villas miserias*. The layoffs following the worker strikes

* The Sorcerer.

and the arrests of trade union leaders had not helped matters. Entire households were now living in the most degrading poverty.

"How can we accept that right next to the wealthiest neighborhoods, entire families are dying of hunger!" protested Rosa.

"We all live in ghettos, we just don't realize it," said Father Mugica. After a moment's silence, he added: "Just off Plaza San Martín, a stone's throw from Torre de los Ingleses, there are families who do not eat every day. I'm worried the only reason López Rega has been appointed to the Ministry of Social Welfare is to get rid of them."

"Isn't there something we can do?" asked Julia, visibly moved.

"Something can always be done," Rosa replied.

Father Mugica continued: "López Rega thinks you can eradicate poverty and hunger by eradicating the poor. We think people who live in poverty are different, feel differently, because they are used to being destitute. They bother us because they mar the beauty of our capital city. Gradually we forget that they're human beings. It's not much of a stretch from there to putting them into concentration camps."

Julia joined Father Mugica's team working in Villa 31. She couldn't believe it was so close to her own home. Just by turning a street corner she found herself plunged into a different world. There were still houses, cars, even electricity poles. But it all looked unfinished and rickety. Most of the buildings were made of big hollow concrete blocks stuck together with mortar that had dripped and dried down the sides, as if the urgent need to get them up had rendered unnecessary any thought of giving them a proper finish. Second, third, and even fourth stories were stacked haphazardly on the foundations. Where they existed at all, roofs were made of sheets of corrugated iron, plastic, or asbestos, never the right size, unattached, half balancing in midair. The noises were different too, as if the world of the millions of poor had gone to live on the streets. The aggressive odors betrayed the lack of basic amenities. And there was the human swarming, constant, desperate, peculiar to the hopeless, and the hordes of children in the streets, and the unspeakable chaos of a permanent construction site.

The young team was in the grip of conflicting emotions. Only Father Mugica remained unruffled. He talked to the people he visited with the same consideration, the same attitude of restraint and attentiveness, that had struck Julia at the d'Uccellos' house. But there was something more: an energy, a kind of barely suppressed elation, that he didn't have elsewhere. He flourished in this underworld, at one with himself; his rebellion against the system was fueled by love, not resentment.

Julia had just come to this conclusion when an elderly woman, who seemed to have been following them for some time, interrupted her thoughts.

"Are you related to Josefina d'Annunzio?" she asked with a hesitant smile.

"Mama Fina, you mean? Yes, of course, I'm her grand-daughter!"

"I thought as much," the woman said happily. "You look uncannily like her."

She went on with a secretive air: "You know, I'm very fond of your grandmother, and grateful to her too. You could say it's partly because of her that I'm still alive."

The old woman began laughing, a hand over her toothless mouth. Her small eyes shone intensely in their deep-set sockets, intensifying the hundreds of furrows plowed in her rough skin.

"Oh! It's quite a strange story," she continued. "Maybe she'll tell you about it."

Then, delighted with the effect she'd had, she added: "You can tell her the girls in the cooperative have worked hard this week; this time she'll really be satisfied with the quality."

That was how Julia learned that Mama Fina was a regular visitor to Villa 31 and that she'd known Father Mugica for years. She had set up a cooperative for unemployed young mothers. They took turns looking after the little ones while the others made children's clothing. Smocking was their specialty—that explained the long dress Mama Fina had given Julia, which she'd worn to Anna's eighteenth-birthday party. Mama Fina took the dresses to storekeepers in La Boca and San Telmo. The profits were shared equally among all the young mothers who were members of the cooperative.

When Julia returned home, she went straight to Mama Fina and threw her arms around her neck. It didn't occur to her to be upset with her grandmother. Full of admiration, she told her everything she'd learned about the cooperative, the old lady, and her social-action activities. Julia understood that, in a way, Mama Fina's discretion about her good works was the same as her own efforts to conceal their gift. All the same, Julia was excited. She told Mama Fina she wanted to work with her at the cooperative and with Father Mugica in Villa 31.

"Good timing," Mama Fina answered. "I want to set up a health center at the cooperative. I know Father Carlos has connections with some pharmaceutical wholesalers. If you want to help me, I'll give you a small budget. You'll have to draw up a list of essential drugs, and you can run the shop after school."

One month later Julia had invited everybody she knew, including Theo, Gabriel, and Rosa, to the opening of her health center. They had all helped her, especially Señora Pilar, the old woman who was a friend of Mama Fina's and who did the accounts for the cooperative. Gabriel had made up a list of drugs to stock. He had also agreed to train Julia in first aid and how to offer basic medical advice. Rosa, for her part, had offered to take turns with Julia to make sure there was always someone at the health center.

Julia's work in Villa 31 brought her even closer, if that was possible, to her grandmother. When Theo came to call for her

on May 1, 1974, on his way to the demonstration in the Plaza
de Mayo, Julia took care to ask Mama Fina her opinion and left
only after she had gotten her blessing.

The Plaza de Mayo was packed to bursting, and columns
of Montoneros were chanting slogans against the government's "gorillas," El Brujo and the vice president, Isabel. Despite all this, there were no violent incidents. Perón appeared
as expected on the balcony of the Casa Rosada. In his speech
to the workers, he violently disparaged the Montoneros,
calling them "stupid" and, once again, "beardless." The public
insult resulted in a spectacular retreat by the ranks of Montoneros, who withdrew with military precision. Julia and Theo
returned home earlier than expected, despondent but un-
harmed.

Even the maté* with which Mama Fina welcomed them did
nothing to lift their spirits. They stayed up all night setting the
world right, realizing that their loyalty to Perón had now vanished for good. They eventually fell asleep wound around
each other on the living room sofa, physically drained and de-
moralized.

Julia woke at dawn feeling stiff all over, her throat parched.
She was walking to the kitchen to fetch a glass of water when
she felt the premonitory tremors come over her. She collapsed
onto the tiled floor and, in the nearly instantaneous awakening

---

* Traditional Argentine beverage—an infusion of yerba maté leaves also known as
"Jesuit's tea," served in a gourd and drunk through a *bombilla*, a silver straw.

of her inner eye, saw a burly man sporting a small, clipped mustache standing in front of her. He was wearing a brown parka and black pants, his body half-hidden behind a blue Renault. The man was emptying his 9 mm submachine gun into her.

In shock, Julia saw the blood spurting out as she watched herself falling to the ground. She had just enough time to glimpse the man with the thin mustache get into the front seat of a green Chevrolet and speed off before she was disconnected from her source. When she came to, she was staring at her hands and crying, struggling in Theo's embrace as he tried in vain to soothe her.

Mama Fina arrived immediately afterward. She crouched down next to Julia, took firm hold of her hands, and asked Theo to leave them. Then, once she was sure they couldn't be heard, she asked Julia in the same firm voice she would have used with a child: "Julia, what did you see?"

8.

THE SOURCE

Austral Autumn
1974

Instantly she calmed down. Now she understood. She refused to say anything, claiming she'd simply felt faint. She wanted to give herself a moment to recover her composure. Above all, she didn't want to arouse Theo's suspicions. He was waiting anxiously for her, puzzled by Mama Fina's brusque reaction. Julia went back and snuggled up in his arms again, reassured him, and pretended to fall asleep.

It was only after Theo had left the house that she confided in Mama Fina. Julia was extremely pale. "I'm certain it was his car," she said.

"I'm sure you're right, but that doesn't mean he was your source."

Julia racked her brain with painful intensity. "In any case, the car wasn't parked in a slum. I can see the street clearly, and it's not in Villa 31. It looks more like a street in Liniers . . . or Mataderos. I don't know, maybe it's someplace I've never been."

"What about the man with the mustache? Would you be able to recognize him?"

"Absolutely, if he were standing in front of me!" Julia answered without hesitating. "But I'm sure I've never seen him before. I could try to draw him if you like."

He was a man with delicate features—quite a good-looking fellow, with big eyes and thick, dark eyebrows. He had his hair parted on one side, an impeccably drawn mustache over thin lips, and a slight double chin that aged him. Mama Fina went out with Julia's sketch in her pocket. She left her some freshly brewed maté and orders to rest. But Julia did nothing of the sort. She couldn't just sit there. What if it was already too late?

Julia headed to Retiro, near the railroad line, where she knew she might find Father Mugica. She went into Villa 31 and wandered through the maze of shacks piled up against each other, bag clasped firmly under her arm. By now she was a regular visitor. She recognized faces; a few children called out to her by name. She went up to them, one after another, to ask if they knew where Father Mugica was. No one had seen him. Then she went to the Chapel of Christ the Worker but had no luck there either.

Julia realized it was already quite late. She glanced at her watch. Theo would be arriving at Mama Fina's any moment now. He went with her every day to the cooperative to open up the health center. She had no way to get in touch with him. Never mind. She would just have to do the return trip twice.

When she got home, it was Theo who gave her the information she needed. "He's probably at home, at his parents' place in calle Gelly y Obes," he told her.

He wanted to know why she was in such urgent need of Father Carlos's assistance. Julia claimed that some drugs had gone missing from the health center and she needed him to go with her to the police station.

"You go to Retiro," Theo said, taking charge of the situation. "I'll see if I can find him at his place. We'll meet up at the health center."

Theo knew nothing of Julia's journeys or the strange lineage to which she belonged. She hadn't attempted to explain it to him for fear he would think she was mad. Theo knew Julia had occasional fainting fits, but he simply thought she suffered from low blood pressure, quite common in young women, according to Gabriel.

In fact, it had taken Julia a very long time to accept that she was normal. She had kept to herself as a child, fearing she would go into a trance at school and people would think she was crazy. It was only recently that she'd really begun to open up to other people, and this mainly because of Theo. But her newfound confidence was also the result of maturity. She had learned to exercise some control over her departures into trance, and Mama Fina, who embraced her role as mentor, pushed Julia increasingly to take the initiative and make contact with her sources.

A few months previously, Julia had been tempted to share her secret with Theo. Each time she'd hinted at it, though, Theo had made fun of her, until one day he had rebuffed her outright. "Look, I'm a rational being. Only fools buy all this stuff about premonitions and clairvoyance!"

Julia had been shaken, and all her childish insecurity had resurfaced painfully. It had even occurred to her that perhaps she had inherited a deformity, not a gift.

She had only recently managed to articulate her unease. How could she not rebel against being involuntarily projected into the critical moment in another person's life? Why should she agree to get mixed up in somebody else's private life? It was no longer the fear of being judged by Theo that dogged her. On the contrary, since she'd decided to keep her secret from him, Julia felt more adult, so to speak. It was the realization that her power was backfiring on her and profoundly affecting her own freedom.

This latest journey had been a traumatic experience. Did she really have a choice in the face of the terrible crime she had foreseen? Could she escape this appointment with someone else's fate, the outcome of which filled her with such dread?

Mama Fina had turned up at the cooperative health center. She wanted to tell Julia what she'd found out so far based on her sketch but instinctively realized her granddaughter was in no state to listen to her. Julia had launched into a self-accusing monologue. Mama Fina stayed stone-faced, waiting for the right moment to speak up. But Julia mistook Mama Fina's silence for condescension. Confused, she paused, struggling with mixed feelings of shame and anger.

Mama Fina broke in before she could get any more bogged down. "We're on our own, my little Julia," she said. "There's no instruction manual. With or without the gift, we all face the same difficult condition of living with the awareness of our own mortality, even as we believe ourselves to be eternal. We all have a longing to break free from the shackles of time. But you and I know from experience that there are escape routes, that freedom is possible."

"But I don't feel any freer than anyone else!" Julia retorted.

"You might not be freer than anyone else, but you know you can be. Each time you go on a journey, the other person's prospect gives you a different perspective on your own life. What you see affects your own feelings and feeds your innermost thoughts. You have learned to recognize elements of your own existence in that of your source. And because you've already acted as a catalyst, you know that destiny does not unfold before our eyes like a predetermined musical score but like a spring of ever-changing possibilities. It's within this choice that we fashion our own identity. We are masters of our destiny, in the truest sense of the term."

"But I *don't* have a choice! I'm subject to the whims of an inner eye that barges into my happiness to project me into other people's unhappiness!"

"Make no mistake, Julia, you always have a choice. You can refuse to make use of your inner eye. Or you can develop your gift."

"I didn't choose it, Mama Fina, and neither did you, so how can you talk about freedom?"

"You didn't choose to be born, either, or to be a woman. But that doesn't make you any less free. Because regardless of the kind of person you are by nature, you exercise your freedom by making the fundamental choice of who you want to be. It is because we can reinvent ourselves at any time that we are free—to act and react, to feel, and to think in a totally different way."

Theo arrived. Carlos Mugica hadn't been at the church of San Francisco Solano all day. But Theo had left a message for him in the hope that he would call back later. Julia felt unwell and went to sit down. Theo assumed it was a repeat episode of the morning's low blood pressure. She buried herself in his arms, relieved he had come up with his own explanation.

"Let's go and say hi to my parents," Julia suggested. "We can stop by Villa Luro on the way and see if Father Carlos is there. That way I'll feel I've done something useful with my day."

Theo knew the route by heart. He often went with Gabriel to San Francisco Solano, where Father Mugica said Mass. They took the bus and got off a few stops early. The city was bathed in gold, perfect for an evening stroll, but to Theo's disappointment Julia was in a hurry. As they walked up calle Zelada hand in hand, Theo could feel Julia trembling. He stopped and looked at her: pale skin, black hair streaming over her shoulders, black eyes. He held back from kissing her. Julia didn't notice his emotion; she had caught sight of the church spire and quickened her step. The doors were closed and the building was in darkness. The sidewalks were empty. Julia spun around and her heart jumped: she was standing in the exact spot where the man with the thin mustache had emptied his gun into her.

"What's wrong?" Theo asked, taking her by the arm to steady her. "You're not pregnant, are you? The timing isn't exactly perfect, but I'd be the happiest man alive. . . ."

Julia's eyes sparkled with a strange intensity. She let him kiss her.

They spent the rest of the evening at Julia's parents' house. Anna was transfixed by her sister. She had to admit that Julia was completely transformed. She and Theo made an unsettling couple; they gave off so much energy it almost made Anna feel uncomfortable. From the moment of her arrival, Julia had been monopolized by her brothers, who fired questions at her from every angle. Eventually Anna took her sister off into the kitchen. They embraced with heavy hearts, not really knowing why. They wanted to talk to each other but couldn't recapture the language of their intimacy, perhaps in the confused sensation that their childhood was over.

The only one who understood their emotion was their father. He had been watching them and guessed at Anna's conflicting feelings because they resembled his own. Julia had become a woman, and he felt in this realization something of a paradise lost.

The next morning Julia was up at dawn. She wanted to stop by the Chapel of Christ the Worker again before going to school to see if she could speak to Father Mugica. This time she had better luck. She saw him from far off, in jeans and an old turtleneck, busy helping the *villeros** transport building materials to the site of a planned new community canteen. She suddenly felt stupid, unable to remember what she had come to say. The sun was climbing higher in the sky, giving the world a substance that diluted her visions.

Father Mugica saw her approaching and once again mistook her hesitation for embarrassment. He went up to her.

"Father, I'm sorry, but I have to talk to you. It's a matter of urgency and importance."

Father Mugica's eyes widened. "Do you want to meet me after school? I could come to the health center if you like. Or

* Inhabitants of the *villas miserias*.

you could come to Villa Luro this evening. I'll be saying Mass at San Francisco Solano."

Julia thought for a moment. "Father, I think I'll come to see you in Villa Luro. There'll be fewer people there, right?"

He smiled at her. "If you feel more comfortable in Villa Luro, that's fine by me."

Julia thanked him, adding: "I'll bring my grandmother along, if you don't mind."

Julia found a satisfied Mama Fina waiting in her green velvet armchair in the living room. She had gathered some new information. A high-ranking police officer friend, Commissioner-Major Angelini, had helped with her search. Mama Fina explained that they had known each other for years. She had warned him about a bombing conspiracy, which had been foiled as a result, and he had subsequently informed her of a raid by security forces to evict her *villeros* friends. She had seen to it that urgent measures were put in place to head off a potentially bloody clash. They were both from Naples, which gave them a sense of solidarity, given that the vast majority of *porteños** were of Genoese origin. Both were also members of the San Juan Evangelista parish in the neighborhood of La Boca.

* Inhabitants of Buenos Aires.

"It's possible your man is a small-time crook," Mama Fina burst out. "If your sketch is a realistic likeness, it bears a strong resemblance to a man known as El Pibe.* He has close links to the minister for social welfare."

"El Brujo, you mean?"

"Yes, exactly. He was kicked out of the police force a few years ago and reinstated recently out of the blue. He's just been promoted to subcommissioner. It's rumored he's recruiting professional marksmen for an organization they call the Triple A, which they want to keep under wraps."

"Mama Fina, I recognized the place. It's calle Zelada in Villa Luro, right across from the church of San Francisco Solano, where Father Mugica celebrates Mass on Saturday afternoons."

Mama Fina didn't hesitate. "We have to warn him."

"We're meeting him in two hours."

They arrived half an hour ahead of schedule. The blue Renault was parked diagonally on the sidewalk a few yards from the door of the church. Much as she wanted to, Julia didn't feel brave enough to confront her source. They agreed that Mama Fina would introduce the subject and then Julia would quickly describe what she had seen.

---

* Nickname given to Rodolfo Eduardo Almirón Sena, the principal suspect in the murder of Carlos Mugica and head of security for José López Rega ("El Brujo") at the time. He died in 2009 in a hospital in the city of Ezeiza, near Buenos Aires, while in prison awaiting trial.

Father Mugica was finishing a meeting with a number of couples preparing for marriage. He spotted Julia and Mama Fina and beckoned to them to come and join him in the sacristy.

He was sitting on a bench against the wall. The chasuble he would put on to celebrate Mass hung from a coat hanger on the door of a wooden cupboard. Dressed in his cassock, Mugica sat waiting for them, his hands resting on his knees. He pulled up a wicker chair, gestured to Mama Fina to take a seat, and invited Julia to sit beside him on the bench.

Mama Fina got straight to the point, offering as little explanation as possible and then drawing Julia into the conversation, so that all she had to do was describe what she had seen. Carlos Mugica listened attentively, without a single interruption. When Julia had finished her account, he remained silent for a long time, staring at the floor, breathing heavily.

"Yes, I've received threats." He got up and began to pace the room. Then, smiling almost defiantly, he added: "I'm not afraid of dying. I'm more afraid my bishop will expel me from the Church."

He started to laugh, then fell suddenly silent. He tried to look elsewhere and avoid what could only be a distressing train of thought.

"I respect Perón, and I know he respects me . . . but there are others who don't feel the same way."

He took a few minutes to recover his habitual calm, then

said slowly, "It would be a great honor for me to give my life in the service of those who are suffering. The Lord knows that I am ready."

He opened the door of the sacristy and gave them a dazzling smile. "Thank you for coming. I know you bear great love for me. That is the best gift you could give me."

9

THE NIGHTMARE

May 11, 1974

Julia hadn't slept a wink all night. She got up very early, even though she didn't have school that day, and went and sat by the fountain in the courtyard while she waited for Mama Fina to wake up. The sound of water chuckling over stone soothed her. She heard the clatter of plates in the kitchen and felt relieved. Her grandmother came out to join her just as a flock of sparrows invaded the courtyard. Mama Fina went up to the birds, the pockets of her apron filled with yesterday's rice, which she scattered with a practiced hand, then kissed her granddaughter. She too seemed quiet.

"We have to go and talk to him again," said Julia, on the verge of tears.

"*Mi amor*, we've done our part. He knows what he needs to know, and he is free to choose. If he wants to fight, he'll have to start by changing his habits. But it'll only be a reprieve, because the people who want to kill him won't give up. He'll have to leave Argentina."

"Then he must leave. We have to tell him! He's got no right to die; he has to be alive to help change things. If he dies, he'll be forgotten."

"Sometimes it's the memory of martyrs that gives others the strength to resist. A great nation cannot be built without examples of greatness."

"But it's awful to accept death like that, Mama Fina! It's selfish to sacrifice everything because you want to be a hero. Two years ago no one would have believed that Perón would come back to power. Two years from now maybe the people who are trying to kill Father Mugica will have every reason to want him alive. He'll have one moment in his life to escape death, one single moment, like Anna and Señora Pilar and Commissioner-Major Angelini, and all the other people you helped. You shouldn't despise life!"

"*Mi amor!* Don't be judgmental. No one can measure someone else's thirst for life. Knowing what's in store for us a little ahead of time gives us greater responsibility, not less. Whether it's now or later, everyone has the same choice in the face of death: to desire it, accept it, or try to escape it. I'm telling you this because it's important for you to learn not to feel guilty about the choices your sources make, even if you think they're wrong."

"I think I'm mad at him more than anything else. I'm disappointed in him. I thought he'd be more of a fighter."

"I have a lot of admiration for Father Carlos. I've seldom seen anyone so passionate. I can assure you he doesn't despise life. On the contrary, I think he holds it dearer than anybody else. But I also think he's made a fundamental choice, namely to give his life for others. Leaving the comforts of the Recoleta neighborhood to go into the slums is as powerful a cry of freedom as refusing to be afraid."

"He could refuse to be afraid and park his car somewhere else."

They left together, knowing exactly where they were going without the need for discussion. They made their way through La Boca, boarded a bus in San Telmo, and drove past the Obelisk as far as Plaza San Martín, where they got off and walked the rest of the way to Villa 31.

Father Mugica was playing football with a group of teenagers on the vacant lot behind the church. It had rained the previous day, and the ball kept stopping dead in puddles. The players were spattered with mud from head to toe. Large covered trucks moved along cautiously, swaying from side to side across the huge holes that littered the dirt road. Small children covered in soot, bare chested, and wearing battered shoes, backed away laughing and holding their noses, caught in the cloud of black smoke coming from the vehicles. A few older women stood looking on, hands on hips.

Mama Fina and Julia soon reached the health center. There

was no one there. Julia began to make an inventory of the drugs while Mama Fina went through the account books. The routine tasks masked the horrible sensation of watching over a person condemned to death.

In the afternoon they went back the way they had come, to attend Father Mugica's service. Sitting in the very last pew of San Francisco Solano, they observed every new arrival at the church. They stayed there until the little blue Renault had left calle Zelada. They took the same route each day that week, careful to keep out of sight so they wouldn't cause trouble for Father Mugica.

On Friday Theo was waiting for them as usual in Mama Fina's kitchen with cups of bitter maté. He usually got there before them, found the key in the flowerpot, and made himself at home. He had added a few leaves of fresh mint to the boiling water and was stirring it with a *bombilla*. As always, they ended up talking about politics.

"You never know what to think," said Theo. "Take Allende's death, for example . . ."

"We'll never know if it was an accident, suicide, or murder," Mama Fina replied.

"The justice system will never know because it doesn't want to know. But the people know."

"It's not impossible that he decided to kill himself, you know," Mama Fina added. "Perhaps he'd already considered it, and when he was faced with the facts, he took it as confirmation of what he'd planned."

"I don't believe that. There were far too many reasons for him to carry on living. The people loved him. . . ." Theo paused, then went on: "Closer to home, take the death of Juan García Elorrio. It was apparently a car accident. But a lot of people wanted to silence him. He was the editor of *Christianity and Revolution*. Either way, the magazine didn't survive his death."

"So your theory is that he was assassinated?"

"Yes. Everyone knew he was very influential. He was the one who named the first Montoneros cell after Camilo Torres."

"Camilo Torres?" asked Julia.

"Yes, the Colombian priest. He joined the guerrillas but was gunned down by the army during their first ambush."

Julia began to sweat profusely, even though it was a cool evening. Theo and Mama Fina exchanged a knowing look and put her to bed. Theo said good-bye, feeling worried.

The next day Mama Fina and Julia spent the morning at the Villa 31 cooperative. Señora Pilar had resigned, and they urgently needed to find someone to replace her. Mama Fina was backing one of her former recruits who had applied for the position, but the woman clearly did not have the respect of her coworkers. The matter dragged on.

Julia was growing impatient. It was a gorgeous day, and she didn't want to be stuck indoors. Besides, she was keen to watch a football match that the *villeros* were playing in Retiro that same day, Saturday, May 11. The match was due to start at half past two and she had just enough time to get there. She gathered up her things and left a note for Mama Fina.

All the players on Father Mugica's team, La Bomba, had found themselves uniforms. They looked good. By the time Julia arrived the match had already begun, and the atmosphere was festive. The whole neighborhood had turned out. Street vendors were selling fried food and soda. Small groups of stout middle-aged women were standing around, bundled up in sweaters. Old men, beers in hand, smoked with an air of rediscovered youth, while children played alongside them, throwing an imaginary ball to each other and performing amazing acrobatics. Everyone had managed to wear something in their team's colors. The fans were going wild, waving banners and chanting insults about the opposing team. La Bomba broke every record and Father Mugica played like a professional, weaving in and out, sidestepping, and jumping better than the younger players.

He left after the match, dripping with sweat and obviously in a hurry. He teased Julia as he went by with a "Hello, my guardian angel!" which made her blush. All the same, she took the opportunity to tell him she would also be coming to the seven o'clock Mass that evening.

"Like you have every day for the past month," he said, giving her a wink. He was in an excellent mood. He took her by the shoulders and walked some of the way with her. "Don't worry about me," he said. "It's too beautiful a day for it to be my last."

———

Julia was about to leave for Villa Luro when Mama Fina opened the door. She came in like a whirlwind of energy, wanting to hear all about the match. Mama Fina took football very seriously, even local amateur games. She had witnessed the growth of the Boca Juniors, nicknamed Los Xeneizes, in her own neighborhood and had long been a member of La 12, the team's *barra brava*.* Julia checked her watch. It was ten minutes to seven. With a bit of luck, they would get there before the service ended.

It was already dark by the time they got the bus to Villa Luro. The traffic was moving slowly. Julia hadn't accounted for that possibility. As they neared the church, they realized something had happened. Police cars blocked the street. Bystanders were talking about a murder attempt. Father Mugica had been taken in an ambulance to Salaberry Hospital in Mataderos. He was still in the operating theater. People were saying the outlook wasn't good. A growing murmur filled the street. Agonized members of the congregation were explaining to the many curious passersby that he had been riddled with bullets by an unknown man as he left the church after evening Mass. The man had fired his submachine gun at point-blank range and wounded two other people in the process. A woman who seemed to relive the scene as she

* Overzealous supporters of the Boca Juniors.

talked described the stranger as a man with a Chinese-style mustache.

Father Mugica's death was announced to the crowd at ten o'clock that night. The multitude that had gathered outside the church of San Francisco Solano made no move to leave, frozen in stubborn, irrational expectation. Finally, at midnight, a few members of the Movement of Priests for the Third World, which Mugica had belonged to, said Mass in front of the ever-growing crowd, which stayed there until the following day.

At dawn Julia made her way to the d'Uccellos' house. Tears stuck strands of her hair to her face, but she made no attempt to remove them. Mama Fina wiped Julia's cheeks before knocking on the door. She looked straight at her with her clear eyes. "You did everything you could."

Julia shook her head. "No, I should have been there."

10.

THE COUP D'ÉTAT

March 29, 1976

Julia and Theo found a room to rent in the Saavedra neighborhood, in a boardinghouse run by an old woman who
was sullen and uncommunicative at the best of times. Rosa
had told them about the place. The rent was cheap, and the
window of their room looked out on a pretty little square
with a solitary tree, huge and beautiful, and a bench.

After Father Mugica's death, Julia and Theo's life took an
unexpected turn. The press reported that Mugica had had a
public quarrel with Mario Firmenich, the leader of the Montoneros, a few weeks before he was murdered. Public opinion
immediately turned against the organization, and its leaders
began to be persecuted. With the death of Perón three weeks
later, at the beginning of July, the situation worsened. He was
replaced by Isabel Perón in her capacity as vice president,
and El Brujo took control behind the scenes. The Triple A

stepped up its criminal activity, and the number of disappearances increased.

In September 1974 the Montoneros went underground. Julia and Theo found their lives turned upside down. Friends were arrested by the security forces and then disappeared. Sinister stories began to spread; there was talk of torture and murder. It was said the Triple A was being trained by former Gestapo officers. The order was given to compartmentalize information, to minimize contact between members of the organization, and to change addresses.

Some of Theo's fellow engineering students at the University of Buenos Aires had been detained. Fear gripped the campus. It was clear that the government was carrying out a raid, and the students were the first in line. Theo dropped out and Julia began looking for a job. They decided to live together, not only to obey orders but also to protect Mama Fina. Julia and Theo moved in together in September 1975, exactly one year to the day after the organization had gone underground.

Mama Fina insisted on celebrating Julia's eighteenth birthday before she left the family home. She wanted to mark the occasion, not only because Julia had come of age but above all because her granddaughter was about to start life as part of a couple, and without getting married at that. It wasn't a question of propriety as far as Mama Fina was concerned. She understood that the younger generation had made freedom in love their credo. But she was convinced that one's choice of partner was a fundamental decision that necessarily involved a change of identity. This change was not confined to a new name, as people were inclined to believe. It involved primarily a transformation in the personality of each partner. To become one with another through love required a process of reflection. And the ceremony, the vows, the preparations, the family gathering—all of it helped construct this new identity. From experience, Mama Fina believed that words exchanged at crucial moments of life worked in a mystical way, as shields against adversity or catalysts for doubt and difficulty. She would have liked Julia and Theo to have this time for reflection, not so they would have the opportunity to back out but so they could become grounded.

For this reason she was adamant that Julia should at least receive a priest's blessing. She wanted to see them start their new life bathed in words that would protect them in their love, surrounded by people who would do them good. Mama Fina invited the whole family, as well as a crowd of neighbors and *villeros*. Neither Gabriel's school friends from the days of the meetings with Father Mugica nor Theo's college friends were invited. Mama Fina made a point of keeping politics out of it. Only Rosa made the cut, because she arrived on Gabriel's arm.

The girls from the cooperative had filled the house with yellow roses and hydrangeas. The courtyard had been arranged for dancing and strung with blue and yellow streamers that fluttered in the wind. The tables were decorated with pretty baskets filled with mixed candies dusted with powdered sugar. Mama Fina was wearing her midnight blue dress and a flower brooch set with yellow amethysts and diamonds. She had hired a youth from the neighborhood football club to be in charge of the record player. He came dressed in the colors of the Boca Juniors.

Julia knew Mama Fina hadn't done it on purpose, but it wouldn't have taken much to make her think she was at a gathering of the *hinchada*. It was a good thing she had chosen not to wear the blue flowered dress the cooperative had given her: she would have felt like part of the decor.

Theo stood off to the side, watching her. Julia looked sublime. She was wearing a red satin dress that flared at the hips, emphasizing her bosom and waistline. With her pearly skin and black hair, she was bewitching. He asked her to dance, determined to keep her to himself for the rest of the evening. Julia spotted Mama Fina deep in conversation with her father in the living room. She slipped away when the next dance ended and went to join them, out of breath. Crouching down beside them, she kissed their hands.

"You are our most precious treasure," her father told her. Theo tugged at her arm and then she was back in the courtyard, dancing on a cloud. The stars were aligned that day.

Anna and the twins arrived shortly afterward, escorted by a group of musician friends. The young people took over the courtyard and sang Mercedes Sosa songs until dawn.

Julia's father came to see her at Mama Fina's a few days later. They spent an entire afternoon strolling around together, hand in hand. He wanted to convince her to enroll at the college and study medicine. Julia came straight out and told him her fears: even though she had never committed any acts of warfare, she was considered a member of the Montoneros, and Theo was the head of their network.

The previous year, Theo's cell had been asked to collect information about the movements, habits, and daily routine of the brothers Juan and Jorge Born. They later realized that this information had been used to facilitate the brothers' kidnapping. The Borns were the majority shareholders in one of the country's largest grain companies. Two people had been killed during the operation: the Borns' driver and a friend who was with them when they were kidnapped. The Montoneros had secured an enormous ransom of more than sixty million dollars for their release, and now the military was after them.

Julia's father understood. He didn't utter a word of reproach or ask her any more questions. His only request was that she go and work with his brother, her uncle Rafael, who owned a large pharmacy on the corner of Plaza de Mayo. Rafael was an extremely cautious man and a Peronist sympathizer. Julia's father could think of no one more appropriate to watch over his daughter.

Julia accepted the idea on the spot. Her experience running the Villa 31 health center was ample justification for being hired to work in a pharmacy without arousing suspicion.

Theo and Julia entertained the hope that the organization's security measures would be enough to wipe out their traces. They constructed a sealed-off world with no visitors and no outings, not even on weekends. Their sole luxury was the purchase of a secondhand guitar. Theo played and Julia sang, and they spent their free time practicing as a duo. But their isolation was beginning to weigh on them. Even their food had lost its flavor.

One evening Theo and Julia plucked up the courage to travel all the way from Saavedra to La Boca to surprise Mama Fina. It was the end of summer. The temperature had dropped a few degrees, and the weather was mild. But the city was deserted. When they got to Mama Fina's, they found her glued to the radio. Isabel Martínez de Perón had just been overthrown by a military junta under General Videla's command. Mama Fina looked distraught. Julia intuitively felt that the situation was serious, though she couldn't say exactly why. Theo went to prepare maté. The three of them drank in silence, listening to the news bulletins that kept repeating the same official statement. They agreed it would be safer for Julia and Theo to spend the night at Mama Fina's.

When they woke, Mama Fina took Julia aside. She seemed anxious. Her eyes were unnaturally pale, as if they had been leached of all color.

"Leave your guitar here. It'll be an excuse for you to come back."

Night had just fallen when Julia returned to calle Pinzón.

11.

THE VISE

———

Austral Winter
1976

Elegantly dressed in a navy suit and white blouse, Mama Fina sat toying with her pearl necklace as she waited for Julia in her living room. They sat facing each other, so close that their knees were touching.

"It's the inner eye again, *mi amor.*"

"Yes, I thought so. Tell me."

"It was you. I recognized your face. You were walking toward a toilet bowl at the end of a long, narrow room. You bent over it. I saw your face reflected in the water."

"Are you sure it was me?"

"Absolutely certain. There was a skylight above your head, and your reflection was clear. You threw up. Everything. Bile and blood."

Julia gave a faint smile.

"When you turned around, I realized it was a prison. A man opened the door of the cell; he was wearing a uniform. I think he was a police corporal. I went to check this morning with my friend Angelini, but he wasn't at the station. I'll go back tomorrow. I'm not as good at drawing as you are, but I'll do a sketch. I got a good look at his face. He had a round head and pockmarked skin. It must have been evening, because the corridor light was on."

They leaned even closer to each other.

"He spoke to you very harshly and you crouched down on the floor. He kept striking you with the butt of his rifle. Then he turned around abruptly and left, leaving the door ajar. You hesitated for quite some time, then you climbed onto the toilet and looked out through the skylight before going out into the corridor. There was another cell next to yours with two women lying on the floor, covered in blood and with open wounds. They must have been unconscious, because when you shook the bars of the door, they didn't react. There were several doors on the other side of the corridor. You pressed your face against the three doors at the far end and whispered into each cell, then you ran to the fourth door and banged on it furiously. You stopped suddenly, raced back to your cell, and sat down where you'd been sitting before.

"Three guards came running. The one who'd hit you locked the door of your cell while the others hurried to open the fourth door. You could see everything from where you were sitting, because it was diagonally across from you.

"*Mi amor*, I'm sure I recognized Theo. But he was totally disfigured. He must have been conscious, because he was trying to say something, but his eyes and lips were swollen, and his nose had been broken. He couldn't walk on his own. Two of the guards held him up while your guard hit him repeatedly. They dragged him to the end of the corridor, to the top of a staircase. . . ."

"And then?"

"That's all I saw."

Julia was livid. She felt overcome by an inexplicable anger. All she wanted to do was run away and shout that it wasn't true, that it wasn't her, and it wasn't Theo.

"What do you expect me to do about your vision, Mama Fina? I don't even know what you're talking about!"

Mama Fina hugged her close, despite Julia's reluctance to be held. She had done as she always did. She couldn't spare her the shock.

"There's no room for emotions in this equation. We both know that what I saw you will see in the future. We have to prepare for it."

"Yes," Julia conceded, trying to pull herself together.

"It was a prison: a cell, guards, metal bars."

"Yes," Julia repeated.

"We also know that Videla has seized power and that his objective is to wipe Peronism off the face of the earth."

"Yes."

"Therefore, if Theo and you are arrested, you won't come back alive."

Julia remained silent.

"My vision could become reality the moment you leave here. We don't know if we'll have another chance to discuss it."

"Yes, Mama Fina," Julia said, realizing her grandmother had already come up with a plan.

"First you'll need to memorize the images I just described. That way, when you're throwing up in your cell and you see your reflection in the water, with the light from the skylight behind you, you'll remember that on the night when the corporal comes to beat you, you'll have a few minutes to make your escape."

"I won't leave without Theo."

"Okay, but you know where he'll be and in what state."

"I won't leave without him."

"Focus on getting out, period. Even if you and Theo are both stark naked. In my experience, it's little things like these that can block our survival instinct."

"You think these are little things, what you're describing to me?"

"Fear of being cold, wet, thirsty, of cockroaches, of hiding . . . They know how to break a prisoner's morale. You'll have to fight against yourself if you want to make it out of there."

"Right, okay," Julia said, concentrating, "the skylight, the cell door . . ."

"You'll have to become invisible. Don't talk to anyone; don't ask anyone for help. When the police get their hands on escaped prisoners, it's always due to some informant. . . . And above all, you must not come back here, because the police or the military will have posted agents throughout the neighborhood."

"Okay, I understand."

"Now we need to find ourselves a go-between. Because you'll have to leave Argentina."

"What! Leave Argentina? No way! I'm going to fight right here, in my country. I'll go into hiding, they won't find me, I'll . . ."

"You see how hard it is, *mi amor*? All the same, you and Theo will have to go and live somewhere else. And we must start looking immediately for a way to smuggle you out. Ideally you'd be able to leave before they come looking for you."

"Theo would never agree!"

Mama Fina remained lost in thought for a moment. She rested her washed-out eyes on Julia: "We have no choice."

They decided that, for want of a better solution, their two go-betweens would be Señora Pilar and Rosa. They agreed not to say anything to Theo until they had something more concrete to go on. He had no inkling of danger. He was convinced that by moving to Saavedra he had become like a submarime retracting its periscope.

———

Everything changed the night Gabriel knocked on their door. It was nearly two in the morning. His face was twisted with anxiety. He had walked nonstop all the way from Posadas Hospital to their place.

"They arrived in several cars, before midnight," he explained in a halting voice. "I was heading back from the bathroom; they didn't see me. Rogelio was at the front desk. They hit him, hard. Then they handcuffed him, pulled a hood over his head, and shoved him into a car. They also took Vlado, who was on the second floor, and Augusto, who was working in the hospital's print room. He's a friend; he came to a lot of our meetings with Mugica. Do you remember?"

"I know exactly who you mean," Theo murmured.

"He was working later than usual. We were supposed to be going home together. He lives in Mataderos too. The fourth car stayed behind while they searched all the departments. I hid in a basket of dirty linens in the laundry room. I'm sure it was me they were looking for."

Theo struggled to pacify his brother. Gabriel showered, changed, packed a bag with some clothes Theo lent him, and took all the cash the three of them could scrape together.

"The vise is tightening around the three of us. We have to get out of Argentina," he told them.

Gabriel knew some French nuns who were assisting people in going into exile. He would go see them. He thought they might hide him and help get him out of Buenos Aires. Gabriel asked Theo to inform Rosa. She knew where the convent was; he wanted her to join him there.

When Gabriel had left, Julia spoke openly and for the first time about preparing for their own departure. Mama Fina knew some people at the port and Julia had learned that she had made contact with an Italian network. They needed to make arrangements as quickly as possible. She thought they could probably stow away on a ship leaving for North America or Europe.

Theo felt terribly guilty about what had happened to his brother. He thought it was his fault. As the head of a Montoneros unit, he had placed his entire family in danger. He had to help them all leave at the earliest possible opportunity.

"I'll go to the port tomorrow to explore what options there are," Theo announced. "And I'll stop by Rosa's place after work."

The thought of having a plan lifted his spirits. Julia chose that moment to tell him she was pregnant. "God willing, our baby will be here in time for the new year."

Theo leaped into the air and shouted for joy, taking her completely by surprise. He twirled her in his arms, then drew her into a dance, exactly as they had on the evening they'd first met.

In the morning they went to work full of optimism conferred by their happy news. Julia was going to drop by Mama

Fina's on her way to the pharmacy, and they would meet back at their place to take stock of the situation and make decisions. Theo also wanted to buy a bottle of wine and some flowers for a romantic celebration of the happy news.

It was early when Julia let herself in at Mama Fina's. She found her in the kitchen with a pile of papers and maps spread out over the table. Mama Fina had all the details about an Italian escape network. They would be ferried across the Río de la Plata by Uruguayan smugglers; from there they would set sail for Europe with new identities. An entire network of Italian families, especially in the south of the country, had made arrangements to receive the exiles and help them find jobs and somewhere to live. Their new passports and tickets had to be paid for up front, but Mama Fina would take care of that.

"I'll leave the smuggler's contact details with Señora Pilar," said Mama Fina. "Go and see her tomorrow. You must make the crossing before the end of the week."

Then, on an impulse, she added: "I'll leave some money in an envelope addressed to you with Father Miguel, the one who came to bless you on your birthday. You can then contact my friend Captain Torricelli of the *Donizetti*. You should find him at the port . . . You never know. Best not to put all your eggs in one basket."

"Where does Father Miguel live?"

"You'll find him at the church."

"San Juan Evangelista?"

"That's right."

"Okay, in that case I'll go and ask him for a second blessing. . . . The baby might need one," Julia said, her voice rising almost to a shriek.

"Really? It can't be true! Tell me you're not joking!"

"It is true," Julia replied, hugging her. "You're going to be a grandmother again."

"Great-grandmother, you mean!"

Mama Fina was transformed. She took her granddaughter's hands in hers. "Let's hope it's a boy!"

"Oh, no! I want it to be a little girl! I want her to be exactly like you, with your eyes!"

The two women clung to each other, unable to say good-bye. When Julia finally picked up her bag to leave, Mama Fina stopped her one last time. Making the sign of the cross on Julia's forehead, she said, "I think it is best that you know. From what I understand, there's a young police officer who apparently looks like the man in my sketch. He's just been assigned to the station in Castelar."

"Which means . . . ?" Julia asked slowly.

"That's where the military interrogate political prisoners."

"Oh, my God!" exclaimed Julia.

"You know too that Angelini and I are very close. . . ."

"Since the whole Señora Pilar affair?"

"Oh, long before that, *mi amor*. We were still children."

"So?"

"So . . ."

———

Julia left in a rush to go to the pharmacy. She reached Plaza de Mayo and hurried in, apologizing. Her uncle Rafael, who was waiting for her, looked at her understandingly. She went to get her white coat, which was hanging on a peg in the back of the shop. Hearing the sound of voices, protests from her uncle, and the crash of breaking glass, Julia came out to see what was going on, hastily buttoning her coat as she did so. Two men threw themselves at her, grabbed hold of her, and dragged her out to the big green Ford Falcon parked at the entrance to the pharmacy. They shoved her inside, forcing her to lie facedown on the floor, and took their seats, trampling her with their heavy boots. The car took off before they had shut the doors. As soon as they were moving, the men fell on her, slapping and insulting her, touching her everywhere as they frisked her. One of them grabbed her by the hair, yanked her head back, and spat into her face: "You're going to die, you filthy Trotsky whore. But before you die, we're going to make you talk."

They wanted names, addresses, the whole network. "You're going to tell us everything," they snarled at her.

The car finally came to a stop in an open-air parking lot in the middle of a building site. They forced her to get out, kicking and hitting her with the butts of their rifles. There was another Ford Falcon parked alongside, its trunk wide open. Rosa was standing between the two cars with her hands tied behind her back. Her eyes were swollen and her cheeks were purple, like split figs. Mascara was running down her face.

Some men pushed Rosa into the trunk of the car. She made no attempt to struggle. Julia was kicked in the stomach and again on the back of her neck. Doubled over, she was forced into the trunk with Rosa. Before it was shut, Julia heard them say: "We've found your boyfriend, Trotska. You can thank your friend here."

12.

THE FAIRFIELD INN

Boreal Autumn

2006

The car takes off. The pungent odor of the exhaust fumes makes her throat burn. She has to chase away the memories. She is facing a different time, a different anxiety, a different pain. More intense. Yet Julia knows this is impossible.

Theo picks up speed, brakes, then accelerates again. The first traffic light. Another left turn and he'll be on the ramp to the freeway. The feel of driving on asphalt gives way to the sound of tires on textured concrete. So he is actually going to the office. What if all her suspicions were wrong? What if Theo wasn't the source, and the young woman dressed in black had nothing to do with them? Theo slows down. He takes advantage of the traffic to make a phone call. Julia can hear the phone ringing into the void through the car's stereo system. He redials. No answer—voice mail: "My love, I'll be in meetings out of the office. I love you. I'll call you as soon as I'm done." He turns on some music and speeds up again.

Julia can feel her temples throbbing. She is curled up in a ball; she tries to steady her breathing, as if Theo could hear her.

The car turns, slows down, and stops. Theo waits for a moment, then picks up his phone again. This time the engine is switched off, so the speakers aren't connected. She can hear him texting. Theo gets out of the car. He forgets to lock it. The doors will lock automatically in a few minutes' time. Julia waits, counting the time in her head. Finally she pushes the seat forward a little and manages to peer out. She recognizes the vast parking lot next to the business complex where Theo works.

Her spirits rise. After all, it's quite possible that this is all a series of unfortunate coincidences. She waits in the trunk, ashamed and at a loss for what to do. Should she come out of hiding, go back home, and finish her work? She nods off briefly, exhausted by her emotions, tired of the thoughts going round in circles in her head. She is just about to get ready to get out when she hears voices approaching. The car shakes as the doors are opened and shut. Theo starts the engine and gradually accelerates. The person sitting next to him is a woman. Julia hears her laugh. She can't tell what they are saying; the vibration in the trunk muffles their voices.

After a short but fast trip, the car comes to a stop again. Theo and the woman get out, slamming the doors. Julia listens as their footsteps grow fainter on the asphalt, hears the click of the remote locking system. She quickly pushes the seat forward and pokes her head out, leaning on her elbows. Theo is walking away, hand in hand with a slender woman in a dark green suit, her black hair pulled into a chignon. She walks confidently in black high heels. They push the revolving door that leads into the lobby of an inn. Theo lets the woman go ahead, his hand on her waist. He glances back instinctively.

Julia can't take her eyes off them. She watches them disappear and remains motionless, barely breathing, staring straight ahead, her mind blank.

She looks away, her gaze seeking to alight somewhere else, on her hands, on her ugly gray tracksuit. It hurts less than she expected. She doesn't feel anything, just her heart beating faster. And emptiness. A hollowness in her stomach. She feels her soul seeping out of her solar plexus. She digs three fingers into her stomach to hold it in.

With an effort, Julia gets out of the car, walks toward the hotel, and summons the concierge. *If I come face-to-face with Theo, so much the better.*

The young man in a gray uniform makes a point of speaking to her as if he can't see her.

"Your taxi will be here in a few minutes," he assures her, and plunges back into his routine.

She has to find something to occupy herself, so she pretends to be interested in the financial papers and the real estate magazines. *I'm going to die.* She raises her eyes, surprised to find them brimming with tears. *I'm drowning in self-pity. I can't do this.* She sees herself sliding down; any minute now she'll be curling up on the floor.

"Ma'am, your taxi's waiting."

When she turns to thank the young man, all trace of emotion is gone from her face. She flashes him a radiant smile; intimidated, the employee lowers his gaze.

Julia walks gracefully toward the car. "Drop me at the train station," she says calmly.

Out of the corner of her eye, she notices a young woman in a dark green suit coming out of the hotel and slipping into another taxi just behind her own. She can't help feeling a hint of satisfaction at the thought that she's still one step ahead.

13.

THE RETURN

End of the Boreal Summer

2006

The thirteenth of the month and a Friday, as it happens. She had to find out today, of all days. It's just a coincidence. Mama Fina used to pretend she didn't care, but she made a point never to schedule anything important on that day. No matter. Julia feels serene. She chose to know. It was what she wanted. It's not a stroke of fate. The truth was essential for her. Lying was at its core an act of contempt and unbearable condescension. In a way, she and Theo are even now.

Julia looks out the window as the familiar stations slip by, one after another. This is her train line, the one she takes home from New York after work meetings. The farther they get from the city, the more scattered the buildings become; skyscrapers give way to big houses overlooking marinas, which in turn are replaced by small provincial towns, home to BJ's and Home Depots.

Julia sees the sea recede and then return. Near Bridgeport

the red-and-white-striped chimney pours smoke into a clear sky. The train doesn't stop at the station but loops around at speed, skirting the coast.

Like when she saw Theo again for the first time after all the years of silence, at the beginning of 2002. They needed to go out into the street to avoid being alone together in an intimacy they both feared. They walked instinctively toward the water, passing under the High Line in Manhattan's Meatpacking District. But at four o'clock in the morning, the rusted structure of the abandoned railway had a dismal air. They went past it with relief, but by the time they reached the waterfront, they still hadn't managed to break the silence.

A cold wind began to blow from the north. They moved closer together.

"I've dreamed of this moment so often," Julia said, watching the tossing of the waves. "But now I don't know if it makes sense anymore."

"Let's not overthink it, Julia."

"But I have to try to understand what happened to us."

Theo placed a finger on her lips to silence her. "Look at the sea, Julia. It's been faithful to me for nearly half a century now. It reminds me who I am."

"It's been my constant companion too. But I'm no longer the same person."

The lights of the city were reflected in the water like so many black stars.

"And you? Who are you?" Julia asked him.

Theo stared, fascinated, at the stretch of dark water between the banks of the estuary. "I'm cursed," he murmured, as if he were the only person in the whole world.

Julia shivered and turned up the collar of her coat. "You don't have the right to say that."

"It's not about having the right, Julia," Theo replied.

"You're not a victim. You're a survivor, Theodoro."

He turned to Julia, his face contorted. He was practically yelling. "Don't you get it? My brother is dead, my mother, my father. All because of me."

Julia took his hand: "Not because of you, Theo. Because of their love for you!"

He jerked his hand free and pushed her away. "Love? What is love? It's just a meaningless word."

She watched him for a long time, then walked in pain slowly away, back along the piers toward the lights of the avenue. A taxi went by, empty. The huge billboards from December were still up, brightly lit as if by mistake. When she reached the intersection, blinking under the orange glow of the streetlights, she decided to go home.

Theo ran after her and caught up. He stood in front of her, helpless, panting.

"Please. . . . Teach me again about love."

Julia leans against the window of the carriage as the train passes by the little town of Stratford. The gray blue painted houses flash past, the white clock tower, the bridges, the boats, the roads, the street life. She couldn't care less. All she can see is Theo.

They woke up happy the next morning. They had made plans all night. She would come back and he would meet Ulysses. Finally giving in to hunger, they left the house in Chelsea and headed for the French bakery on the corner, where they sat like lovers at one of the small, out-of-the-way tables. Theo couldn't stop talking. He wanted to buy a house with a big fireplace and a garden full of flowers. He wanted a motorcycle. And he wanted a dog that would sit by his side while he looked at the stars.

"I haven't had a home since. I've been living like a nomad all this time."

Julia kissed him softly. Theo pulled away to add: "Because I could only ever have a home with you, Julia."

Julia felt scared. Life couldn't be that perfect.

They spent the entire afternoon wandering around, getting to know each other again, laughing again like children. Along the way, they stopped outside the gates of Our Lady of Guadalupe on Fourteenth Street. They took the stairs two at a time, clowning around, and found themselves inside the church almost unintentionally. A Mexican couple was getting married, and the families were standing in the chancel. The bride was wearing an organza dress buried under silver sequins and an embroidered mantilla on her head.

Julia and Theo knelt for a moment, then went back out in silence. The noise of the city took them by surprise. Theo sought refuge in the doorway of a building and pulled Julia in with him.

"I just made a wish."

Julia blushed.

"I want to marry you."

"In thirty years' time?" she answered slyly, kissing him.

She steps off the train into the bustle of the station and allows herself to be swept along by the rising tide of people. Lost in her own world, she finds herself alone on the sidewalk outside the station. She turns left like a robot, her feet finding the way home automatically. She crosses roads without stopping and nearly gets run over by a driver who leans on his horn. She comes to a stop in front of some railings with no idea what she's doing there. On the other side rows of cars fill the huge parking lot outside IKEA. Her fingers grip the bars. She is overwhelmed by a feeling of powerlessness. Annoyed, she moves away and makes an effort to fill her lungs with fresh air, resumes her path, steps up her pace.

———

Julia didn't expect the meeting between Ulysses and Theo to go so badly. The three of them met up in the spring. Ulysses wanted to visit New York, and Theo could get there easily. They took the ferry to the Statue of Liberty and stopped at Ellis Island.

Theo was dragging his feet. The idea of sightseeing exasperated him, and he had no interest whatsoever in the history of American immigrants. To make things worse, it started to rain, and the lines became endless. In an attempt to be pleasant, Ulysses pretended to look for Theo's name among the long list of immigrants who had passed through the island. Theo took it badly.

"What does it matter to you? You don't even have my name!"

"Wait a minute. . . . You weren't there!"

"Exactly, so just as well you kept your mother's name."

"What are you talking about?"

"I'm talking about not going digging into other people's pasts. What are we doing here, looking at photos and reading stories of people we don't know?"

"I'm not surprised you feel that way; you're not even interested in your own family's past."

"Stop it, Ulysses," Julia implored.

Ulysses upped the ante: "No, since we're here, let's talk

about it. We'd like to know why you didn't look for us. My mother spent thirty years searching the whole world for you."

"I don't have to stand trial before you, Ulysses. You know nothing about my life. You don't know me."

"Well, this is as good a time as any to get to know each other," Ulysses replied. "We've lived all these years on the love my mother had for you. What about you? What have you lived on?"

Theo was trembling.

"I've lived on hate!"

She'll talk to him. It will only take a second for her to gauge the extent of the damage.

She pulls herself together, annoyed at her own weakness. There's no need to talk to him; she's already aware of the damage! In any case, she can't stay. She'd rather lose him than pretend not to know. And yet for one brief moment she's tempted to say nothing, to fake it, if only to see how far he means to take it. She manages to smile, imagining it.

No. Her choice is made. She wants to be free. Free not to lie. Free to confront her fears. Even to love him in spite of himself.

14.

THE NEIGHBORS

End of the Boreal Summer
2006

The sight of the blue and orange flowers that she planted throughout the garden and around the base of her old tree pains her. Julia turns to gaze at the avenue and, beyond, her sea. Always in its place, smooth, its horizon stretching straight as a ruler. The human universe seems ephemeral in contrast, precarious. Julia will leave; the house and the flowers will remain. She has already left. She will not grow old with a faceless man, like in a Magritte painting.

Julia turns the key in the lock like a thief. Everything seems foreign to her now. She walks slowly toward the cut-stone fireplace in the living room. Theo wanted to put in a vent and install a pellet stove to reduce their heating bill. Julia was against it, and the issue turned into a fight: he would be the one to decide. In the end Julia managed to convince him to put the stove in the basement, because then the heat would rise and warm all the rooms, even the ones upstairs. Theo agreed begrudgingly and got his revenge by insisting on keeping the heat on its lowest setting during the day, turning it up only when he got home. So Julia spent her winters wrapped in a blanket, waiting for a man hemmed in by his obsessions, needing to punish himself and the world.

I've let myself be engulfed by his demands, succumbing to who he wanted me to become.

Their wedding photo has pride of place on the mantelpiece. Standing beside them, Ulysses does not look like their son. Julia is wearing the lace dress Anna brought her from Argentina. Theo looks handsome. He has that same boyish air as when he takes her by the hand and kisses her surreptitiously, as if he might be caught.

A few days before they were arrested, they came to an agreement. The military knew that the leftist youth were distrustful of religious weddings. When the police persecution was at its height, the Montoneros had given orders to marry in churches, because wedding photos would deter the *milicos** from continuing a search.

Holding the photograph, she looks around her and mechanically makes an inventory of all the things that will have to be packed up. Would she have preferred not to know? She

---

* Nickname for the military.

collapses onto the sofa. If she had the energy, she would pick up the phone and call her friend Diane.

Instead, Julia goes to fetch her bicycle. She must steady her insides, which are churning like snakes in a sack. She turns right, with no particular destination in mind, and passes a couple out jogging. They stop in their tracks and call out to her. She recognizes them as two of Theo's colleagues who live in their neighborhood.

"Back home early from the office?" Julia asks, by way of small talk.

"No, we take Fridays off. That way we get to have a long weekend."

"I thought they ended that system."

"No, it's still going. Thankfully!" the young woman says, ready to start running again. Then, jogging back, she adds: "Come over for dinner this weekend. We'll invite Mia too."

"Mia?"

"Yes, the new Korean girl. You don't mind, do you?"

"I don't know who she is," Julia replies, smiling.

"She and Theo often have lunch together. I thought . . ."

Julia cuts her off. "Great! It'll give me a chance to meet her."

Well, it looks like I'm the last one to know.

She gets back home and heads straight for her cell phone.

"Diane, darling, it's me. Yes. I need your help."

15.

DIANE

End of the Boreal Summer
2006

Diane and Julia met by chance during the winter of 2002. At least that's what Diane thought. They became friends following a terrible accident outside the mall in Milford. Diane left her new Jaguar in the parking lot on the other side of Boston Post Road because the lot at the mall was full. She was about to cross the four-lane highway on foot, flouting traffic laws the Latino way. Diane had been born in Buenos Aires and had lived in Spain for a long time, working as a professional dancer. It was there that she had met Max, a wealthy East Coast real estate developer, who had brought her to the States, setting her up in a grand house in New Haven while they waited for his divorce to come through.

Diane was getting ready to cross snow-covered Boston

Post Road when a pretty woman muffled in a fluffy white parka started running toward her, calling out and waving her arms, despite the risk of slipping on the icy sidewalk. Diane assumed it was a comical case of mistaken identity. But the strange woman flung her arms around Diane's neck, exclaiming in a strong *porteño** accent: "¡Vos no sabés lo que te he buscado!"†

The next instant their heads swiveled in unison to watch as a pickup lost control on a patch of black ice and rammed into the undercarriage of a Whole Foods truck coming from the opposite direction. It all had seemed to happen in slow motion. The speeding truck flipped over on its side and slid crosswise down the avenue, carrying off everything in its path amid a terrifying screech of tires, brakes, and crushed metal.

The cacophony gave way to a heavy silence.

"I think you just saved my life," Diane said.

Clinging to each other, Diane and Julia moved away blindly and sat down. They discovered they were both *porteñas* from the same part of La Boca, that neither had been in the United States long, that they'd both spent a significant part of their lives in Europe, and that they lived a fifteen-minute drive from each other. Clearly there was no such thing as coincidence.

Julia didn't say anything about her gift, or the journey that

* Native of Buenos Aires.

† "I've been looking for you for so long!"

had enabled her to foresee the accident, or the sleepless nights she had spent crouching in the bathroom, reviewing the images to find a clue.

In fact, it was by sheer chance that Julia had recognized the intersection where the accident would take place. She had gone to Milford to get one of Theo's suits altered. She had recognized the intersection when she'd done a U-turn on the avenue to get to the shop and found herself smack in the middle of her vision. Julia had then determined that the accident would take place on a Tuesday, because that was the day Whole Foods trucks delivered to the store, and worked out the approximate time based on the usual delivery schedule.

Each Tuesday at the same time for the previous three weeks, Julia had taken up a position outside the parking lot of the menswear store and stood watching for the arrival of a woman she knew hardly anything about, just that she would be driving a metallic-gray car, wearing red nail polish, and toying with a Boca Juniors key ring. She'd had no doubt that Diane was her source when she'd seen her risking her life by charging into the flow of traffic without waiting for the light to change.

By way of explanation, she told Diane that she had mistaken her for a friend she hadn't seen since her youth in Buenos Aires. In one sense it could have been true. Julia had immediately been intrigued by the demeanor of this woman

who, like Rosa, had the unmistakable allure of a girl from Buenos Aires.

Diane arrives less than half an hour after Julia's phone call. She
lets herself in noisily through the kitchen door and finds Julia
sitting curled up in the living room, miles away.

"Darling! Are you sick?"

"No. Yes. Maybe. I don't think I can move."

"Then it must be serious."

"Yes. Theo's cheating on me."

"Oh, my God! How do you know? Are you sure?"

Julia describes the episode in the trunk of the car.

Diane explodes into a fit of giggles and collapses onto the
sofa next to Julia, who begins to laugh as well.

"Tell me you didn't do that, Julia!" Diane squeals.

"Yes, I did."

"But that's pathetic, darling! Theo could have found you.
Can you imagine?"

They double up on the sofa, roaring with laughter.

"Okay, if that's all it is, we're going to celebrate," Diane
says finally. "Let's open a bottle of champagne."

"Stop it. I haven't been able to eat a single thing all day."

"I can see that, but I'm not asking you to eat. We're going
to drink! We're going to celebrate his adultery."

"No way. That's out of the question!"

"But don't you see? You've spent your whole life moping around because of him. Julia, you're beautiful, young, and full of life. He's just set you free! This calls for a celebration."

Julia gets up and, with an air of conviction, takes the champagne flutes out of the sideboard and sets about ceremoniously opening the bottle Theo always keeps chilled in the fridge.

"I've been asking Theo for the past week what happened to the foie gras I brought back from France. Now I realize: he celebrated before us!"

"What are you going to do?"

"I don't think I have any choice, Diane. I'm going to leave him."

The two women look at each other.

"Yes. The fact is the two of you have a serious, fundamental problem, and I'm not sure you can set things straight. We've seen each other practically every day for nearly four years now. I've had plenty of time to observe your relationship with Theo. Anyone would have thought that if one of you was going to tire of the marriage, it'd be you. But there you go. Darling, I think you've just gradually fallen out of love."

"I don't think that's true for me."

"Sure it is. Look, it's very clear. You wanted to be the person you thought he wanted you to be. But he wanted you to be the way you were before. He's not the same person anymore, either. Basically, the person you love is no longer there. And you are both imprisoned in the past. Sorry, darling, you're going to have to let me raise a toast to good old Theo. Now that he's running after that Korean girl of his, I actually think he's pretty impressive."

They hear the kitchen door opening.

It's Theo.

16.

THE BERKSHIRE MANOR

Boreal Autumn

2006

We were just drinking a toast to you," Diane says to him.
Theo quickly puts his things down on the kitchen
counter and walks into the living room to join in the conversation. But Diane glances at her watch and, suddenly remember-
ing an urgent something or another, leaves them. Theo and
Julia look at each other, confused.

"Have you packed your things?" Theo asks finally.

"What things?"

"But . . . we're off to the Berkshires, aren't we?" he stam-
mers, taken aback. "Why do I always have to remind you of
what's going on?"

"Maybe because I had more important things to take
care of."

"Come on, let's get ready quickly. It'll do us good to get
away, Julia, my love."

"Go pack your bag. I'll pack mine."

"Don't you want to help me?"

"No."

Theo doesn't lose his composure and goes upstairs to pack his things. Then he goes out to load the motorcycle onto the trailer. Julia joins him outside and waits for him by the car. She has taken Diane's advice and is wearing her black skirt, a white silk blouse, and her wedge sandals that really show off her legs. It seems like they're in for a magnificent sunset. The clouds are melting away like candy against a pink and green background. Julia isn't sure she has the strength to face what lies ahead.

The bags are now in the back of the car and they're ready to leave. Brushing past Julia, Theo turns and peers at her.

"You look tall!" he says, sounding surprised.

The remark irritates Julia: she's being compared with someone else. She shrugs. Diane was right. He's falling off his pedestal.

They get into the car, get on the freeway, and turn off onto the Merritt Parkway. The idea of shutting herself up in a forest makes Julia feel more at ease. She likes the way this landscape stands up for itself. Theo joins the Connecticut 8 toward Waterbury, heading north to the small town of Lee.

All of nature seems ablaze. Autumn is her favorite season. Julia would like to love this country without him, to come back without him. To see it all again, one last time: the needle-shaped steeple of Lee's little church, its winding river and the old covered wooden bridge. She switches on the radio. A tired old Led Zeppelin song comes through the speakers. The notes travel through her veins like poison, secreting an uncontrollable sadness. She digs her nails into her palms to keep herself from crying. Theo hasn't noticed anything.

But she can feel he's agitated, ill at ease. In the end he asks her to help him look for a CD he's just bought. "It should be in the glove compartment."

Julia doesn't react. He stretches out an arm impatiently and brushes her knee.

"Sorry. I don't know what's wrong with me. I can't stand that music anymore."

"But you used to love it."

Theo flinches. "We're not the same people anymore, Julia."

"I'm not so sure. The tree draws life from its roots."

By way of an answer, he puts the CD in the player. A wave of ear-splitting sounds floods the car. She turns down the volume and turns to Theo. "You like this!"

Theo throws her a black look. "Yes. This music helps me."

Julia would like to help him too. But she no longer knows how.

They leave the Mass Pike and take the little roads that wind westward through the countryside. Night is already falling by the time they finally reach the deserted little town of Lee. They drive down a narrow, leafy road and turn left into a lane lined with huge maple trees. At the far end of a park is a large house with several outbuildings. It is a big Georgian-style farmhouse dating back to the beginning of the eighteenth century. It has been well looked after, repainted all in white with a new gray slate roof. They park the car under the proud trees and go inside with the owner, who has come out to greet them.

He leads them through a maze of little staircases and corridors, stopping in front of a door on the third floor. "I've made up the Blue Room for you," he says courteously.

"Perfect, thank you," Theo replies, placing their bags on the bed.

The man sets about coaxing the embers of the fire back into flames and then leaves, closing the door softly behind him.

Theo crouches in front of the hearth. Julia stares at him, then sits down on the pretty wooden chest at the foot of the bed. The mantelpiece displays a collection of antique plates that give the room its name. She wishes it all could have just been a misunderstanding, and that Mama Fina had been wrong.

"Theo . . . I ran into your colleagues from work."

"Oh, did you? The McIntyres?" Theo says without turning around.

"Yes, the McIntyres."

"And?"

"They were out for a lunchtime jog." She pauses. "They told me they take Fridays off, like you."

"Not like me. I've already explained it to you."

"Stop it, Theo."

Theo turns around and snarls: "So you're spying on me?"

"I know you're seeing one of your colleagues. A Korean girl called Mia."

Theo turns pale and sits down abruptly on the floor. Licking his lips, he avoids Julia's gaze. When he finally speaks, it's clear he's choosing his words carefully. "She's just a friend. I see her at the office. We have lunch together once in a while."

She watches him struggle, his throat dry, his eyes casting about the room. He's suffering, but he carries on talking, gradually gaining confidence.

"You remember, I pointed her out to you at the Fourth of July party. We were in the parking lot for the fireworks."

Julia has stopped looking at him. She doesn't want to listen to him anymore. She is doubled over, her eyes feverish.

"I'm more upset with you for lying to me than for cheating on me."

Theo falls silent, paralyzed. After a moment, she adds: "I wanted so much to help you."

Julia thinks she sees him falter. He runs his fingers nervously through his hair. "You don't understand. I have to break free from the past, Julia. I can't explain."

"Don't explain. Theo, I'm leaving you."

Her words echo in the silence, frightening her. Julia is overcome with dizziness. Long minutes tick by slowly, increasing the distance between them. Theo puts an end to it.

"Are you sure?"

Julia doesn't know. She wishes she could go back in time, wipe it all out.

"Are you going to live with her?"

Theo turns around.

"No. We're not like that."

His words feel like a slap in the face.

17.

CASTELAR POLICE STATION

Beginning of the Austral Winter
1976

Shouldering his bag and his dreams, Gabriel had left. Theo and Julia had shut the door behind him and clung to each other. They were going to have to leave Argentina. The thought had terrified her. She hadn't been able to even begin to imagine their life elsewhere, especially when she'd just told Theo she was pregnant. She had been scared. She had held him tighter, struck by a painful feeling of solitude. What if their escape attempt failed and they were captured by the military and disappeared into one of its torture centers? What if the two of them were tortured or separated?

Theo had placed his hand over her mouth to shush her. "No, my love. Stop it."

But Julia had pulled free, overwrought. "If they torture me,

Theo, I won't be able to hold out. I'll give everyone away and then I'll hate myself as long as I live!"

Theo had sat down on the bed and gripped her firmly, holding her still. *"No. We're not like that."*

Theo's words had seeped into her and calmed her immediately. The "we" had been an epiphany, revealing to her a new identity founded on the strength of love. It existed both inside her and outside, through Theo. Never again would there be emptiness. Mama Fina had been right: there was magic in words. The "we" had eclipsed her fear.

She had slipped her fingers through his and repeated: *"No, we're not like that."*

She repeated the same words to herself as she lay jammed against Rosa in the trunk of the Ford Falcon, rigid with fear. Julia wished she could hug her, to give herself courage and to make Rosa be quiet.

"I didn't say anything, I swear," Rosa was saying over and over again, on the verge of suffocation.

"Be quiet. We're not like that," Julia replied, seeking the echo of Theo's voice in her own.

The car braked sharply. A door opened. *No, sounds more like a heavy gate with rusty hinges.* Orders, insults, men. The car slid slowly through this corridor of shouting and the sound of boots, then came to a stop with a wrench of the emergency brake.

The trunk suddenly opened. Julia blinked, blinded by the glare. A big courtyard, a big building with a metal spiral staircase outside. Julia's brain registered pillars, windows, two stories, a dozen uniformed men.

"Blindfold them, you idiots!" a voice yelled; then she received a blow that brought her to her knees. When she'd gotten her breath back, she caught a glimpse of Rosa, with a hood over her head, being dragged toward a door underneath the metal staircase. Then Julia saw him. Theo was standing motionless and blindfolded at the foot of the stairs.

"I'm here!" she shouted with all she had.

Her audacity met with a shower of blows before a sack was pulled over her head, nearly suffocating her.

She was thrown into a cell and kicked repeatedly by a man who forbade her to take off the hood. A door creaked and she heard the sound of a key being turned in a lock. Then there was silence.

"They've gone," murmured a soft voice from somewhere close by. "You can take off the sack; you'll have plenty of time to put it back on. We can hear them coming from a distance."

Julia lifted a corner of the sack and saw Rosa, still wearing her hood, and a blond teenager sitting next to her.

"My name's Adriana. What's yours?"

They were in a long, narrow prison cell. A few feet away a woman lay motionless, her clothes covered in blood. Adriana followed Julia's gaze.

"That's Paola. She's been like that since yesterday. She's breathing, though."

Not daring to ask any questions, Julia looked around. At the far end of the cell was a dirty ceramic toilet with a cracked rim. Cold light filtered in from the ceiling through a skylight with a mesh grille.

"We're spoiled. We have a toilet. The others have to go on the floor. That's why it smells so bad."

Julia became aware of the foul stench in the air.

"And it comes in handy for a drink of water and a quick wash."

Julia felt like gagging.

"What's your friend's name?" Adriana asked.

"Sorry, my name's Julia. And she's Rosa."

Hearing Julia's voice, Rosa cautiously lifted a corner of her hood. "Where are we?" she asked.

"In Castelar."

Rosa looked horrified.

The three of them crouched close together. Adriana lowered her voice to a whisper. "Upstairs there's a table, two chairs, and a bed. The lights are very bright. First we're interrogated by the *colimbas*.* Then the commanders take over. There's one in particular, El Loco†—he's really bad. It was Paola's second time. She told me everything. She wants me to be prepared."

---

* Military conscripts.

† "El Loco" means "crazy man" in Spanish.

"You haven't been up there?"

"No, not yet."

"And Paola, can we talk to her?"

"She's not answering. She's not even moaning. They brought her back half-dead."

"Have you already seen people die?" Julia asked. "I mean, have any prisoners died?"

"Yes, one. They went too far with *la máquina*. I heard the policemen talking about it when they were cleaning up his cell."

"What's *la máquina*?" whispered Rosa in a thick voice.

"They tie you to the bed and hook you up to it. Then they pass an electric current . . ."

"Oh, my God!" Rosa exclaimed, covering her ears.

Julia took Rosa in her arms and rocked her like a child. "Don't worry, everything's going to be okay," she told her. Then she asked quietly: "Have you had news of Gabriel?"

Rosa hadn't had any contact with him since the previous day. She knew nothing about what had happened at Posadas Hospital or his plan for leaving Argentina. She was convinced there was no reason for them to suspect him. Except his relationship with her, since she'd been captured. Julia decided not to tell her anything.

"I'll crack, I know it," Rosa told her. "I'd rather take a bullet through my head and get it over with."

"That's what we'd all prefer. But we'll hold out, you and me. We'll get out of here."

They heard the sound of boots, a key being turned in a lock, and the creaking of rusty hinges. The three women moved away from each other and covered their heads. They heard one of the guards bark: "Your turn today, you Trotsko piece of shit. Say good-bye to your youth, asshole. When you come back you'll feel a hundred years old."

They heard blows and more abuse, then a long groan. Then there was silence.

My God, don't let it be Theo.

For three days the women were forced to listen to Wagner's "Ride of the Valkyries" played at full volume through huge speakers placed in the corners of the courtyard to drown out the screams of the prisoners. Even the silence of the night after the torturers had gone could not dispel the horror and madness of it.

Like the words of a prayer, Julia kept repeating to herself: *We're not like that. We're not like that.*

18.

THE CELL

Austral Winter
1976

The washing method that Adriana taught them gave the girls some semblance of normality. Julia would remove the panel from the wall that held the flush in place, giving her access to the cistern, the only source of water for drinking and washing. A luxury as far as they were concerned.

Adriana had witnessed the ordeal of a man who'd been brought back from the upstairs room. He'd cried out for water all night long. No one came. Unable to control his bowels, he had lain in his own excrement for two days until one of the duty policemen, a young *colimba* whom Adriana called Sosa, had finally taken him to wash and given him water to drink. The man had died soon after.

Sosa had won the inmates' respect. When he was on duty, they could talk to each other and pass on information. As soon as new prisoners arrived, the veterans made contact with them, from one cell to the next. The stories that made the rounds about El Loco's interrogations, as described by the survivors, were intended to help them bear up under torture. The veterans also said that some inmates were in Castelar only temporarily. They spoke of another even more horrific place: Mansión Seré. People who were sent there did not come back. They all realized it was better to be interrogated by El Loco if they wanted to stay alive.

Adriana introduced Julia and Rosa to the young people being held in the cells on the other side of the corridor. They were all between twenty and twenty-four years old. A few of them were students. Most of the others had worked in the same hospital as Gabriel. Julia realized that the prisoner in the cell right across from hers was Augusto, the friend Gabriel had mentioned the night he had managed to escape—the same friend who'd come to one of their meetings with Father Mugica. Augusto had been working at the hospital print room. He'd known the d'Uccello brothers since high school, but he wasn't a regular member of Gabriel's circle. He didn't remember Julia or Rosa and had only a vague recollection of the conversation with Mugica about Evita and Perón. "An aftereffect of the machine," he joked.

Augusto said that all the other people who'd been arrested with him that night had been sent to Mansión Seré. He was terrified he would meet the same fate. Julia was talking to him, trying to figure out how she could get more information about Gabriel and Theo, when they heard the sound of keys and fell silent.

Sosa came in with the leftovers of the garrison's meal. He went from one cell to the next distributing the food. He was also kind enough to give them water. It was the weekend, and the inmates knew they would get nothing else to eat for the next two days. They were fed once a day, and only on weekdays. Their obsession with the mess tin that the guard would slip between the rusted bars of their cell door kept them alert, even though the paltry rations never satisfied their hunger. As a result, the scraps Sosa brought them were gratefully received. Sosa was the only guard who spared a thought for them, at the risk of being punished. The others gleefully gave the leftovers to the dogs.

Her companions threw themselves at the food, eating with their fingers, choking as they devoured it like animals, while Julia stayed on the sidelines. She had scarcely been able to swallow a thing since coming to Castelar. On the other hand, she was extremely thirsty. She couldn't imagine the suffering of the other prisoners, who sometimes had to wait days for a drink of water. Adriana had told her that they had access to water for only two minutes a day, when they were allowed to wash in a trickle from a rusty tap, and never on weekends. To make matters worse, they had to relieve themselves in a toilet overflowing with filth.

After Sosa had left, Julia tried to resume her conversation with Augusto. But Augusto asked the prisoner in the cell next to his to talk to her. He wanted Julia to hear this man's story.

"We won't all get out of here alive," he explained, "and one day we'll have to tell the families of the others what happened here."

Oswaldo introduced himself. He had been in Castelar for nearly two months. "You get used to it in the end," he acknowledged, with no hint of irony in his voice.

He had spent his first week in the hands of El Loco and had been convinced he was already sentenced to death.

"He hooked me up to the machine after they had beaten me up and broken my arms. But the worst was yet to come: the *submarino*. I can't tell you. At that moment I prayed El Loco would finish me off. I wanted to die. Then he tied my hands together with wire and left me hanging by the wrists for two days. By the time he took me down I had lost all control over my body. He tied me to a chair. I could tell he was enjoying himself as he set a plate of food between my knees. I was just a mass of torn flesh. I couldn't even lift a finger. All I could move was my head and neck. I lowered my head and ate like a dog. He went on hitting me. He broke my toes one by one while I was eating. He was shouting: 'Wild animals have to be tamed!' He could have done anything he liked to me; I just kept on eating."

Julia couldn't bear to hear any more. She knew the interrogations could last for days, even weeks, and that a prisoner

wouldn't be brought back to the cell until El Loco had finished
with them. The inmate they had heard screaming above the
strains of Wagner hadn't returned. It was rumored he'd been
sent to Mansión Seré. Nobody knew who it was because he
had gone directly to the interrogation room with El Loco
without being held in a cell. And Theo had never been in a
cell.

Paola's condition made Julia fear the worst for herself. She
was very weak. She had bruises and burn marks all over her
body. Since her return, she hadn't stopped whimpering as she
lay, only half-conscious, in Adriana's arms. She had finally
dozed off in a corner of the cell, on the cold cement floor.
Adriana rocked her gently to and fro, trying to soothe her.
She stroked Paola's feverish forehead. Her face was covered
with strands of hair stuck together with dried blood and pus.

Julia squatted down beside them. "I'm scared too," Adriana
said in a sad voice. "You see, I'm a virgin."

"What did Paola tell you?" Julia said, finding it difficult to
speak.

"She said El Loco and the other men rape the women up
there. He's a sadist. You've heard about the submarine? It's
even worse. Oswaldo didn't tell you everything. El Loco
shoved his head into a bowl of water and sodomized him with
a metal rod connected to the machine. Look what he did to
Paola. She's got burns everywhere. He must have sent an electric current through every inch of her body."

Rosa had overheard their conversation and taken refuge at

the other end of the cell. She didn't move a muscle all night. The next morning Julia found her trembling and unable to speak, totally dissociated from reality. It was impossible to get her to drink or even to turn over. Julia hadn't slept herself. Ever since arriving in Castelar, she had been wondering when it would be her turn.

There was a screech of brakes in the yard and the brisk thud of boots. They all pricked up their ears. "A newcomer!" someone whispered. Julia stiffened. At the sound of keys, everyone quickly adjusted their hoods. Julia had situated herself against the wall near the door and peered out through a slit in her hood. She couldn't see much, just a small section of the corridor, but it was enough for her to guess that a body had been dragged and thrown into the fourth cell from the end, the one next to Augusto's. They all held their breath, trying to make themselves inconspicuous.

Sosa wasn't on duty that night. Another policeman had taken over from him. Adriana recognized his voice. He was a nasty little corporal who had just been transferred to Castelar Police Station. He'd been nicknamed El Cabo Pavor.*

A long moan came from the fourth cell.

"Shut up, you son of a bitch, or I'll finish you off myself!" El Cabo Pavor roared from the guardroom.

Julia felt almost grateful to him. Maybe it was Theo.

* Corporal Dread.

19.

LA MÁQUINA

Austral Winter
1976

Paola had a very bad night, caught in the grip of hallucinations and delusions. Rosa too tossed and turned in her sleep, and Julia could see that she had fallen into a depressive spiral. Julia and Adriana kept an eye on them.

The two girls washed before dawn and were leaning against the wall watching their cell mates struggle to sleep when they heard the sound of boots approaching, and El Cabo Pavor's voice, addressing his superiors.

"They've come from Morón," Adriana murmured in a weak voice, referring to soldiers from the Argentine air force based at Morón. They were known for their brutal interrogation methods.

The two sick girls already had their hoods over their faces. Julia and Adriana slipped theirs on just in time to hear El Cabo

Pavor bellow, as he turned the key in the lock: "We're going to have some fun today, girls!"

He pushed the door open. "You, blondie. Get a move on," he shouted.

Adriana began to shake from head to toe. Julia squeezed her hand tightly.

"Hope you've washed properly, kid," he sniggered.

Because Julia was trying to hold on to Adriana, El Cabo pulled off her hood and struck her across the face. He dragged her out of the cell by her hair, tied her hands behind her back, and blindfolded her, tying the cloth so tight it cut into her skin. Then he started to kick Adriana so she would come out too and locked the door of the cell.

There were more men waiting for them at the end of the corridor. There was a commotion, fresh abuse, more orders. El Cabo Pavor dragged Julia and Adriana up the spiral staircase, kicked the door open, threw them inside, removed their blindfolds, and closed the door behind him. It was pitch-black. Clinging to each other, they groped around them, trying to find a place to sit so they wouldn't fall.

A harsh glare flooded the room and an iron hand pushed them apart. Julia's hands and feet were tied and she was forced into a chair with a bright light shining in her face. A hand yanked her head up by the hair. Half-blinded, she could just about make out the edge of a table pushed up against her knees and a metal bed to her right. She heard Adriana whimper behind her, then a thud, like a sack of rice being dropped.

Now the groans were muffled. From the sound of their footsteps, she could tell that there were two men in the room. One of them seemed to be gagging and tying up Adriana. The other one kept circling Julia, breathing down her neck.

"You're going to talk," said the voice of the man now gripping her chin and twisting her face.

A blow dislocated her jaw. Julia screamed in pain. The voice said, "You're going to be a good girl and tell us everything, in front of your little friend. She's right here; she can see it all. If you don't want her to get hurt, you'd better tell us everything you know right now."

A second blow, this time straight to the nose. She felt blood trickling down to the corners of her mouth. She couldn't see the man's face, but it wasn't El Cabo Pavor speaking to her. This voice was nasal, almost childish.

"Do you know who I am?" the man asked. "No, you don't know yet, but you will soon, and you won't ever forget me. They call me El Loco. I love my nickname. Because you see, lying drives me insane. I can smell a lie the way a dog smells fear. Finding out the truth excites me. I'm an expert at digging it out."

She felt a burst of adrenaline. The man speaking to her was mentally ill, there was no doubt about it. An animal with a human voice. She could sense his arousal. He had already tied her feet to the chair. He prowled around her, sniffing her, pressing his crotch against her arm. She felt him harden. He panted as he spoke.

He moved away briefly and went over to a record player. He lifted the arm and carefully returned the stylus to the beginning of the LP.

"You're in luck—I'm going to make you sing along to the *Nocturnes*. Ever heard of Debussy? No, of course not. I might as well cast pearls before swine."

He gave a roar of laughter, and the opening bars filled the air. The music coming out of the loudspeakers was fragmented, slow, dissonant. Julia found it sinister. The man approached her again and stroked her hair gently. She had to stop herself from biting him. He hit her again, so hard that she fell to the ground, taking the chair with her.

The man took his time before sitting her up in the chair. Then he began to tie her whole body to it. He went about it meticulously. With each movement he pawed her, as if she were a piece of meat. He tied her up neatly with electric wire, pulling it so tight that it cut into her.

His voice had become almost delicate, his breathing short when he spoke again. "Now you're going to tell me everything. I want your alias, Montonerita. What is your alias?"

El Loco tugged the wire tighter. It felt like a razor was slicing into her skin. He secured the end of the electric wire to something heavy behind Julia, then moved away. Her gaze followed him instinctively. He walked toward a shadowy corner of the room. The music drowned out his voice, but Julia knew he was talking to someone else. Still blinded by the spotlight, she couldn't make out what he was doing. Out of the corner of her eye she could see shadows moving rhythmically.

"What was your role within the organization? Who is your contact person?"

Julia trembled all over. She managed to turn herself around, the wire digging into her wrists. Then she understood.

"No!" she screamed. "Not Adriana, not Adriana!"

"Where did you meet? I want addresses, telephone numbers. I want all the names," the clipped voice continued.

"No! No!" Julia struggled to free herself, her wrists bleeding.

"Talk, filthy Trotska. I want the whole truth about the d'Uccello brothers. I want to know their rank in the organization. Who is the head of your unit?"

Each time El Loco asked Julia a question, El Cabo Pavor struck Adriana violently. El Loco jerked Julia's head up with one hand to make sure she was following his every move. With his other he laid into Adriana in the shadows. Suddenly both men loosened their hold, and the teenager flopped over like a puppet.

"Adriana! Adriana! Answer me!" Julia implored.

Then she distinctly heard El Cabo Pavor's voice. He was accusing Adriana of pretending. He began to slap her to make her get up.

"Enough!" barked El Loco. "I want her to remain conscious, to tell the others."

El Cabo Pavor straightened his uniform. He kicked Adriana's inert body several times, then backed into the shadows and vanished again. Julia had the feeling he was staring fixedly at her. El Loco wiped his mouth with the back of his sleeve and came back to Julia.

"You, on the other hand, you're dead."

He hit her with increasing ferocity. The violence of each blow anticipated the pain of the next. She wouldn't survive. Julia wanted to beg him to stop, but her body wasn't responding anymore, and she was incapable of making a sound.

To prolong his enjoyment, El Loco turned methodical. He was instinctively aware of the level of pain he needed to inflict on her to make her lose her mind, give in, and talk. He always got them to talk in the end; that was his specialty. And his passion.

"I'll make you want to open your mouth, you fucking Trotska!"

He kicked her and she fell to her knees, still tied to the chair. El Loco dragged a large tub of water in front of her face. "You think you can make a fool of me. You don't want to talk. We'll see about that."

Julia struggled with all her might, but by exhausting herself she was only making her torturer's job easier. He shoved her head into the water. She held her breath for as long as she could. She counted in her head to give herself strength. But eventually she gave up and allowed the water to fill her lungs.

When he pulled her head up, she couldn't inhale the air.

She threw up a lot of water before she felt a thin stream of oxygen penetrate her lungs, bringing relief. As she gasped like a fish, her mouth wide open, he pushed her head back under the water. Five, ten, twenty times in a row.

She thought she was already dead, but she came to when she felt a hot object being forced down her throat, suffocating her. Her instinctive reaction was to bite. The man let out a grotesque howl.

There was a long silence. Then El Loco declared: "You're going to die with your eyes wide open, and when you breathe your last breath, I'll be the last thing you see."

He untied her from the chair and dragged her over to the bed. Julia's mind had gone completely blank. She felt him bind her with the same metal wire that cut into her flesh. He threaded the wire between her toes, splaying them out and attaching them tightly to one end of the bed. Then he passed the wire between her fingers and tied them to the other end. Finally he strapped her to a wire mesh base that served as a mattress and gagged her with a rag that he stuffed into her mouth.

Julia heard Adriana screaming over the music playing in the background. She raised her head and saw the young girl struggling in a nightmare. Then came the electric shock. A black hole, and then her whole being shattered under the pressure of millions of needles speeding through her veins in an endless circuit running from her head to her toes and back again. The electric particles split her skin, exploded inside her limbs, and pierced every cell in her body. Julia felt liquefied, crushed from the inside, burned alive as if by a stream of acid.

Suddenly the intensity of the voltage increased, as did the deafening volume of opera music that reverberated inside her head, accompanying the infernal pain that shook her. The current plowed a furrow deep into her bowels. Julia had no eyes, no lungs, no stomach. She was torn apart, impaled, jerked like a hooked fish above the wire mesh; she had no existence outside of her suffering.

Julia heard the man's laugh, his shrill voice between each increase in voltage. Names, streets, times, codes, ranks: all the information was going to spill out of her brain and she wouldn't be able to stop it. She knew she was going to tell him everything.

Then there was emptiness, a descent into oblivion.

Julia opened her eyes and couldn't recognize anything, not even Adriana, who huddled against her, crying. It took her days to emerge from a state in which the only thing she was aware of was a raging thirst. Adriana refused to give her a drink. She told her that after *la máquina*, the water could kill her. In her delirium, Julia accused Adriana of being her new torturer.

Sosa had returned to guard duty. He began to smuggle medicines in to them. Julia gradually came out of her coma.

Then it was her turn to look after Adriana, whose wounds were deeper but less visible. The weekend came like a reprieve. Sosa would be supervising the prisoners on his own. He listened to the girls talking without intervening, especially since most of the old prisoners had left Castelar, and the new ones were not talkative.

"We were very lucky," Adriana murmured.

Julia stared at her in shock.

"Yes. You weren't hooked up to *la máquina* for long. They had to break off the interrogation because they were called by a superior."

"That's bad news," Julia replied in a low voice. "That means it's only postponed."

"Maybe," Adriana said.

"We have to get out of here."

"But that's impossible! We don't stand a chance."

"We don't if we can't walk. That's why we have to get back on our feet as quickly as possible."

"But if they see us up and about, they'll take us back upstairs."

"Don't kid yourself; they'll take us back there anyway. They'll drag us by the hair if they have to."

They hadn't heard Paola and Rosa since they'd gotten back. Neither answered when the girls called out. They were probably being held in a cell farther away. Adriana and Julia were back in the cell with the toilet. Even Sosa refused to tell them what had happened to their cell mates.

"Maybe they've been transferred elsewhere?" Julia suggested. "Or legalized?"*

"I don't think so."

"But all the old ones have left. Maybe they got lucky?"

"The one who got lucky is our neighbor across the corridor. I overheard the guards say he's come back from Mansión Seré."

"I thought nobody ever came back alive."

"Exactly. He moans sometimes. I think he's coming to. If he recovers . . ."

"Do you know who he is?"

"I think it's a student from the sciences faculty, or maybe an engineer. Sosa told me he's in very bad shape. El Loco tortured him here before sending him to the pilots. Apparently there's a particularly vicious officer—a captain, I think— whom they call El Diablo.† He throws the prisoners out of planes himself. El Loco suspected this prisoner had something to do with the kidnapping of the Born brothers. That's why they handed him over to the air force."

Julia became unsteady on her feet and had to lie down. Her head was spinning.

* Refers to disappeared prisoners who reappeared as political prisoners.

† "El Diablo" means "the Devil" in Spanish.

Monday came. The silence in the courtyard at Castelar was absolute. Even Sosa was no longer on duty. The stench from the cells across the corridor was becoming unbearable. When the prisoners pissed, they directed the urine outside their cells. Some couldn't hold their bowels any longer and piled up their excrement in the hope it would be cleaned away.

At dawn El Cabo Pavor's voice was heard in the distance. He turned a deaf ear to the prisoners' pleas for water and went away. It was noon before he returned to take them to the toilet.

At five in the afternoon, a commotion shook the building. The sound of boots running through the courtyard sent the two women into a panic.

Feeling increasingly ill, Julia couldn't control the spasms that shook her. She went to throw up in the toilet just as she heard the key turning in the lock.

Bending over the toilet, she saw her face reflected in the water together with the overhead skylight. Exactly like Mama Fina had described it. The stream of bile and blood she vomited reminded her that she was also pregnant or that maybe she wasn't any longer.

She turned around as El Cabo Pavor entered the cell. He laid into her with the butt of his rifle because she had forgotten to wear her blindfold. With his pockmarked face he looked like a bloated toad. "We haven't finished with you, Maoist whore. You'll die here like a dog."

Julia instinctively crouched down and curled into a ball to avoid the blows.

The noise of an engine stopped El Cabo Pavor in his tracks. The main gate clanked open. The whole building seemed to go into a state of frenzied agitation. A voice shouted, giving the order to fall into formation. The officer rushed out, forgetting to shut the cell door.

Julia knew she had only a few minutes.

20.

THE ESCAPE

Austral Winter
1976

She spun around and raced over to Adriana, who was huddled at the other end of the cell, her face covered. Julia
ripped the hood off her face and tried to pull her to standing.
The teenager resisted with all her might, eyes shut in anticipation of a blow.

"They're coming back to get us," she whimpered.

"We won't be here when they do. Hurry, we've got three
minutes!"

Julia's confidence jolted Adriana into action. She jumped
up, ready to run. Julia made sure the corridor was empty and
went straight to the fourth cell. Adriana understood and tried
to unbolt the others, her hands stiff with panic. All the doors
were padlocked. Julia, however, had no difficulty sliding open
the latch and opening the metal door of cell four. At the same

time, their eyes fell on the body that lay there. His face was disfigured, his nose a mass of blood. Julia recognized Theo's eyes in the swollen flesh.

"Too bad, we'll just have to drag him," Julia said. "We're out of time."

Theo tried to speak, but all that came out of his broken jaw was a gurgle. He made a superhuman effort to stand up, holding on as best as he could to the two women. They didn't have too much trouble getting him out of the cell; he was nothing but skin and bones.

The corridor was still empty, and the door at the end was ajar. Julia was counting backward mechanically in her head. Without knowing why, she turned and rebolted the cell door while Adriana pulled Theo along toward the exit. Theo's breath made a whistling sound. Every movement aggravated his wounds.

They soon reached the door to the courtyard. Julia could feel her hair standing on end in fear. She took a deep breath and sneaked a peek outside. The coast was clear. They crept along the wall under the rusty spiral staircase and reached the courtyard. There were three police vans lined up between them and the large outer compound where the garrison was being drilled.

An officer wearing dress uniform and all his stripes was barking orders at the troops standing to attention. He was striding up and down the ranks inspecting each of his men. He was the only one who might see them. For a brief moment Julia thought he had, and a surge of adrenaline glued her to the spot. But the man continued on at a steady pace without hesitating. The troops had their backs turned.

In two minutes' time, El Cabo Pavor would be back. They would have to walk the length of the police station and the guardroom to reach the main gate. They had only a slim chance of slipping behind the vans without being spotted. Seizing the opportunity at once, Julia gestured to Adriana to move forward. They bent down instinctively so they could drag Theo along with them. They stole silently behind the convoy and passed safely under the guardroom windows. The rusty main gate was open, blocked by one of the vans.

Looking outside, Julia became suddenly aware of her fear. Her breath came in jerks; her eyes were wide. But there was no time to think about it. The street was deserted. Julia suppressed the urge to run and walked out, holding Theo around the waist to support him. Adriana did the same. They had to get out of sight as soon as possible. They walked up the right-hand side of the street, then crossed and turned left at the first intersection. As soon as they were out of range, the girls quickened their step, almost breaking into a run. Adriana, the stronger of the two, was bearing nearly all of Theo's weight, since Julia was ready to collapse at every step. They didn't meet a soul. It was as if the city were under curfew again. All around them curtains were drawn and shutters closed.

Adriana forced her two companions to keep pace. The farther they got from Castelar, the more the young girl feared recapture. The empty sidewalks provided no reassurance. Julia was struggling to continue. Hearing the noise of an approaching engine, Adriana made them jump behind a low wall. They just managed to hide in the bushes of a small garden before a police car drove by, combing the neighborhood. A powerful beam of light swept the path and played over their heads, brushing past them without giving them away. The car moved off.

The garden, full of bracken and construction waste, belonged to a house that appeared to be abandoned. Adriana wanted to go inside. She had no trouble finding a way in: two of the ground-floor windows were broken. The house was in a sorry state. All the furniture had been overturned. They bumped into it as they ventured through unlit rooms, eventually huddling in the dark under a large staircase in the hope that the police would give up searching this area.

Once they had regained some strength, Adriana and Julia plucked up the courage to explore. Night had fallen, and moonlight filtered into the house. Fumbling around in one of the upstairs rooms, they found some clothes and shoes for Theo to wear. They were too big for him but even so would make him less conspicuous.

In the basement they found a few dirty clothes in what must have been the laundry room and brought them back up. The rest of the house had been ransacked.

"It's the *milicos*," Adriana said. "They did the same at my place."

"You never told me why you were arrested."

"They wanted to get their hands on my brother, but they only found me. So they took me to Castelar. I'll have to let my family know I'm out, so my brother doesn't give himself up. My parents are old. They won't survive without him."

"You can't do that," Julia whispered. "They'll flood your neighborhood full of informers, and your parents' phone must already be bugged by now. They'll be waiting for us to contact our families. You have to disappear completely. Like a mole."

"But I have to let them know!"

"You'll put them at too great a risk. They'll kill all of you. . . . We have to split up. We'll have a better chance of staying alive if we're not together."

"No way! You're not getting rid of me that easily."

"Listen to me," Julia ordered. "Theo and I couldn't have escaped without you. Now you have to keep going and succeed. We're not only fleeing the government and the military. We're running from El Loco, El Cabo Pavor. . . . This is a manhunt. Do you understand?"

Adriana huddled as close as possible to Julia.

"I'll leave before daybreak," Julia continued. "I'm feeling stronger now; I'll be able to find my way. You're going to stay here with Theo until he can walk. Then you go to La Boca. Go to San Juan Evangelista church and ask for Father Miguel. Remember what I said: La Boca, San Juan Evangelista, Father Miguel."

Adriana repeated: "San Juan Evangelista, Father Miguel."

"Don't take Theo when you go to see him. It could arouse suspicion. Go alone, and ask him to hear your confession. Are you with me?"

"Yes, Julia."

"Good. Tell Father Miguel that Julia d'Annunzio, the granddaughter of Josefina d'Annunzio, sent you. He'll ask you for dates. Give him my birth date, August 6, 1957, and Mama Fina's, September 1, 1900. You have to learn those dates by heart; it's important. Remember: Mama Fina was born at the turn of the century."

"September 1, 1900, and August 6, 1957. I won't forget," Adriana promised.

"Good. Father Miguel will give you an envelope that Mama Fina left for me. There'll be money inside. We'll need it to leave Argentina."

"Leave Argentina?"

"Unless you want to stay behind and wait for El Cabo Pavor or El Loco to get their hands on you."

Adriana shrank into herself.

"Take the money and go to the port. Look for the captain of the *Donizetti*. It's an ocean liner making its final crossing. The captain's name is Enzo Torricelli. Everyone knows where to find him. Tell him that Mama Fina's children are ready to leave. Follow his instructions. You'll have to find a way to keep Theo hidden while you go to the church and the port. Don't walk around on your own in the streets or at the port—wait until it's busy. I'll join you the day after tomorrow. I'll go straight to the captain and find you on the ship. If for some reason I don't turn up, don't wait for me. You'll have to leave with Theo and get out of Buenos Aires."

Adriana nodded, tears pouring down her cheeks.

"One last thing. Don't go home. Don't go to Theo's house. Don't talk to anyone, on the phone or in the street. Don't ask for help; don't answer if anyone speaks to you. Go straight to the church, then to the port. Don't use public transport: no metro, no buses, no taxis."

Adriana acquiesced.

Close by, Theo was burning up with fever, tossing and turning uncontrollably in the grip of a nightmare. He was delirious and kept calling out El Diablo's name. Julia wished she could clean his wounds but didn't want to turn on a faucet, for fear of activating the meter and unintentionally drawing attention to their presence. She huddled close to him for a long moment, to warm him and to give herself the strength to leave.

"I'll meet you on the ship," she whispered in his ear.

Theo seemed to calm down at the sound of her voice. He didn't open his eyes, but he slipped his fingers through Julia's.

21.

THE TRAP

Austral Winter
1976

Julia slipped out of the house like a cat. It was cold, but she had found a man's sweatshirt with a hood to protect her from the weather and any prying eyes. She stayed close to walls, keeping to the shadows where possible, and walked silently along the asphalt. She continued in the same direction for over an hour, hands in pockets and head down, with no real point of reference, her only objective being to get away from Castelar. The sun was already rising above the rooftops when she heard the hum of turbines. Planes were taking off and landing somewhere ahead of her, to the left.

She shuddered. It could only be Morón Air Base. So she hadn't made much progress and wasn't really heading in the right direction. She quickened her pace, feeling the nausea return. She couldn't get El Loco's words out of her head, the ones he'd screamed into her ear as she lay on the metal bed, over the background music that was now engraved in her memory. She rubbed nervously at her ears to cleanse herself of his presence. El Loco had talked about El Diablo. And Theo had spoken El Diablo's name aloud in his nightmares. El Loco had told her El Diablo would push her out of an air force plane into emptiness, above the Río de la Plata. He would hold on to her for a moment to hear her beg, then let go, and her body, her name, and her entire existence would disappear for all time, swallowed up by the dark waters of the estuary. Julia didn't know what she was more afraid of: being hooked up to *la máquina* again or being thrown alive from an airplane into the sea.

Julia was so lost in her thoughts she hadn't noticed that the streets were now crowded with passersby. She snapped back to reality as she reached a neighborhood that was all too familiar, where the townhouses had slender windows and crenellated roofs. She slipped through the narrow streets she knew only too well, trying to get out of Liniers as quickly as possible and to avoid her parents' house at all costs. Only then did she feel mistress of her fate.

Julia kept walking all day long, steering clear of bus stops, metro stations, and busy streets, which would be swarming with informers. She avoided the colorful neighborhood of La Boca and headed north instead, past the handsome buildings and along the leafy avenues of the diplomatic quarter. She was careful to bypass Plaza de la Constitución and the station, with their crowds of bystanders.

Night had fallen by the time Julia reached Villa 31. Her feet were sore and swollen, but they were the least painful part of her body. Setting foot on the dirt path that led into the slum, she felt as if she'd finally escaped enemy territory. The older women were still outside, and a few kids were kicking a punctured football under a lone streetlight. A few blocks farther up, a van swayed as it straddled a dusty road punctured with deep potholes. Julia made swift work of the labyrinthine alleyways and went straight to Señora Pilar's house.

She knocked tentatively on the door. It gave way with a creak. Julia poked her head inside and called out softly. She was met by silence. The house was empty. Totally empty.

Julia felt like running away. This room without furniture, a dusty floor all that remained, this silence, this door left open— it was all so different from what she had expected. *Maybe she's dead; maybe she's gone to live somewhere else.* Julia threw a glance over her shoulder. But there was the familiar distant hubbub of the city, the familiar youths smoking on street corners, the familiar women sitting outside on chairs leaned back against doors, sweaters wrapped tight around their chests, the familiar stale, humid air.

The normality of it all reassured her. She pushed open the door and went in to sit down. She needed a roof, a rest, a moment to catch her breath. All of a sudden, it was as if she collapsed inwardly. Tormented by thirst, hunger scalding her stomach, she fell asleep propped up in a corner, her legs sticking out in front of her.

The shouts, the screams, the blows to her ribs, her shoulder blades, her skull, they were all part of a forgotten dream, a different world.

And yet they kept pulling her insistently toward a hot, intense, cruel, unbearable light. She opened her eyes to find herself in a reality more devastating than her worst nightmare.

She was tied up and blindfolded again, in a room, a bedroom. The upstairs bedroom? Was it El Loco hitting her where she was already wounded, on her nose, ribs, shoulder blades, and head? Was she back on the wire mesh bed, hooked up to *la máquina*?

"Thought you'd sneak away quietly, did you, you Bolshevik bitch? Where were you going? Who were you planning to kill? When's your next attack? We're stronger than the lot of you! You're dead; you don't exist anymore. But before you go to join your friends at the bottom of the Río de la Plata, you'll talk, you filthy Trotska!"

It wasn't El Loco. She tried to hold out, to think clearly. She remembered walking—she had gone through Parque Avellaneda and Flores and reached San Telmo. She remembered her route. She was sure of it. Yes, the old women in Villa 31. She had gotten to Señora Pilar's house. She didn't know what had happened after that. Was it a trap? How long had she been in their clutches? What about Theo and Adriana?

The blows rained down incessantly, all over her body. She

preferred this to *el submarino*. She would rather suffer thousands of blows than suffocate, millions of blows than face *la máquina* again.

"Names, give us the names! Who was waiting for you in Retiro? Who was your contact? Where are the guns? Where are you hiding the ammunition?"

The man held her head and dealt her a sharp blow to the hollow of her ear with the knuckles of his right hand. Julia felt the world spin. She couldn't take any more. She had to end this right now, push the man over the edge, and find release in death.

She regained consciousness with the feeling of coming up from a bottomless well, unable to breathe. There was a plastic bag over her head; it was sticking to her face like a suction cup. She could feel herself going mad. She had to die soon. But the man was splashing her with a substance that sizzled as it touched her skin. He was burning her alive while simultaneously beating time to an aria.

Julia lost all control. Unable to die, she shouted out names, dates, and places, everything she kept in her memory, swept along in a paraphrenic hallucination. All the names, all too distant, all already dead, all the fruit of delirium. In her madness Julia clung to a thread, a strained, secret voice from the other side of the mirror, in a world beyond her psychosis, a voice as sharp as a sting: Theo's voice.

When the man drew a razor blade across her body and began to peel the skin back, magnifying her torment, she finally passed beyond the limits of what she could endure. Her voice was an endless piercing wail. There was nothing left but death. She dreamed she was thrown from a plane into emptiness, and the idea of finally escaping him consumed her as much as her suffering. But death did not come. Merciless, the man subjected her to life.

Then, once again, there was nothingness.

She was sure she was dead, because she could no longer feel her body. Except for the pain, which was now part of her being, and not confined to any particular part of her anatomy. The only thing that lived in her was pain. And, perhaps, that imperceptible quiver in the pit of her belly, like a butterfly fluttering its wings, still clinging to her somehow. Through her nightmare Julia recognized Paola's distant voice. Then there was renewed absence.

She came to several days later, in the very same cell she had escaped from. The same toilet at the end, the same skylight above it. Unable to move, she cried with rage, trying to drink the tears to quench her thirst. For weeks she cried at the realization that she was still there, alive, that she still had a body they could torture.

"There's some good news," she heard Paola say one day.

Julia didn't understand.

"El Loco has been transferred. We don't know where to exactly, but the guards think he's now in charge of Mansión Seré."

For the first time since her return, and in spite of herself, words made sense to Julia.

Mansión Seré was a few minutes away from Castelar Police Station. All the members of the organization knew that the air force had turned it into a secret interrogation center. Julia remembered passing it once. It was a curious late-nineteenth-century European-style building planted at the end of a park. The carved stone facade framed large arched windows on the first floor. Wrought-iron balconies decorated the second floor, and the external walls were clad with geometric redbrick shapes, which produced an odd overall effect.

The building had been uninhabited for a long time, and with its front entrance on the corner situated between two wings, it looked like the prow of a ghost ship. Julia recalled once hearing that it had been used for witchcraft ceremonies and that the house was cursed. Whatever the truth, people gave it a wide berth.

Julia shuddered. A madman in a haunted house. Only Paola could think it was good news.

"Have you heard anything about the others?" Julia asked with difficulty.

Paola paused for a moment, taken by surprise. When she answered, she chose her words carefully: "No, there's no news of Adriana. But I have to tell you about someone else."

Instinctively Julia slowed her breathing. She was afraid she would learn Theo was dead.

"It's about your friend Rosa. . . . After you escaped, El Loco moved on to her. She was already delirious when they took her out of here, but when she came back . . . Even that madman's music couldn't drown out her screams. She screamed so hard she lost the use of her vocal cords. And then she was transferred. I don't think she'll survive."

Julia was crying. She was ashamed of her unmentionable sense of relief.

22

THE FATHER

Boreal Autumn

1981

Ulysses had waited for her before going to sleep, sucking on his comforter. Julia sat down on the edge of the bed. This was his favorite moment of the entire day. Nothing else mattered to the child except the pleasure of having his mother all to himself. Julia gave him a little nudge to make room for her. He moved over with a mischievous smile, a corner of his bedsheet in his mouth. He'd had the habit since he was a baby and Julia had let him continue, unable to judge if it was good or bad, normal or the result of trauma.

She thought Ulysses had seemed overexcited after school that day. She had tried to get him to calm down before bedtime, because he had put on his red rubber boots, a sign that he was in the mood for a fight. He hadn't stopped racing around the little apartment and jumping all over the place.

Julia had forgotten all her good intentions and chased him, rolling around on the floor with him and tickling him. Then she'd seized the opportunity to grab hold of him, had rolled him up in a towel and given him a bath, and finally had gotten him into bed. But Ulysses wanted the full bedtime ritual, so Julia had returned with a picture book.

"Mom?"

Tired, Julia tried not to become impatient. She stroked his hair. "What is it, angel?"

"Dad . . . is he dead?"

Ulysses' question caught his mother off guard. She became distraught as all her own doubts suddenly resurfaced. And yet she should have expected it. During her last visit, Mama Fina had expressed concern about the child. Ulysses had asked Mama Fina several times where his father was, and she'd sensed her answer hadn't satisfied him. Then Ulysses had taken to dressing up as a firefighter. He wanted to wear boots, even inside the house. In the end he had thrown such a tantrum that Mama Fina had agreed to buy him the red boots he'd set his heart on, even though it was the height of summer.

Ulysses insisted on wearing his red boots to the park, complete with shorts. Julia often took him to the park, hoping he would make friends. But Ulysses would give his spade and bucket to the other children and sit in a corner with his back turned, surrounded by twigs and carefully chosen pebbles. Then he would become absorbed in his solitary war games. The twigs came to life in his hands, flying off into an imaginary

cosmos and colliding with the pebbles to his own soundtrack
of explosions, crashes, and violent deaths.

"I'll protect you, Mom," he had told her the first time he'd
dressed up as a firefighter. This consisted of pulling on his red
boots and running off, small fists clenched. He would then
fight an invisible enemy, launching into a series of flying kicks
that usually ended in an equally spectacular fall. Julia had decided it might be a good idea to sign him up for karate lessons.
Even when he was asleep, Julia could sense that the child was
anxious. Every night he would come into Julia's bedroom,
half-asleep, and climb into bed with her. Sometimes he would
be wide awake and sweat soaked after a nightmare.

"I'm scared of the dadashes," he'd once told Julia while she
changed his pajamas.

"What are the 'dadashes,' angel?" she'd asked, without expecting a proper answer.

"The dadashes that fly in the sky and go *boom!*" Ulysses had
replied, gesticulating widely.

It had taken a big thunderstorm for Julia to realize that he'd
been talking about flashes of lightning.

Shortly after their arrival in France in the spring of 1977, while
listening to the radio in order to improve her French, Julia had
stumbled upon a series of programs presented by a pediatric
psychoanalyst that had convinced her of the importance of
telling children the truth.

So she had set out to make Theo a familiar figure in Ulysses' life. Strangely enough, Julia had never sensed in the child any real interest in his father. Even at the age of five, when he started elementary school, he had remained indifferent to the subject. As soon as Julia started talking about Theo, he would run off to play somewhere else, shouting: "I know, Mom!"

Ulysses settled into school without any problems. He was happy to go there each morning, and his teacher, Mademoiselle Leblanc, was full of praise for him. She said Ulysses was an intelligent child, bursting with energy and eager to learn. It was probably in his character that he most resembled Theo, Julia thought. Everything else he had inherited from Mama Fina. People often stopped them in the street to admire his eyes, and passersby would irritate Julia with their sidelong glances, confirming he hadn't inherited his looks from his mother.

Julia hadn't anticipated that tonight her little boy would make her relive her own nightmares.

She took a deep breath as she tried to decide how to answer.

"No, your father isn't dead. He's alive."

The child turned toward her and squeezed her cheeks with his little hands. "What does 'dead' mean, Mom?"

Now Ulysses was really making her think.

"Dead is when your body stops working."

"Does it hurt to die?" Ulysses asked, stuffing a huge piece of his sheet into his mouth.

"Not necessarily," Julia replied cautiously.

"What about me? Am I going to die?"

"We're all going to die someday," Julia answered.

"But if I die, who'll look after you, Mom?"

Julia looked at her son. He was so beautiful. She hugged him close and stroked his curly little head. Ulysses' wide-eyed gaze was fixed on her.

"I'll always be here, right next to you, and you'll always be right next to me," she told him.

Ulysses kept staring at her. "Why doesn't Dad live with us?"

Julia hesitated.

"Is it because of me?" Ulysses asked.

"Of course not! Where did you get that idea?"

"That's what Malo said."

"That Malo again! He's a naughty little boy, that friend of yours."

"He's not my friend and he's not little. He's big!"

"All right, don't get upset, Ulysses," she said more gently. "What's this Malo been saying to you?"

"He makes fun of me at recess."

"And why does this Malo make fun of you?"

"He asked me what my dad does."

"And what did you say to him, angel?"

"I told him you were looking for him."

"So what's funny about that?"

"Malo said Dad ran away when I was born because he was scared I was so ugly."

Julia suppressed a laugh. "He's just jealous."

"No, he's not jealous. His dad is a firefighter and he saves people."

"Okay, well, great. But he shouldn't make fun of you."

"He makes fun of me and he takes my snacks."

"But why didn't you tell me?"

Ulysses looked as if he was about to cry.

"I'm not scolding you, my angel."

"He hits me too."

"Have you told the teacher?" Julia asked, indignant.

Ulysses began to sob.

"Are you scared of him, angel?"

Ulysses shook his head, wiping away his tears.

"How old is Malo?" Julia asked.

"He's seven!"

"But you know how to defend yourself, Ulysses! You're as strong as a lion and you do karate! Show me your Choku-zuki."

Ulysses brought one small fist out from under the covers, extended his arm, and rotated his wrist, sucking his comforter all the while.

"Well, there you are! Tomorrow you can give him a taste of his own medicine."

"No way! I'm never going to do that," Ulysses answered, taking the sheet out of his mouth.

"And why not?"

Ulysses replied after a pause: "Because I'm not like that."

Julia stared at him, stunned. After a while she said, "Well, actually, you're right."

Ulysses wasn't looking at her. Lost in thought, he kept rolling a corner of the sheet between his fingers, until it looked like an arrow tip.

"I'm very proud of my son," Julia said, as if she was talking to someone else.

Ulysses went on happily sucking the corner of his sheet. He snuggled a little closer to her. Now he was thinking about something much more important.

"Mom . . ."

"Yes, angel."

"Tell me a story about Dad."

23.

HAEDO

Austral Spring
1976

The prison gate opened. Paola held her breath and signaled to Julia not to move. She climbed onto the toilet seat and looked out through the skylight.

"A lot of cars have arrived," she whispered into Julia's ear. "It must be a general again. The day Adriana and you escaped, it was Angelini who'd come to carry out an inspection."

"Angelini?" Julia asked. "Commissioner-Major Angelini?"

"Do you know him?"

"No, not really. But I've heard of him."

"He's the one who's ordered El Loco's transfer."

Her thoughts racing, Julia asked: "Has he been promoted?"

Paola shrugged. "I don't know. In any case, he's going. Sosa seemed to say that Angelini had reviewed all of our files. There was total chaos when they found out you'd run away.

Actually, I've been meaning to ask you: who was the other prisoner?"

"I don't know. We split up soon after. It was the only cell that hadn't been padlocked. The man was half-dead; he'd come back from Mansión Seré. They must have thought that even if they left the door wide open, he wouldn't be able to take as much as a step outside."

Paola was looking at Julia with a strange intensity.

"You've just come back from Mansión Seré too. You know that, right? Sosa told me when they brought you back. So you met El Diablo. . . ."

Julia was stunned. "I don't know. I don't remember anything."

The sound of keys opening the door at the end of the corridor put them on the alert. They adjusted their hoods and waited, holding their breath, leaning against the wall.

El Cabo Pavor's voice made them jump. He opened the door of their cell and barked: "You, the brunette. Over here. We're going to finish you off once and for all."

Julia was trembling all over. She found Paola's hand and dug her nails into it as if to anchor herself there. El Cabo Pavor separated the girls and herded Julia out, spewing a torrent of abuse. He shoved her into the corridor and slammed the cell door shut. Back in the trunk of a car. The journey seemed short. She was sweating profusely despite the cold. Morón Air

Base, where the death flights took off from, and Mansión Seré were both near Castelar, although located in different directions. Julia couldn't hear the sound of jet engines. It could only be an escalation of the nightmare: she was returning to Mansión Seré.

The trunk was opened. The sound of boots, kicks, insults. She was dragged unrelentingly down a set of stairs, then flung into a dark hole. A metal door closed heavily behind her. Then nothing. She waited. The footsteps moved away. Then there was silence.

She couldn't see a thing, not even her own hand. She began to feel her way around. It was an airless cell that seemed to be particularly narrow. From where she was sitting, Julia could touch the walls on either side by stretching out her arms. The room felt damp, like a cellar. She couldn't stand up without her head touching the ceiling. She estimated that the distance between the metal door and the far wall was barely ten feet. There was no water, no toilet. She sat down again on the cold concrete, trying to control the wave of claustrophobia welling up inside her. The absence of light was particularly hard to bear, as was the viscous silence that gnawed away at her brain like ultrasound, preventing her from thinking. She hugged her knees and rested her head on top of them. She had learned to sleep in this position to minimize contact with the cold floor, but now it irritated her wounds, and she heard herself moaning.

Hours passed, and she no longer knew whether she'd been

asleep or not, having lost all sense of time. She missed the cell in Castelar. She was thirsty and she needed to pee, but she didn't dare call out. They were going to torture her again. She had escaped and they were going to finish her off, as El Cabo Pavor had said.

There came another moan. Sure it wasn't her this time, Julia pinched herself, then dug her nails into her palms. No, she wasn't asleep. She couldn't see anything, but she was definitely awake. The sound came again. It was coming from the other side of the wall. Julia pressed her ear up against the damp concrete, trying to locate the source of the groaning.

Somewhere very close by, someone was crying. She felt her way around her cell again, pressing her entire body up against the walls as she listened. The sobbing was coming from her right when she faced the cell door. She took heart and began knocking a rhythm on the wall: three short knocks, a pause, then three long ones. She repeated the sequence several times.

The moaning stopped. Then a man's voice said from the other side of the wall: "Who are you?"

"My name's Julia. Who are you?"

"They call me the Ant."

"Oh."

"Did you get here today?"

"I think so," Julia said. "Do you know where we are?"

"Yes. The police station in Haedo."

"Do they interrogate us here?"

"No, don't worry. There's no more torture here."

"Are you sure?"

"Obviously, because I'm telling you!"

"So why were you crying?"

"I'm alive because I'm a degenerate, a traitor."

"They're the degenerates!" Julia practically shouted, choking back sobs.

After a lengthy silence, the voice said: "Did they torture you?"

". . . It's better now."

"It's going to get even better. We're allowed visits here. We're being held under PEN."*

"How do you know?!" Julia exclaimed.

For Julia, being detained under PEN was nothing short of a miracle. Prisoners who were handed over to the National Executive Power were "legalized." They were no longer "at the disposition of" the military authorities, and their files were converted into criminal records. They would, of course, have to stand trial, but they escaped the torturers.

"That's the procedure," the Ant replied. "It takes a while, but once they bring you under PEN, things start to change. First they authorize you to receive letters. Then, if all goes well, they agree to let your family bring you food."

* Poder Ejecutivo Nacional (National Executive Power).

"My family doesn't know where I am."

"Give me a name and a telephone number to memorize. I'll give them to my family. They'll tell yours."

Julia spent two weeks in Haedo. She suffered from terrible cramps and had no choice but to urinate in her cell. She believed she was still pregnant and would stay very still listening to her body, incubating her hopes.

A guard came to let her out for a few minutes once a day. She never saw him, because she was always blindfolded. She was forced to relieve herself in front of him while he hurled obscenities at her. She didn't wash for the entire two weeks she was detained in Haedo. Her body stank of excrement and of the fear she couldn't shake off. Being alone in that black hole, feeling the rats scurrying across the floor, the cockroaches crawling over her skin and becoming tangled in her hair, terrified her.

Julia's only moments of respite came when her neighbor broke his silence. He was riddled with remorse. He had been selling out his friends, one of which, he told Julia one day, was seized while trying to flee Argentina disguised as a priest. He knew his friend had been brought to Haedo immediately after his capture. "It was one of the d'Uccello brothers," he said. He explained he had gotten the information from the torturer with whom he'd made his deal, and who made a point of updating him on the results of his collaboration to feed his guilt.

Julia wished she could hate him.

She consoled herself with the thought that if Gabriel had passed through Haedo he must have been automatically transferred to PEN custody, which could only be a lesser evil.

One cold morning Julia was finally taken out of her cell. She saw natural light for the first time in weeks. It was particularly cold, and even though she didn't know where she was being taken, the idea of never coming back was a relief. She was coughing, each spasm a frightening reminder of her swollen belly.

Julia didn't see the entrance because, as usual, she was transported in the trunk of a car. The khaki pants and boots that she glimpsed by peeking under her blindfold disappeared once she was inside the building. The footsteps grew fainter, not a word, then silence. She stayed standing at attention, paralyzed by panic, not knowing whether she was alone or facing an execution squad. After what seemed like an eternity, a woman's voice asked her for her name, birth date, and place of birth. Julia answered hesitatingly. The voice ordered her to take off her blindfold and step forward. Julia found herself in a huge room with a ceiling so high that the echo of her voice came back to her. A chair and table sat redundantly in a corner; she got the impression they had been placed there temporarily. Behind the table sat a stout, stern-looking woman with a fixed expression, wearing horn-rimmed glasses and a spotless gray uniform, her shiny hair pulled back into a bun. She was busy tapping rapidly with two fingers on a prewar typewriter.

"Profession, address, telephone number," the woman continued in a monotone.

For the first time since her arrest, Julia felt like a human being. She had a name, she had a life. She fought back tears. This uniformed woman was "legalizing" her.

Julia tried to maintain her composure, but her voice kept cracking, and she had to blow her nose on her sleeve.

"Why are you here?" the woman went on coldly.

Julia couldn't answer.

"What are you accused of? What did you do? Why are you under arrest?"

Nothing. Julia knew nothing. She didn't know what she was accused of, and she was crying with joy because at last she was under arrest.

The woman raised her head, took off her glasses, and looked at Julia.

"You're in Villa Devoto prison, my girl," she said in a tired voice. "It's Tuesday, June 22, 1976, and the time is 1:35 P.M."

24.

VILLA DEVOTO

Austral Spring
1976

There were three other inmates in the cell Julia was placed in. They were all serving long prison sentences. Coco was an active member of the Communist Party. Her real name was Claudia, but her cell mates used her activist nickname. The oldest woman, whom they referred to as La Veterana, was a Montonera like Julia, and Maby, the shiest of the three, had been active in a far-left organization called Revolución del Pueblo.

As far as Julia was concerned, it was sheer luxury: a sink, lights, a proper bed, a mattress. But best of all, a big jug of *maté* every morning, along with a ration of fresh bread for each of them. The height of indulgence: every other day the guard distributed food that the common-law prisoners shared with the political detainees. Sometimes there was even chocolate.

The prison building had six floors. It was made up of three large wings in a *U* shape. Julia's wing was reserved for political prisoners, the one opposite for common-law prisoners. Julia's cell was on the fifth floor, which housed women who had been sentenced to more than ten years in prison. The floor below was allocated to men serving a similar sentence. Lower down, on the second and third floors, were prisoners awaiting trial. On the top floor, above the women's floor, were the punishment cells. This infamous uppermost floor was known as the *chancha*.

One night they were awakened by screams coming from above. The screaming continued for at least two days, during which they found it impossible to do anything at all. Then, one night, there was a heavy silence.

"Maybe they've brought him downstairs," Coco said the next morning.

"Maybe he's dead."

"No, I can hear the guard delivering his tray."

Maby climbed on one of the bunks and thumped hard twice on the ceiling. They were surprised to receive two knocks in reply. Eagerly the women set about inventing a basic alphabet. The number of knocks corresponded to each letter's position in the alphabet. The man must have had the same idea, because in no time at all they had devised a system of communication. Information trickled down slowly, one knock at a time, stopping whenever a guard approached, and this was how Julia learned, to her astonishment, that the man communicating with them from the punishment cell was none other than Augusto, Gabriel's friend and her neighbor at Castelar. When he realized Julia was part of the group below, he informed her that Rosa was apparently also at Villa Devoto and might even be on the same floor as her.

Another equally simple and effective secret communication network had been operating in the prison for a long time. The women would climb onto the top bunk to reach the window. From this vantage point they had an unobstructed view of the neighborhood rooftops, the street, and the windows of the common-law prisoners' wing. These prisoners could communicate with their families and were therefore constantly in touch with the outside world. Julia's cell mates used them as a post house to send and receive news. The prisoners had invented a sign language of their own for the purpose.

This means of communication became vital for Julia. She had no way of knowing whether Mama Fina was aware of her predicament, but the common-law prisoners could let her know via their relatives. This was how Julia was given the first piece of good news: informed of Julia's reappearance at Villa Devoto, Mama Fina and Julia's mother had begun the procedures to come and visit her.

But the women were unable to obtain any information about Theo or Adriana. All of Julia's attempts led to a dead end. One evening, though, when her companions were sleeping, Julia witnessed a strange sight. La Veterana, the longest-held political prisoner in Villa Devoto, was on all fours with her arm stuck down the toilet up to the elbow. She was flush-

ing the toilet while holding on to the end of a rope leading into
the sewage pipe.

Maby explained it to her the next morning. La Veterana
had been communicating with her Montonero superiors on
the floor below. Maby described in detail the way messages
were sent and received through the plumbing system. It might
be a way for Julia to get some news. But persuading La Veterana to act as an intermediary would not be easy.

Julia had struck up a friendship with young Maby quite
naturally, since they were both pregnant. She knew that some
prisoners on the lower floors got information straight from
Montonero headquarters. She had heard that the organization
had put together a file on each of its disappeared members and
wanted to know who was being detained and legalized in Villa
Devoto.

La Veterana was a hard-bitten, solitary woman. She didn't
take part in discussions, ate by herself, and never complained.
Julia could sense the other woman watching her constantly but
had never managed to catch her eye. Whenever Julia turned
around, La Veterana seemed to have her head in a book. She was
a great reader with a huge collection of books under her bunk.

A few days after the nighttime incident with the plumbing,
La Veterana began to read a book entitled *Teología de la
liberación*,* which piqued Julia's curiosity. She had heard Father
Mugica talk about it. He had even mentioned meeting one of

* *A Theology of Liberation.*

the leaders of the movement during his visit to Europe. In-trigued, Julia took advantage of the arrival of the maté to ap-proach La Veterana. She asked if she could take a look at the book. They were surprised to discover that they had both known Father Mugica and attended the prayer vigil on the night of his assassination. Julia found out from La Veterana that Father Mugica had taken part in the May 1968 protests in France. Julia knew nothing about France, and even less about its recent history, but she had found a good avenue. La Vete-rana was delighted to find a serious pupil.

In a rare show of confidence, she lent Julia some more books, and Julia devoured them. La Veterana then undertook to broaden Julia's cultural horizons and scheduled discussions on subjects of her choice. In the course of their conversations, Julia had plenty of time to talk to her about the d'Uccello brothers. La Veterana had no trouble alerting her network. A few weeks later she called Julia over: she had had a response from her superiors.

"Listen, I think I know what happened to the elder d'Uccello."

"Gabriel?"

"Yes. You told me he got himself arrested when he was try-ing to escape disguised as a priest, right?"

"Yes, it was the Ant who told me about it. . . . Have you heard anything about Theo?"

"Not so fast. For the moment I've only been given informa-tion about Gabriel d'Uccello."

"And?"

"The leaders have confirmed the specifics with various sources."

"Well?"

"He was arrested and taken to Haedo."

"I knew that."

"From there he was transferred to Mansión Seré."

"Oh, God!"

"We know they sent him to ESMA* after that."

Julia felt her legs give way and sat down on her bunk.

"Go on, I'm ready. Tell me everything," she mumbled.

"They threw him out of a plane alive."

Julia was so shaken by the news that her cell mates asked for her to be transferred urgently to the prison hospital, for fear she was going to miscarry. But nobody came for her.

Julia lay prostrate, refusing to get up, eat, or speak. She felt she was responsible. She was the one who had brought Rosa into Gabriel's life, and Rosa was a member of the clandestine military wing of the Montoneros. She knew only too well how strongly Gabriel had disapproved of their violence, but he had agreed to treat their wounded, especially after the Ezeiza mas-

* Escuela de Mecánica de la Armada, the Argentine naval mechanics school in Buenos Aires: the largest of the five hundred clandestine detention centers that operated during the military dictatorship, where an estimated five thousand people were tortured and killed and hundreds of children born to detainees were forcibly removed at birth.

sacre. And particularly because of his feelings for Rosa. The organization had given the order to avoid the emergency services because the military was drawing up lists of suspects based on the information obtained in hospitals, and he was determined to protect her.

In retrospect, Julia felt she had lacked common sense when Gabriel had turned up at their flat after the police raid at the hospital. She should have sent Gabriel to the port straightaway to make contact with Mama Fina's connections. Why hadn't she thought of it? He had seemed so decided, so confident of his plan to escape via the convent! It had all seemed so simple. She had stupidly believed their luck would hold, when in fact the vise had already closed around them.

And then there were Theo and Adriana. No one could give her any news of them. Maybe Gabriel's death was just the beginning of the horror. Julia didn't know if he had died before or after their escape from Castelar. If Adriana and Theo had been recaptured, they had probably ended up in El Diablo's hands and been dropped into empty space over the estuary, like Gabriel.

The thought drove her crazy.

Dismayed at the impact the news had on Julia, La Veterana surmised that the dead man must be the father of the child. She was distressed too, but in a different way, as if her convictions had not been strong enough to help curb the debasement.

At least she had managed to get word to Mama Fina, who was now pestering the authorities incessantly. A visit was authorized for the end of September. This was the only thing that seemed to get through to Julia.

The day eventually arrived. A middle-aged woman with a bleach-blond crew cut, rigged out in a gray uniform that was too tight for her, barked for Julia to follow her. Julia walked with difficulty through the maze of corridors, up and down staircases, through gates and doors that were opened and closed. Her stomach was huge and she held on to the walls for support as she walked, her head spinning. Unable to make sense of the route they were taking, she was taken aback when she suddenly found herself in the visitors' area.

The room intimidated her. It was filled with a crowd of prisoners she had never seen. There was a row of narrow booths, open on the side of the guards' corridor and cut down the middle by a thick glass partition that prevented any physical contact with visitors.

The uniformed woman pointed to a booth. The allocated space was minimal and offered absolutely no privacy. Julia stared straight ahead, making an effort not to eavesdrop on the other conversations. On the other side of the glass partition was a chair identical to hers. A tube through the middle of the glass functioned as an intercom. Prisoners and visitors had to take turns speaking into the tube and listening. Julia wiped her hands nervously on her pants and patted her hair. What if Mama Fina didn't come?

She smoothed out the creases in her uniform again to keep

her hands from trembling as the guard looked on impassively. Finally a door opened. But it wasn't Mama Fina. Julia tried to hide her disappointment and conjured up a bright smile to greet her mother.

"Mother . . ."

"*Mi Julia mia*, it's good to see you. You can't imagine what we've gone through."

"I'm sorry, Mom."

Her mother stared at her as if to make sure it really was her daughter. Her expression twitched slightly as she noticed Julia's belly.

"Your grandmother wanted to come, but she wasn't given permission. They kept promising until the last minute that she would get it."

"Oh."

"But the whole family's behind you. Your father sends his love. And Anna and Pablo, and the twins."

"Thank you, Mom."

"Mama Fina asked me to tell you she's claiming your dual citizenship. We hope you'll be allowed to leave Argentina with your Uruguayan passport. She thinks we can obtain refugee status for you in a European country. She's in contact with a French organization called France Terre d'Asile."

For some reason Julia found she was crying.

"And Mama Fina also wants you to know that she's looking for the father of your child."

A sudden tension accentuated the lines that were beginning to form at the corners of her mouth. "You know your
grandmother. She didn't give me any details."

"Oh, Mom!"

Julia clung to the tube, but the guard had already taken her
by the shoulder to lead her away.

25.

RUBENS

Austral Summer
1976

W hen you have the baby, make sure you don't register it under the father's name," Maby had advised her.

She had explained to Julia that under Argentine law, fathers were granted full rights over children, including custody. In the event of Theo's continued absence, Theo's parents would receive rights over the child. In practice, this meant not only that the child would be taken from her six months after its birth and given to Theo's family but also that Julia wouldn't be able to take her baby with her if her asylum application was accepted.

During her second visit, Julia informed her mother that the procedures for leaving Argentina urgently needed to be completed. Her asylum application had to be accepted before the baby was six months old. According to Julia's calculations, the baby would be born in January. She would have to leave by July 1977.

Her mother reassured her. She and Mama Fina were doing the rounds of the European embassies, but they still thought France was the country most likely to accept her. They had been told that a French consulate official had applied for authorization to meet with Julia in the prison. This was part of the procedure, and it meant the asylum process was already under way.

This time Julia's mother had brought her a bag of things. Julia had been wearing the same uniform ever since her arrival in Villa Devoto, even though the prisoners weren't required to wear a uniform. There was also a selection of baby clothes, which her mother held up on the other side of the glass.

Julia seized the opportunity to raise a thorny subject. "Mom, my baby won't be able to take its father's name."

Her mother looked up. "I'm relieved you've come to the same conclusion as us," she said. "So it'll be a little d'Annunzio. Your grandmother's convinced it's a boy. I'd like a little girl myself, but never mind. She says you should baptize the baby with a good strong name, something like . . ."

"Like Josefina," Julia interrupted mischievously, "since I'm hoping it'll be a girl too."

Her mother refrained from comment. After a moment she said, "I don't like this glass between us. It reminds me that I stupidly allowed distance to grow between us. You were always so strong and confident. Even when you were a child, it was hard for me to think of myself as your mother. I sometimes felt like you were already an adult."

She placed her hand on the partition. Julia did likewise. Their hands were identical.

"I wanted you to know that."

On December 21 a guard came to take Julia to the maternity unit. It was the first day of summer, which she took as a good omen. She would have liked to slip on sandals and wear her hair down. She collected her things and kissed her cell mates.

The hospital was on the first floor of a separate building. They had to go through several gates and checkpoints to get there, as each floor was sealed off from the others. Julia crossed the large courtyard in which she had been "legalized" on her arrival and entered a long, gloomy corridor painted creamy yellow. She followed the guard in silence, her footsteps echoing in the emptiness, as if they belonged to someone else.

The door to the hospital opened onto a fenced-in lobby area. Farther on, behind another barred door, was the maternity room. It was a sort of enclosed yard with a pillar in each corner, and between the pillars there were around thirty beds lined up along the walls in two rows facing each other.

More than half the beds were empty. There were only about ten detainees in the room. Julia could take her pick and settled on a bed close to the barred door that separated the room from the lobby area. By leaning against one of the pillars, she could keep an eye on what was going on outside while remaining hidden from sight, if she wished.

In the bed next to hers was another woman who looked to be just a few weeks away from giving birth. They exchanged a smile. The young woman helped her put her things away in a small locker between the two beds. At the far end, next to a sealed-up window, Julia counted three patients on drips. She could tell at a glance that they were in a critical condition. In another corner sat a mother with her back to Julia, rocking her baby, while other women chatted in low voices.

The room was lit by a long, narrow plate-glass window at ceiling height, so it was impossible to see what was going on in the street outside. There was a row of six showerheads behind a partition wall. The bathroom consisted of two squat toilets.

A short man in a white coat with a nervous walk made a conspicuous entrance. He headed straight for her without looking up from his papers, followed by three nurses.

"I suppose this is Julia," he said, reading his notes.

"Yes, sir," Julia answered.

A pair of steel-blue eyes behind round glasses looked hard at her.

"She'll give birth at the end of the month," he announced. "Or rather, she'll shit out her runt. You lot don't give birth, you shit."

Julia swallowed. "I'm due in January."

"We'll see about that," the little man replied with a fixed grin.

He continued his rounds, instructing the nurses in a haughty tone and with deliberate and noticeable brevity, then left the way he had come.

"You'll have to get used to it," Julia's neighbor said when the procession had gone. "All the women in this prison have C-sections. We're guinea pigs. They test drugs on us. If we don't die, they put them on the market. Everyone wins: the pharmaceutical companies and the government, because it means more money and fewer opponents. . . . Oh, sorry, I haven't introduced myself. I'm Valentina—Tina to friends. I'm with Poder Obrero.* What about you?"

There were all kinds of women in the same room: women who had returned after torture, mentally ill women who had not recovered from the abuse, and a few pregnant women.

"That poor girl in the far corner, the one who keeps humming to herself . . . she's lost her mind. She's just had a baby, born two months early. He's in an incubator, but they're going to give him up for adoption. She's still waiting for him, poor thing."

"Isn't she rocking a baby?"

"No. It's a doll."

Tina went on: "The nurses are quite nice, and the food is better than in the cells. There's more of it, at any rate."

"When are you due?" Julia asked.

"Rubens is the one who determines the due dates here. I'll

* Workers' Power.

reach full term in mid-January, but he's decided it'll be earlier. I don't care. I just want to make sure my baby is healthy. As for the rest, I know he'll butcher me."

"What do you mean?"

"Rubens is a nasty character. A torturer in the making. It's a good thing we're in the hands of the PEN, and there are nurses around. But don't expect him to stitch you back up nicely."

Dr. Rubens scheduled Julia's delivery for December 31, one month before her due date. He seemed to have a fixation on dates, since Tina was scheduled to give birth on Christmas Day. It was rumored that he was taking revenge on a group of nurses who had denounced the maltreatment he inflicted on the inmates, two of whom had died after he'd operated on them. He had immediately given their babies to his colleagues to adopt.

To prepare as best as she could, Julia began to read out loud, as Tina had suggested, so the baby would recognize the sound of her voice. She wove a tiny bracelet to put around the baby's wrist as soon as it came out of her womb. She sifted through the things her mother had brought her. She wanted only white cotton linen for the baby at first. She washed it, rinsed it, and hung it to dry next to her bed. She filed her nails right down so she wouldn't accidentally scratch the baby. Finally, she asked Tina to cut her hair to shoulder length and washed herself thoroughly on the night before the big day.

A nurse came to get her after lunch. She was made to wear a green hospital gown that tied up the back and to swallow some pills that made her head spin. Then she was led into a large, cold room. There was a rudimentary birthing bed, old and rusty, in the middle of the room, with a spotlight on either side of it. Julia was alarmed. She didn't understand why she was being made to put her feet in the stirrups if Rubens was planning to do a C-section.

"Be quiet and do as you're told," a nurse told her as she filled a syringe.

Dr. Rubens made his appearance, impeccable in his white coat. He looked at Julia lying on the bed, her feet in the stirrups under a sheet that was too short, as he pulled on his gloves. "Filthy Trotska," he murmured. "This is the last time you'll be shitting a Bolshevik into the world."

26

THE YOUNG KOREAN

Boreal Summer

2006

He saw her come in wearing her gym clothes, a towel around her neck. She glanced at her watch and walked over to the exercise machines. Theo pretended to be tying his shoelaces so he could observe her at his leisure.

He had seen her once before at the company's annual staff conference. A young Asian version of Julia, he'd thought. Theo had taken advantage of a break in the program to stand behind her in the drinks line and then offer to pour her a cup of coffee. They'd exchanged a few words before she went back to her seat. He now knew that her name was Mia Moon and that she had recently joined the accounting department.

The young woman tossed her towel into a corner, hopped on one of the few empty treadmills, adjusted the settings, and began her workout. She was wearing a black crop top that showed off her toned stomach and a pair of matching capri leggings. Her black hair, pulled back into a ponytail, accentuated her athletic appearance. Theo, who was busy lifting weights, couldn't take his eyes off her.

She got off the treadmill in a sweat and passed him on her way to the water fountain. Theo seized the opportunity to do the same. He acted surprised to see her as he said hello.

"I saw you when I came in, but you looked busy," she said jokingly. "I've forgotten your name. It's Tom, right?"

"Almost. It's Theo. Theodoro, really. But Theo's easier," he said before downing a plastic cup of cold water.

"Oh, right. I remember now. You're Italian."

"No. Despite the name and the accent, I'm actually American."

"Yes, of course. I meant to say of Italian origin."

"No, wrong again. And I bet you that you won't be able to guess where I'm actually from."

"Aha! I like bets. But I should warn you there's a strong chance it'll end in a tie. You'll never guess where I'm from."

"With a name like yours?"

"You remember my name?"

"Mia Moon. Hard to forget such a pretty name."

"Good memory—one point for you."

"And I don't think I'd be too far off the mark if I said you were of Korean origin."

"That's what everyone thinks."

"Does that mean yes? If I've won, let me buy you a drink."

"You've lost."

Theo made a gesture of disappointment.

"But you can still buy me a cup of coffee after work," the young woman added, picking up her towel to leave.

They met at the end of the day in the parking lot and drove out of the office complex one behind the other. There was a pub near the train station that Theo liked. It was always packed, but hardly anyone from the office went there. They sat down at a small table that had just become free, wedged in between the restrooms and the bar.

"You're even prettier than you were this morning," Theo said, pulling his chair closer to hers.

"I'm married," she said, raising an eyebrow.

Theo burst out laughing. "That doesn't change anything. You're still beautiful!"

"What about you?"

"Are you asking if I'm beautiful?"

"No, if you're married."

"I see you're really applying the recommendations made at the annual conference."

"What do you mean?"

"The speaker said that it was important to know how to ask the right questions."

"He also said you have to know how to listen. So. I'm listening."

"Okay, but first we have to resolve our little bet."

"It's over. You lost," Mia replied, laughing.

"I'd say we're equal. I'm not Italian, and you're not Korean. Give me a hint."

Her husband was of Korean descent, but he had never set foot in Korea and he didn't speak the language. He and Mia considered themselves American. They had met in college, while she was studying accounting and he was getting a master's in finance. Now he worked for an investment bank.

"All right, so he's Korean, but you're the one I'm interested in. And I'm still none the wiser."

"You haven't told me much about yourself either. You're not Italian, but surely you're of European descent."

"I'll give you that. Not that it'll help you."

"Oh, okay. Is it really that complicated?"

"Not really. I'm from a country that experienced massive European immigration."

"In that case, shall we say . . . Argentina?"

Theo looked at her with admiration. "Wow, I'm impressed."

She opened her eyes wide and leaned toward him, resting on her elbows.

"Don't tell me you're Argentine."

"I am indeed. I was born in Argentina."

"But that's impossible," Mia said, crossing her hands over her chest. "It's too much of a coincidence."

"A coincidence? What do you mean?"

"My maiden name is Mia Matamoros Amun."

"Matamoros Amun . . . Amun? That's an indigenous name, isn't it?"

"Yes. My mother was Mapuche."

"So you're Argentine on your mother's side!"

"Yes, and Spanish on my father's side."

Mia's cell phone started to ring.

"Oh, my goodness, it's really late. Where did the time go? I have to get home."

Mia stood up, picked up her bag, gave him a little wave, and left.

The gym became Theo's number one priority. Every day he would track Mia down there and then head back upstairs with her to heat up his lunch. They would sit at a small table by the vending machines and drink coffee.

"What's that you're eating?" she asked him one day.

"Why? Doesn't it look good?"

"Sure, I guess so, but I'm not sure it's all that good for you."

"I'm not on a diet."

"Me neither, but I still watch what I eat."

"So what exactly is wrong with my lunch?"

"Too many carbs, not enough protein."

"I don't need more protein!"

"Yes, you do, to build muscle," Mia said, pointing to her flat stomach.

"But they say meat clogs your arteries."

"There are other sources of protein. Egg whites, for example."

"I don't see myself becoming a connoisseur of egg whites."

Mia burst out laughing. "You have no imagination."

"Do you have any recipes?"

"Tell you what: why don't you come over to my place for dinner? Kwan went to New York this morning. He won't be back till late. I'll make you my specialty. Egg-white curry. It's delicious."

Theo gave her a sidelong glance.

"And besides," she went on, "I hate eating alone."

Back in his office, Theo called Julia from his cell phone and told her not to wait for him. He was going out for dinner with some colleagues. Luckily, Diane had just called to invite her to the movies.

Theo had gotten into the habit of keeping some clean white shirts in the bottom drawer of his desk. He went down to the gym to take a shower and change.

It had been a long time since he'd felt this pleasant sensation. He couldn't wait to be alone with Mia in her apartment. He lingered under the shower to prolong the pleasure and lost track of time. On his way out, he ran into Ben, a coworker and neighbor, who had just finished his workout. His wife, Pat, who also worked for the company, happened to be out of town.

"Let's go for a drink," Ben suggested.

"Not tonight. I've got dinner plans," Theo replied, eyeing his watch.

The gym door slammed open. Mia burst in, said a quick hello to Ben, and pulled Theo aside.

"I've been looking for you. I left you a voice mail. Then I saw your car was still in the lot."

Mia was fiddling nervously with her keys. "I'm really sorry. I have a project that's due tomorrow morning and I need to pull an all-nighter. Shall we see each other tomorrow?"

"No problem," said Theo with a broad smile.

She rushed out of the gym, leaving a trail of perfume in the air.

"Well . . . looks like we can go for that drink after all," said Theo, staring at the door.

The weeks that followed were a torture. They saw each other only at the gym. Theo had to make an effort not to call Mia. He had wanted to send her flowers at home and talked himself out of it just in time. Instead he bought an anthology of Argentine poems and left it on her desk with a bookmark tucked inside marking a sonnet by Francisco Luis Bernárdez. The last lines were underlined:

Porque después de todo he comprendido
Que lo que el árbol tiene de florido
*Vive de lo que tiene sepultado.**

Unable to understand it, Mia sent the three lines to her father. He wrote back straightaway with a translation, adding a note at the end: "This was one of your mother's favorite poems. Where did you get it?"

Mia sat down. Her hands were shaking. She had to stop seeing Theo. Finally she picked up her cell phone.

"Let's have dinner tonight."

Mia made a reservation at a sushi bar in the center of Westport, a ten-minute drive from the office. It was also one of Kwan's favorite restaurants. She felt safe there. She planned to tell Theo that she needed some space.

Instead she found herself talking about her life throughout the evening.

"My mother died soon after I was born. I have no memory of her. Dad hardly ever talks about her. I think he resents her for committing suicide."

"I thought she died during childbirth."

* Because after everything I have understood
  That what the tree has visibly in bloom
  Thrives of what is buried beneath.

(Translation by Sarah Salazar, http://theenglishcenterblog.tumblr.com/post/
113527898559/poem-translation)

"Yes, that's what I always say. The word 'suicide' scares people. It's okay. It hasn't affected me, since I never had any emotional bond with her. I couldn't even tell you what it means to be part Mapuche. I have her eyes, that's all. I prefer to have people think I'm Korean. That way I don't have to explain about my mother."

"Do you know why she did it?"

"I know her family never forgave her for marrying my father. She was some sort of Mapuche princess. I believe she was very beautiful."

"Do you have any photos of her?"

"No, none at all."

"What about your father? Did he keep any?"

"It was a very hard blow for him. He left Argentina, and he's never wanted to go back. He made a new life for himself here. He married Nicole when I was barely two and then became an American citizen. She helped him to stop drinking. She didn't want to have any more children, so she could take care of me. She's my real mother. We were very lucky."

"How did he meet Nicole?"

"Nicole? She's the sister of his best friend. That's how they met. Uncle George is a captain in the air force; he's the one who helped me get this job. If it wasn't for him, I never would have been hired at Swirbul and Collier."

"True. Not just anyone can get a job with Swirbul and Collier," Theo said, stirring the ice around in his glass. He reached out and stroked Mia's cheek. She stopped him.

"No, Theo."

"We have too much in common for us to stop here."

"I don't want to."

"I'll only go as far as you want, Mia. I can wait."

Newark airport was very busy and the traffic was moving slowly. Cars were lining up to drop off passengers, then struggling to negotiate their way out of the congestion. Theo was impatient. He had just said good-bye to Julia, who was leaving for a month to visit Ulysses.

After one final maneuver to overtake a long line of taxis, Theo forked off in the direction of New York City. He took the New Jersey Turnpike and then turned onto a congested freeway through the Bronx, telling himself that yet again he'd made the wrong decision. Finally he passed the toll plaza and sped toward the Connecticut Turnpike, heading up the coast in the direction of Trumbull. He still had an hour's drive ahead.

By the time he'd parked in front of Mia's building, the sky had already turned red. A flock of birds flew overhead, chirping loudly. Theo looked out and saw the white streak of a plane crossing the blue sky. He hesitated for a moment, then got out of the car.

Mia opened the door wearing a simple green wrap dress tied at the waist and black stilettos. Theo watched her as she walked over to a carefully laid table. The lit candles in the center were reflected in a large picture window. Everything had its place in the room, a minimalist space uncluttered by ornaments or photographs. Mia poured a glass of champagne and offered it to Theo.

"What are we celebrating?" he asked, putting an arm around her waist.

"Our first weekend on our own," she answered, moving closer.

"And I thought you'd asked me over to sample your famous egg-white curry."

"There's something else on the menu," she murmured in his ear.

She took him by the hand and led him down the hall.

The next morning he was awakened by a ray of sunlight falling across his face. Mia was curled up against him, her lips slightly parted as she slept.

He recalled their conversation from the night before. He shouldn't have talked so much. He had shared his life story, or rather the official version of it: his childhood with Gabriel and his brother's death during the Dirty War. He had told her—out of habit—that the Montoneros had kidnapped him during the terrible years of violence in Argentina. Mia had no idea who the Montoneros were and couldn't have cared less.

Besides, he hadn't revealed anything of real consequence. But it had done him good. For the first time his past seemed far behind him.

Since arriving in the United States, Theo had not mentioned his brother's name to anyone other than his uncle Mayol and Julia. He hadn't told a soul that the real reason he had wanted to work at Swirbul and Collier was to track down Gabriel's killer and not, as everyone assumed, to obtain U.S. citizenship.

He had joined the company as a systems engineer, hoping the position would give him access to classified files. He was very young when he was hired and had just arrived in the country. From his earliest meetings with the CIA, when he was trading information for protection, his contacts had realized he was exceptionally skilled in the field of IT security. He had been steered in the direction of Swirbul and Collier, where he could remain anonymous. He quickly rose through the ranks, under the close watch of the CIA.

As head of his department, he was now in charge of servicing all of the computers in the company. He had gone through all the available archives with a fine-tooth comb. He knew his target was hiding in the United States, but it had proved impossible to track him down. He had spent thirty years driven by hatred, obsessed with revenge. Even Julia hadn't been able to set him free. But this morning he felt elated.

———

The sun was barely above the horizon when Theo and Mia climbed hastily into the car. They gulped down a backpackers' breakfast in the first open diner they found, before stopping off at Theo's to get the motorcycle out of the garage and pull on leather jackets. They headed north at full speed, free on an empty highway. Theo wanted to reach Rhode Island by lunchtime, but Mia wanted to go farther.

They arrived at Cape Cod just as the sun was setting. The beach was deserted except for a woman and her young daughter. The girl, who was wearing a straw hat that was too big for her, was staring at them disapprovingly as they chased and splashed each other in the waves. They bought freshly caught and fried fish on the waterfront and ate it with their hands, licking their fingers, before making their way home slowly, exhilarated, their heads in the stars, arriving in time for bed at dawn with no desire to sleep.

Theo woke first. He loved this moment, when Mia belonged to him in spite of herself. He lay there, captivated, then got up gently so as not to wake her and went to get dressed. Mia had hung a gallery of family photos in the hallway leading from the living room to the bedroom. Theo ran his eye over them. All the pictures were of Kwan and his parents except for their wedding photo, in which a radiant Mia kissed her husband, her parents on one side and Kwan's parents on the other.

Theo made himself a cup of coffee and went to sit in the

living room, opposite the large window with its view of the sky. He took out his cell phone and scrolled distractedly through his messages.

All of a sudden he stopped short, put down his coffee cup, and hurried back into the hallway. He found the wedding photo again and peered closely at it. A shiver ran down his spine.

27.

ULYSSES

Austral Summer
1976

E scorted by a nurse, Julia made her way into the maternity unit, empty-handed. She found it difficult to walk. She winced as she sat down on the edge of her bed. Tina thought she looked different. There was something of an Italian madonna about her.

"Well?" asked Maby, who had been transferred to the maternity unit during Julia's absence.

"It's a boy!" Julia said breathlessly. "I wasn't allowed to bring him myself. He weighs five and a half pounds. He took his first breath at precisely 3:27 P.M."

"Is that important?"

"I don't know," Julia said, lying down. "The nurse put him on my chest as soon as Rubens had gone. He lifted his head and looked at me. I'm sure he wanted to see what his mother looked like. He fell asleep straight after that. I think he was relieved, poor thing!"

Tina and Maby laughed as they sat down next to Julia.

"What about Rubens?" Maby asked.

"Like with Tina. Horrible. But not enough to ruin the moment."

"Did the nurses help you?"

"There are two of them. Only one helped me. She cancels out Rubens. The other one is a complete witch, even worse than Rubens. They all hate each other."

"That's reassuring," Maby said, before adding: "Was there a lot of damage?"

"Yes, serious damage. Ulysses will be my only child."

There was a brief silence.

"Ulysses?" Tina asked. "That's a tough name for a kid!"

"Couldn't you find something more . . . local? Like Juan, or Pablo? Then we could call him Pablito. Try saying Ulissito, just to see!"

The three of them burst out laughing.

Julia bit her lip, lost in thought. After a while she said, "I think the name will suit him. Ulysses never lost hope. I want my son to be like him."

Tina pulled a face. "I should have thought about it, like you did, before calling my daughter Dolores!* Dolores . . . I guess it was my subconscious playing a dirty trick on me."

* "Dolores" (and by extension the nickname Dolly) means "pains" in Spanish.

They were crying with laughter when the door opened and two nurses came in, each carrying a newborn. Dolly had spent a few days in an incubator, and Ulysses was being allowed a few minutes with Julia.

The young mothers sat up and got ready to hold their babies.

Without warning, the crazy woman from the corner darted forward and made a lunge for Ulysses.

"That's my baby!" she cried, looking around wildly.

Julia had never really paid any attention to the young woman, who was always seated in her corner with her back turned. Now she had suddenly burst into Julia's life, sparking panic and a general effort to reason with her. Julia moved slowly toward her.

She was slight and probably very young, but her salt-and-pepper hair accentuated the effects of premature aging. Everything about her evoked the fear and fragility of a wounded bird. She stood hunched over, as if expecting a blow.

"That's my baby," the woman repeated, becoming louder each time.

At the sound of her voice, Julia stood rooted to the spot. Impossible. It couldn't be. Despite the rictus that twisted her mouth and the paralysis down one side of her face, despite the wrinkles, the receding hairline, and the unfocused gaze, Julia had finally recognized her. It was Rosa. Her friend Rosa.

The one Julia had pulled from the hell of the Ezeiza massacre, the one Gabriel had nursed back to health and fallen in love with. The one on whom El Loco had unleashed his fury after she had escaped with Adriana. It was Rosa, her friend.

Her torturers had stripped her of everything, but not of her heart.

"Rosa . . ." Julia said as the other women fell silent. "Rosa, my darling, listen to me."

Rosa turned her blank gaze on Julia.

"That's my baby. . . ." she replied.

"No, he's not your baby. His name is Ulysses. But you can hold him."

Rosa took the baby carefully and walked slowly to her bed at the far end. She sat down and rocked Ulysses, singing to him in a soft voice, a picture of serenity and fulfillment. The baby fell asleep in her arms.

In the days that followed, Julia tried several times to strike up a conversation with Rosa, to no avail. She then experimented with sitting next to her in silence for hours, looking for a flicker of recognition in her eyes, an emotion, anything that could bring her back. In the end she decided to talk out loud, convinced that her words would somehow reach Rosa's heart. She told her about everything that had happened since Castelar, about Paola—whom she no longer had any news of—and Adriana and Augusto. She sensed that the young woman was listening to her, because the rhythm of her breathing changed slightly when Julia described events they both had witnessed. But she could never be sure, as Rosa had mastered the art of absentia. When she finally told her about Gabriel, about his death, Rosa didn't even blink.

Rosa was the only one who didn't receive any visitors. Julia couldn't recall her ever mentioning her family. She knew that Rosa had grown up in foster care. Julia remembered Gabriel talking at some point about Rosa's parents and how he had met them. They had been destroyed by alcoholism, lived on the edge of poverty, and had lost custody of Rosa because of their violent behavior. Gabriel had been shocked by the way Rosa's parents blackmailed their daughter. They were constantly asking her for money, even though she was making just enough for herself. As a child, she had been shunted from one foster family to another, ineligible for adoption because her parents refused to sign the forms surrendering custody. As soon as she was old enough, Rosa had taken charge of her own life, working several part-time jobs to put herself through college. She had been co-opted at a very young age by a clandestine network of the Montoneros, who valued her for her extraordinary memory. Julia knew she was impressive in passing on vast quantities of information without writing any of it down.

She took to giving Ulysses to Rosa to rock every day. Rosa did exactly as she was told but refused to talk. Rosa had never been one to open up, but Julia trusted her, and her help with Ulysses was invaluable. Dr. Rubens hadn't spared her, and Julia was left with an angry red scar that caused her a lot of pain and severe headaches—a side effect of the drugs he had tested on her. Julia spent most of her time lying in bed, battling her migraines. Tina had her hands full with little Dolly, and Maby, who would be giving birth any day, had been transferred to the intensive care unit.

One morning as Julia was lying on her bed, she heard Rosa murmuring as she rocked Ulysses: "Muse, tell me of the man of many wiles, the man who wandered many paths of exile. . . ."*

The words flowed out of her mouth. Her speech, usually so incoherent, had now acquired a clear rhythm. She went on, stopping only to draw breath: "Men are so quick to blame the gods: they say that we devise their misery. But they themselves— in their depravity—design grief greater than the griefs that fate assigns."

"Rosa, what are you saying?" Julia interrupted.

Rosa turned and looked at her calmly, then said in an even voice, "I'm rocking him to sleep."

Julia sat up on the bed.

"You're rocking him?"

"Yes."

"What were you reciting?"

"*The Odyssey.*"

"You know *The Odyssey* by heart?"

"I learned it at school."

"Rosa . . . And me? Do you know me?"

* *The Odyssey of Homer*, translation by Allen Mandelbaum (New York: Bantam, 1991).

Rosa didn't respond.

"Look at me, Rosa."

Rosa looked away.

"Rosa, do you know where we are?"

"Yes, at home," she replied without emotion.

Julia made as if to embrace her, but Rosa placed the baby gently on the bed and walked away.

The following week Rosa had another unexpected fit. She went after Rubens, ripped off his glasses, and bit his hand.

"You crazy bitch!" he spluttered, backing away. "You'll pay for this!"

Not long after, Julia was informed that her mother had obtained permission to visit her again. They wouldn't let her into the ward, but Julia knew that physical contact through the bars was tolerated.

When Julia saw her mother outside the room, she lifted Ulysses up off the bed, removed his gray flannel blanket, and slipped the tiny bundle between the bars and into her mother's arms. Julia was surprised at the emotion she suddenly felt as she looked at Ulysses nestling into her mother's shoulder. It was as if something had been released inside her, as if the baby had at that precise moment become her son in the eyes of the world.

Her mother spoke after a few minutes. "Mama Fina's waiting outside. If it's all right with you, I'd like to introduce her to her great-grandson and have her hold him."

Julia asked the guard who had been listening to the conversation.

"The child can't go out," she said gruffly. "But you can let the grandmother in. Just for a minute."

Clothed with the sun, Mama Fina made a striking entrance. With her blue gray suit with white piping, her matching straw hat, her smile, and her voice, she managed to fill the place with a breath of spring air. Julia was embarrassed to be seen in her old gray tracksuit. She patted her hair into place and moved closer to the metal door, a lump in her throat. Mama Fina took her hands through the bars, unable to say a single word.

"Here," Julia's mother said, flustered, handing the baby to her.

Mama Fina held him to the light and studied him carefully.

"He's perfect," she said.

She turned back to Julia with a broad smile. "So, what's his name?"

Julia relaxed. "Ulysses Joseph d'Annunzio," she said proudly.

Mama Fina's eyes grew wide.

"Ulysses Joseph! Thank you, *mi amor.* I'm very touched. And relieved that Joseph is his second name, not his first. Fino is an unfortunate nickname for a man."

"So is Ulissito, for that matter," Julia joked.

Mama Fina suddenly became serious. She turned away from the guard as she handed the baby back through the bars.

"The French consulate is going to send an envoy to start the asylum process. The procedure is already under way. Your guardian angel is helping us obtain authorization for the visit."

Julia looked blank.

"You know . . . the one who was inspecting the troops that evening."

"Ah! . . . of course, I see. When?" Julia asked, taking the baby in her arms.

"*Señora*," came the stern voice from behind them, "you'll have to leave now; it's the end of your visit."

"Be patient," Mama Fina murmured.

"*Señora!*" the guard repeated.

"Let's go," Julia's mother said, tugging at Mama Fina's arm.

"You can stay for a few minutes more," the guard told Julia's mother as Mama Fina was shown out.

"Mom, I need to ask you a favor," Julia said.

Julia gestured behind her to where Rosa was sitting, crouched in the far corner. Her mother listened, ill at ease.

"I want you to help Rosa. We have to find her family. She was Gabriel's fiancée. She went mad after being tortured."

"After being tortured? You mean . . . My God!"

Deathly pale, she moved closer to the bars and took Julia's face in her hands.

"Oh, my God!" she said again.

———

Things moved quickly from that point on. The French consulate sent an envoy to the Villa Devoto prison, but he was not allowed to meet with Julia. France then granted political asylum to Julia and her child. A safe-conduct pass was issued in their names authorizing their entry into French territory.

On the day Rosa was transferred to the psychiatric unit, Julia was sent to Block 49, the block for mothers and infants. That same day, Julia also learned that the Argentine government had ordered her into exile. She was given the information while she and Tina were discussing a recent change in the law reducing the time prisoners were allowed to keep their babies with them from two years to six months. With the news of the deportation, Julia realized that her life had been split in two. Of all the people her new destiny would force her to leave behind, it was the separation from Mama Fina that caused her the most anguish. She didn't know how she would ever find Theo again without her help. When the time came to pack her belongings, the only thing she insisted on taking was the bundle of blue letters that Mama Fina had sent her every week since her arrival at Villa Devoto. They were her only treasures.

Julia arrived at Ezeiza Airport wearing the red satin dress she had worn on her eighteenth birthday. There hadn't been any space left for it in the one small suitcase she'd been allowed, so she had resolved to wear it under her old gray coat.

She walked with her head held high, pushing the baby carriage with one hand, the other handcuffed to the policeman escorting her to the plane.

People stared at Julia as she walked through the endless corridors of the airport with the baby carriage and the policeman. Julia found some consolation in the officer's obstinate silence.

Five minutes before boarding, Julia was given permission to see her family one last time, through a window in the corridor leading to the gate. Her white-haired father and her mother were pressing their faces against the glass. Anna was sobbing in the arms of Pablo, who stood behind her. The twins had brought their guitars and were playing something she couldn't hear. She spotted Mama Fina last and burst into tears. The policeman pushed her forward as she held up Ulysses for them all to see. She went meekly, looking back over her shoulder until she could no longer see them.

Julia wiped her cheeks hastily as she boarded the Aerolíneas Argentinas plane. She felt the weight of eyes on her as she made her way down the aisle, and she kept her gaze lowered. She busied herself with pointless tasks, trying to appear composed, while the policeman handed her travel documents to the chief flight attendant. Then he removed her handcuffs, clipped them to his belt, and motioned to her to sit down. He left just before the aircraft doors were closed. A flight attendant passed Julia and gave her a condescending look. She stopped, pushed Julia's suitcase under the seat with her foot, and ordered her to fasten her seat belt.

The plane took off. Julia gazed out the window as her world shrank. Ulysses was already asleep in her arms. She sighed, leaned forward to pull out her suitcase, and rested her feet on it.

It's all I have, but I don't need anything else.

28.

THE MOVE

Boreal Winter
2006

Julia shuts her suitcase and looks around. There's nothing left, no trace of her time in this house. Even the photo on the mantelpiece is gone. In front of her is a pile of about twenty storage boxes ready to go, filled with useless objects she cannot bring herself to throw away.

If she had used the coupons Theo had left out for her, Julia could have saved 10 percent on the boxes. She has left them in full view on the kitchen countertop.

When the movers arrive, they'll have only a few items of furniture to cover and dump in the container for shipping to France. She lays her small suitcase on its side, sits down on the edge of the bed, and rests her feet on it. She certainly has more possessions than when she left Villa Devoto, but the only ones worth keeping are in her case. She still has the neatly tied bundle of blue envelopes containing Mama Fina's letters.

The movers will arrive in an hour's time. She has nothing else to do. She had pictured this differently: the two of them waking up early, having time to look at each other, to feel pain together. Theo helping her pack.

Maybe it's better this way. She has stopped waiting. She spent the night on her own and managed to sleep. It's more than she'd hoped for: she hasn't been able to sleep for weeks. And this constant stomachache is exhausting her. She feels worn out. Existing has become a chore in a dull world. Even the pounds she has shed fail to give her any satisfaction.

Theo has already begun his new life. She too would like to be excited, in love. She wishes sometimes that she could be angry with him, hate him. But she can't. For now, she still loves him, until the day comes when she can remember the pain but not the attachment. She hopes she will love him forever, but in a different way. She needs that certainty in order to heal. *Love is so short and forgetting so long.*

Finally she makes up her mind. She can't refuse to go there any longer. Even though she'd wanted so much to be the exception, to prove the predictions wrong, to experience the grace to depart from destiny. She opens the suitcase, unties the envelopes yellowed by time, and pulls out one of the letters at random. Mama Fina's voice comes back to her with each word, distinct, powerful, real.

Julia allows herself to slide onto the floor. The convulsions come quickly. She has learned to travel at will. She knows what she wants. It is not the future that interests her now; instead, she is eager to go back, to see again, to understand. She plunges into the thick white substance with confidence, her inert body abandoned behind her. She glides forward, carried by her emotions. Julia knows the circuit through the stages of consciousness, the potential connections and openings. She has learned that the emotions are a universal force, subject to the same laws as energy, working through connected vessels. She advances backward, seeking the inflection point at which contact with the other moment in time becomes inevitable. She knows she is close, very close.

Done. She just made it. All of a sudden, she resurfaces.

The fountain in the patio is just confirmation of the mastery she has attained. Julia looks on, satisfied. She knows. She wants to take her time, immerse herself once again in this world that belongs to her. Her host's eyes suit her. Julia walks through each of the rooms. She leaves the patio to go in search of the *calabaza*, the *bombilla*, and the *maté* that awaits her on the large cherrywood table in the dining room. She crosses the living room, where the upright piano on which she learned to play, like her father before her, stands in its usual place. A folded newspaper on Mama Fina's armchair tells her the date: August 6, 1984. Her birthday. Of course. It is obviously no coincidence.

In Mama Fina's room the bed shows signs of a recent siesta,

but the curtains aren't drawn. It's still early. She moves over to the bedside table, on which a large framed photo of her kissing Ulysses in his firefighter outfit stands beside a photo of her parents. The little wooden drawer opens. A rosary, glasses, pills. Julia sees Mama Fina's hand rummaging around and then taking out a large magnifying glass.

She goes back out into the corridor. Julia knows that Mama Fina is heading to her old room. She could count the number of steps. Everything is still there, intact, as if it were only yesterday that she'd moved out to live with Theo. Her bed, her poetry collection, her sketchbooks, her old magazines, her dressing table, her desk.

Mama Fina switches on the light and sits down at Julia's desk. She opens the middle drawer, takes out a folder, and puts it down carefully in front of her. She opens it. A jumble of papers and newspaper cuttings. She begins to sort through them methodically with the help of the magnifying glass: recipes, movie flyers, articles. Mama Fina comes across a child's drawing and sets it aside on a corner of the desk. Julia recognizes it. It is the drawing she gave Mama Fina to explain her first "journey" when she was only five years old. Mama Fina places a hand on it as she returns to her filing.

She has already gone through half of the file's contents when she stops at a newspaper cutting and holds it close to the light. It is a clipping from a society magazine. It is about the wedding of an air force captain—Ignacio Castro Matamoros, Julia reads in the caption—to a pretty girl named Mailen

Amun. Mama Fina looks at the picture and inspects the faces of the newlyweds with the magnifying glass. Julia cannot help noticing that the young bride resembles her. She is probably the same age as Julia too. But Mama Fina's gaze lingers on the face of the bridegroom. He is a big, muscular man with a buzz cut, petrol blue eyes, and a scar on his temple. Mama Fina places the cutting on Julia's drawing and carries on sifting.

Suddenly she stops, stands up, and walks back across the corridor. She returns to the living room, switches on the light, and sits down in her armchair to answer the telephone. The newspaper she places on her knees, El Clarín, is open to the crime section. A photograph shows a group of policemen in front of a row of identical houses. Julia thinks she recognizes Commissioner-Major Angelini, Mama Fina's friend. The barely legible caption says the police are looking for the killer. Her grandmother drums her fingers nervously on the armrest of her chair. Julia knows she is looking for her source.

Mama Fina contemplates the receiver for a moment before hanging up. Julia wishes she could be there to work with her. She goes back to Julia's room and puts the folder away in its drawer, leaving the press clipping and the drawing on the corner of the desk. Then she sits down, takes out a few sheets of blue paper and a fountain pen from the side drawer, and begins to write. Julia knows the contents of the letter by heart. It is the one she is still holding in her hand.

A sudden jolt brings her back into her own body. Julia is disconnected with a snap. She is projected into nothingness, despite struggling to stay with Mama Fina. Her being is sucked forward. Her body is calling her back. It is time. Very well. Her eyes flick open instantly. A burly man in blue overalls is bending anxiously over her. She can smell the cigarette smoke on his breath.

"You okay, ma'am? Are you feeling all right?"

"Yes, I'm fine, thanks. I must have nodded off. I'm sorry."

"I saw the door was open and everything was all packed up, so I thought . . ."

"Don't worry, you did the right thing."

Julia gets up, runs a hand over her hair, and smooths down her pants. She looks at Mama Fina's letter in her hand. She'll have to read it again carefully.

But not now. First she has to move out.

29

THE RULE

Boreal Winter
2006

Julia watches from the window as the movers struggle with the art deco piano. It is a George Steck. It followed her all the way from Argentina to Connecticut, and she has no intention of leaving it behind. Not only is it rare, with its inlaid wooden case and oval soundboard, but it used to be in Mama Fina's living room.

The movers will be asking to take their break soon. Julia glances at her watch. As if reading her thoughts, the man in the blue overalls begins to stride across the lawn. Julia rushes downstairs. Too late: he's trampled through the flowerbeds.

"We're just taking a half-hour break," the man says.

"Yes, of course, go ahead," she answers, eyeing the muddy footprints on her parquet floor.

The men are already sitting in the big truck with their

sandwiches. Julia feels strange. She sits down too, at the foot
of the staircase, and allows the river of images to flow again.

The dimly lit room, the half-open door. The eyes of her
host travel from the bathroom to the bedside table. In the half
light, Theo reaches out for an object. He unlocks a cell phone
and reads a three-line text. He scrolls briefly through his messages, then switches off the phone. His eyes swing back to the
bathroom. The young woman is putting on her makeup, leaning close to the mirror. She's wearing black stilettos. The hotel
towels lie discarded on the floor. The young woman is about
to pick up her purse, wave, and slam the door.

Feeling the need to splash some water on her face, Julia
gets up, stopping to pour herself a glass of cold milk on the
way. She shakes her head as if trying to get rid of the images.
The thought that Theo might burst in at any moment makes
her nervous. She doesn't want to see him. Not now. She checks
her watch again. There are jobs where people are always on
time. Her movers probably don't fall into that category.

She casts a final eye around and pulls a face. *Damn, I forgot
the china.*

She'll have to ask them to pack it up. They won't be
pleased. Her mind has definitely been elsewhere. She opens
up the cupboards.

Too bad, I'll leave it.

The sound of her cell phone ringing startles her. She goes
to look for it. She can't find it anywhere, and now it's gone
silent. Julia searches behind the boxes, under the cushions, on

the window ledges, and in the fridge. In the end she decides to use the landline phone to dial her own number. She hears it ringing upstairs; she must have put it in her suitcase. But instead she finds the phone waiting for her in the bathroom, vibrating and ringing at the same time, on the edge of the sink.

It's a message from Theo. Julia makes a gesture of annoyance.

She jumps again. This time it's the doorbell. The gang must be getting impatient on the stoop. She hurries downstairs, cell phone in hand, to open the door. Now it's the boss who comes in, solemn and wearing a suit. Julia has to fill out and sign about a dozen forms. The other men have already dispersed throughout the house and begun packing up what's left. She has to intervene to explain that the remaining items belong to her husband.

The boss leaves. Julia suddenly feels more relaxed, and so do the men. One of them comes back with a large black and yellow building-site radio, made to survive a cataclysm, he says. He asks if he can turn it on while he packs up the books. She can't refuse. The sound explodes into the house, startling Julia yet again. This time she laughs about it.

"We like to follow the news. Have you heard about the plane?" asks the man, seemingly unable to keep quiet for longer than a minute.

Julia raises her eyebrows. She hasn't paid any attention at all to the outside world for the past few days. She's happy for them to listen to anything they like; she just wants to take a quick look at Theo's message.

"No," she answers politely, trying to find a quiet corner.

"There's a private jet heading from New York to Boston. They're going to try to land not too far from here. Apparently there's an airport in Stratford."

"Oh, right," Julia says distractedly.

"Yeah, I'll find the live coverage for you," the man continues, overeager. He fiddles with the radio dials. A woman's voice fills the living room, describing the movements of the distressed plane and the various measures being taken to allow it to make an emergency landing on the runway of the small airport in Bridgeport.

". . . Sikorsky Memorial, which is actually situated in Stratford," the voice adds, before launching into a lengthy discussion of the reasons for the long-standing confrontation between the two towns on the subject of the airport.

Julia is miles away. She is totally focused on Theo's message. Three lines asking her to forgive him. He calls her "my love."

"What a moron!"

All heads turn to stare at her. No, she doesn't supply an explanation. Instead she heads to her room. She's going to re-read Mama Fina's letters.

The yellow radio goes on providing details of the emergency. The aircraft is still reporting difficulties. There is now talk of a forced landing.

Julia returns to the kitchen, hands on hips. Hell, no. She's going to take all the crockery too. And all the pots and pans. She takes out piles of plates, large, medium, small; the cups, the saucers, the teapot, the coffee maker, milk jugs, saucepans, frying pans. She lines them all up on the counter with military precision.

"Guys, I forgot about all this."

The movers look at one another. The man in the blue overalls walks around Julia in a circle, raises his cap, scratches his head, and declares in the voice of an expert: "That will take at least another hour and a half."

Julia agrees. The bill will be substantial, but that's the least of her worries. She still can't believe Theo's nerve.

"If I hadn't seen it with my own eyes, I'd still be here waiting, telling myself the reason he didn't come home all night was because he had too much work!" she mutters, stationing herself by the front door.

The movers have nearly finished. They're rolling up carpets, taping the last boxes shut. The radio is still broadcasting live updates. The plane is now a few miles from Fairfield. It is flying over the Connecticut Turnpike and has begun to dump fuel. It won't be able to reach Stratford. The pilot is asking for the highway to be cleared, and the authorities have given evacuation orders.

Julia is impatient to have them finish. The house is empty,

except for the yellow and black radio that has taken center stage in the room. *Can't they just shut this radio off!* Julia freezes, then turns slowly to look at it, as if she was just discovering it. The voice continues: the highway, Fairfield, the plane.

Her world starts to spin in slow motion. She hears Mama Fina's voice speaking from afar: "Julia, repeat back to me what you have to remember."

To serve others. She turns deathly pale. "Oh, my God!" she shouts, and rushes outside. She wants to call for help, to set off at a run. She races back into the house, takes the stairs two at a time, fetches her car keys from her handbag, and grabs her cell phone.

The moving truck is blocking the driveway.

"It's a matter of life or death," she calls out to the man in the blue overalls.

The others, who are standing to one side, grumble among themselves. *They must take me for a lunatic. Who cares.* The man flicks his cigarette away, turns on the engine, and starts to move the truck.

Julia is already behind the wheel of her car. She calls Theo while the truck is backing out of the driveway. She tries his number once, twice, twenty times.

"He's turned his phone off!" she yells, banging the steering wheel.

30.

THE LIE

Between Boreal Springs
(1977–1980)

I n the event of a loss of cabin pressure, oxygen masks will automatically drop from the ceiling, the flight attendant had
said. Mothers were required to secure their own masks before
assisting their children. If she hadn't been given that instruction, Julia would have done exactly the opposite—and yet
Mama Fina had always insisted that she needed to be in the
best shape possible so she could help others. The reasoning
was the same.

"Your body is only limited by your mind," Mama Fina used
to say.

Right now that didn't seem very real. Going into exile,
alone, with her baby in her arms, Julia questioned her abilities
and strength of mind. The flight attendant was no help. She'd
probably never see her again, but this girl was Julia's first con-

tact with the outside world, and she wanted to get off to a good start.

Julia looked up and smiled at the young woman as she went past. She had nothing to be embarrassed about. The flight attendant didn't deign to return the smile, but Julia noticed the set of her mouth softening and took heart. Yes, she'd been through a lot, and she was crossing the Atlantic for the first time in her life to arrive in a country where she didn't know a soul. But she didn't want to feel scared anymore.

When the flight attendant had finished serving the passengers, she crouched down beside Julia to ask if Ulysses needed his bottle warmed up. Julia repaid the gesture by thanking the girl profusely. They began to talk, and Julia ended up telling the girl some of what had happened to her. The young flight attendant's curiosity had gotten the better of her reticence. Although Argentine by birth and from the same generation as Julia, she knew nothing about politics, let alone the extermination campaign that the ruling military junta was carrying out against the left.

"I'm Alice. Is there anything I can do to help you?"

"I don't know. I know nothing about France, or what will happen when I get there."

"Your family must be worried sick about you having to leave like this. I make the round trip every week: I'd be happy to be your go-between. I could take your letters and bring you theirs."

The mail service was particularly slow, and phone calls

very expensive, but thanks to the flight attendant's offer, she would be able to communicate easily with her family. And she'd just made a friend. The thought gave her renewed courage.

Julia landed at Roissy Airport on a foggy spring morning. She was met by a representative of the French foundation Terre d'Asile, a young Chilean woman called Conchita who worked as a translator. She had been following Julia's case for the past six months and had been in constant contact with her family and the French embassy in Buenos Aires. Julia immediately felt at ease.

Conchita lifted Ulysses deftly into her arms, and the baby gurgled contentedly as they rode the futuristic escalator tunnels that led to the exit. The airport was like nothing she had known before. Julia was mesmerized, as though she'd stepped into a flying saucer.

"For the first six months you'll be staying at a center for refugees in Fontenay-sous-Bois, and you'll have intensive French lessons at the church at Porte de Choisy. After that, we'll see," the young Chilean woman told her.

There were Brazilians, Chileans, and other Argentines at the center, all refugees like her, fleeing the dictatorships of South America. Julia didn't have time to be bored. In the evenings, after lessons and once Ulysses had fallen asleep in their small room, Julia would meet up with Conchita and the priest who taught them French in the church. As she was learning very quickly, they had decided she should become an interpreter for new arrivals.

At the end of the six months, Julia was able to rent a small apartment using her single-parent housing allowance and her wages as a part-time worker at a chemical plant in Fontenay-sous-Bois. Her work as an interpreter was voluntary. And she still had time to chat with all the people who came to see her, just like the stream of visitors to Mama Fina's house in La Boca.

Julia no longer felt alone in her new world. She had also struck up a friendship with a French student who helped her out with Ulysses. He obviously had a crush on her. But Julia was living on standby, waiting for the moment when she would be reunited with Theo.

Unfortunately for her, the news from Argentina wasn't encouraging. Alice regularly brought her letters from her family, including the much-awaited blue envelopes from Mama Fina. But there was still no news of either Theo or Adriana.

Her fellow refugees had discovered a phone booth right in the middle of Avenue de la Grande Armée that had been cleverly tampered with. By dialing a particular set of digits, they could make free long-distance calls to South America. Julia had been tipped off about it by some friends. It was the only way she could afford to speak regularly to Mama Fina, Anna, and a few school friends, and it made her exile far more bearable.

"I'm coming to see you this summer," Mama Fina announced shortly before Ulysses' second birthday.

Julia spent the next few months in anticipation of this re-
union. She was also hoping Mama Fina would arrive with some
confidential information she couldn't share over the phone.

The thought that Theo might be alive helped Julia keep her
head above water. If no one had been able to confirm that he
had left Buenos Aires with Adriana on the *Donizetti*, it was simply because their escape plan had worked so well that they had
managed to disappear without a trace. After all, Mama Fina
said she'd lost all contact with Captain Torricelli, and the *Donizetti* had never returned to South America. This seemed perfectly normal: it had been the *Donizetti*'s last crossing, and the
ship had been scrapped in 1977. That said, Father Miguel, the
priest Julia had sent Adriana to, was among the junta's most
recent *desaparecidos*. He had been suspected of being in contact
with the Montoneros, though Mama Fina knew, through
Angelini, that it wasn't because of Theo's escape. Therefore, if
Theo was still alive, why hadn't he tried to find out what had
become of Ulysses and her?

"I'm starting to fear the worst," Julia admitted to her friend
Olivier.

"Yes, it's strange that you haven't had any news for over a
year."

"It isn't like him. He would have found a way to communicate if he could," Julia said, keeping a watchful eye on Ulysses
as he waddled between the table and the kitchen door, ready
to catch him before he fell.

One evening, shortly after the football World Cup, Olivier turned up in a state of great excitement. He had heard that Montonero militants were trying to sneak back into Argentina in a bid to end the dictatorship.

"It's incredible, isn't it?"

"Are you sure it's not just speculation?" Julia asked.

"Listen, I know what I'm talking about. I have contacts too, believe me!"

"Really?"

"If you must know, there was a Montonero delegation at the last socialist youth conference. Let's just say the Socialist Party has a good relationship with them."

"Meaning?"

"Well, they have the support of Europe's Social Democrats. Their leader has met everyone: Willy Brandt, Felipe González, Olof Palme, even Mitterrand!"

"That's precisely why I think it doesn't make sense. Look, if they have all these backers, why are they walking into the lion's den instead of fighting from the outside?"

"So, according to you, they should take it easy abroad while the others are getting themselves killed? If I was in their shoes, I'd do the same!"

Julia fell silent. Olivier stared at the floor, holding a glass in his hand.

"Let's not talk about it anymore. Anyway, I shouldn't feel concerned," he said finally.

"Do we know who they are?"

"Of course not! It's not the kind of thing that's printed in the papers!"

"Well, you're pretty well informed, so it can't be all that secret!"

Olivier left, slamming the door behind him.

He broached the subject again a few weeks later.

"Do you remember what I told you about the Montoneros?"

"What, you mean the Normandy landings?" Julia quipped as she got Ulysses dressed for preschool.

"That's not very nice, Julia. But, in fact, I think you were right."

"What about?" she asked, hastily pulling on her coat.

"They were arrested by Battalion 601 as soon as they set foot in the country. Does that mean anything to you?"

Julia pulled Ulysses' hat down over his ears and stayed crouched next to him. "How do you know?"

"I just know."

"Do you know where they are now?"

"*Desaparecidos.*"

Julia dabbed at the beads of sweat on her forehead. "Will you come with me to drop Ulysses off at school?"

Olivier took the child in his arms.

"Do you have any names?" Julia asked as they left the building.

"Not really. All I know is that the son of an actor called Marcos Zucker has fallen into their hands."

"Who?"

"Marcos Zucker."

"I haven't heard of him. Who else?"

"We don't know much. What we do know is that they've been sent to El Campito."

Julia turned pale. She kissed Ulysses, smiled at him, and handed him over to his teacher.

Prisoners never returned from El Campito: an innocuous-sounding name for the concentration camp inside the military school at Campo de Mayo. Julia knew as much. In the Devoto maternity unit she'd heard people say that the military was especially keen to send pregnant prisoners there. There was a list of military officers wanting to adopt their babies. After giving birth, the mothers were executed and the babies given to new parents.

Overcome by anxiety, Julia didn't want to talk about it anymore. She knew that casting doubts could become a deadly poison. Mama Fina had warned her against the temptation to give voice to her apprehensions, because, she said, the energy in words can transform our fears into reality. So Julia didn't say anything, but it was a possibility she couldn't exclude. If Theo had agreed to return to Argentina and been captured again, that would explain his silence. Her attitude toward everyday life changed. She lost her appetite and developed a taciturnity that even Ulysses could only dispel momentarily.

Alerted by Alice, Julia's parents decided to lie to her. They led her to believe that Theo was being held in the Unidad 9 prison in La Plata, which was in itself good news. She was told Theo wouldn't be allowed to write to her but that he could receive her letters.

Julia's life changed overnight. She began to make plans for the future and to try to get her career on a firm footing so that she could support Theo when he got out of prison.

"We have to stop seeing each other," she told Olivier.

"But I can still help you, you know."

"It's better if you don't. Please understand me."

"I don't want Ulysses to go out of my life like this, Julia, and besides, you don't even know if Theo will want to live with you again. Prison changes people."

"Not him. And he is Ulysses' father, Olivier."

"Let me help you," he persisted.

"The best way to help is for you to leave us."

The separation from Olivier proved harder than she'd thought. She didn't feel any closer to Theo, and in fact found herself more alone than ever.

Anna was mortified too. In a way she thought it was disrespectful to lie to her sister, even if it was to help her. So she began to do what she thought Julia really needed: she discreetly searched for Theo.

First she went to the d'Uccello house. It was empty, but she learned from one of the neighbors that Theo's uncle, a man named Mayol, had looked after the house for a while.

"Señora d'Uccello's brother, I believe," the woman told her. "They're the ones with the money, you know."

"I see. And this gentleman . . ."

"Señor Mayol? He's gone abroad. He went to work for a big American company. From what I hear, he's a highly skilled scientist."

Anna did not find out anything else at the Colegio Nacional de Buenos Aires, where Theo and Gabriel had gone to high school. The cold reception she was met with deterred her from asking any more questions. She obviously made sure to avoid the universities, which were under surveillance by the intelligence agencies, and finally went to Father Mugica's church, more in the hope of renewing her courage than because she expected to glean any new information.

"You should go and talk to the Jesuits at the Colegio Máximo de San José," the sacristan told her.

He knew the d'Uccello family well. The children had been baptized there, and he also remembered Julia because he had often seen her in church before Father Mugica's assassination.

"If Gabriel or Theo were at any time seeking refuge, that is probably where they would have found it," he told Anna.

There was an atmosphere of suspicion at the Colegio Máximo de San José. Anna had to explain her case to a number of people before being allowed to talk to the prefect of the congregation. Everyone she spoke to confirmed that neither of the d'Uccello brothers had taken part in what they called a "spiritual retreat."

"Give me some time to ask around," the bursar told her. "I'll let you know if I find anything out."

In the end the only thing Anna was able to ascertain was the itinerary of the *Donizetti*. The ship had set sail from Buenos Aires on June 26, 1976, and called at ports in Brazil and the Caribbean before returning to Genoa, where it had been sent to the shipbreaking yard the following year, as Mama Fina had already learned. The captain, Enzo Torricelli, was retired, and the passenger manifest wasn't available.

But a few weeks later she got a call from the bursar of the Colegio Máximo. "Come and see me," he told her. "I have something for you."

Anna realized as she walked into the bursar's office that she wasn't going to be told what she hoped to hear.

"I have some information that should interest you," he announced, offering her a chair. "We think we've traced one of the d'Uccello brothers."

Anna gripped the purse she'd just placed on her lap.

"Gabriel d'Uccello. We believe he was murdered four years ago."

Reeling from the news, Anna walked out of the bursar's office not knowing which way to go. She could not believe such an atrocity had taken place so close to her. She knew the rumors, of course, but the description she had just heard was much worse than anything she could have imagined. She had no idea whether Julia knew.

Since her sister's departure, Anna had become aware of the

insidious fear that permeated the whole country. It was now taboo to mention Julia's situation. The fact that Julia had disappeared for so long, that she'd been arrested and then expelled from the country, was never mentioned at social gatherings, not even with very close friends. Besides, nobody in the family really knew what Julia had gone through during the months of her absence, and none of them dared to openly ask her about it.

Then Anna remembered Rosa. They had tried to help her when Julia was in prison. If Rosa was back in her right mind, she might turn out to be the only link left. She decided to go to the psychiatric ward in the Devoto prison. It was the only thing she could still do for her sister.

The guard who let her in looked astonished. "No one ever visits her, and today there are two of you!"

Anna turned and saw a young blond woman in a blue gingham dress sitting next to Rosa in the courtyard of the ward. She seemed to be talking to her very affectionately. Anna approached quietly, not wanting to interrupt them.

She heard the young woman say, "Rosa, it's me, Adriana. Tell me you recognize me."

31.

ANNA

Boreal Winter

1985

Ulysses had been in elementary school for several years when Julia received a long, thick envelope with a black border from Alice. Her friend left her so that Julia could read the letter privately.

Seated by herself in a café, Julia lacked the courage to open the envelope. For years she had refrained from asking questions because it was more bearable to live with a lie. Eventually she had come to the realization that Theo's silence couldn't be due to an administrative ban, since his status had been "legalized" in an official prison. She continued to write to Theo, for the letters were as much to herself as to him, and this rigor and discipline helped her stay the course, even if she no longer expected a reply.

Her diligence was rewarded, she felt, by the wonderful

version of Theo that Ulysses was turning into. True, he had the d'Annunzio features. Ulysses looked a lot like Julia's father and had inherited Mama Fina's transparent eyes. But he had Theo's character: proud, passionate, hungry for life.

No, she wasn't ready to read the letter. Not now, when she had to go to her job at the Institut Gustave-Roussy, and afterward rush to pick up Ulysses from school.

"Mom, I've got lots of homework!" Ulysses said, leaping into her arms.

Lost in thought, Julia kissed him.

"Will you help me?" Ulysses asked, clinging to her.

"I don't feel up to it right now, angel. Besides, my French isn't that good."

"But it's math, and also I have to do a drawing. Please."

"No, you don't need my help."

"Come on, Mom!" Ulysses said, tickling her.

"Stop it! Everyone's looking at us," Julia said, laughing. "All right, I'll do the drawing, but you must do the rest yourself."

Ulysses skipped along, swinging his schoolbag.

"Mom, have you heard from Theo?"

"I've told you to call him Dad; he's your father."

"But I've never seen him!"

"You've seen photos."

"Mom!"

"No, I haven't heard from Theo."

Without letting go of his bag, Ulysses gave his mother a big bear hug and looked up at her.

"So why are you making that face, Mom?"

"I got a letter."

"From Theo?"

"No."

"Do you want us to read it together?"

"No, love. I think I'd rather read it alone."

The boy began to play a game with one of his pencils as he walked along. He stopped short outside a bakery, where the baker was placing trays of piping-hot golden brown galettes in the window. Julia looked at Ulysses, pretending to be cross, and went into the bakery.

"And a chocolate croissant too!" Ulysses shouted.

That night, when everything around her was silent, Julia went to sit on the floor in a corner, next to the bed where Ulysses still slept with her.

The letter was from her father. She could hear his voice as she read the carefully penned words. She had been expecting the worst. But not this.

In a way, news of Theo's death, however harrowing it might be, was the event she had been bracing herself for all these years. She knew she would have to face up to the truth one day. But in her headlong rush into the future, she had decided to live her life choosing to believe that Theo was still being held in the Unidad 9 prison in La Plata. And yet things had changed. The election of Alfonsín* a year and a half earlier had put an end to the dictatorship and, inevitably, to the lie. Julia understood her family would be forced to tell her the truth. And in her heart of hearts she knew it would come as a relief.

But not this. The shock made her numb. The words began to dance in front of her eyes, as if she had suddenly forgotten what the letters signified. She had to reread her father's letter out loud before she could take it in. She had been completely unprepared for Mama Fina's death.

Unable to slow her racing heart, she wondered why she couldn't cry. Even as her mind began to function again, her heart remained frozen. Mama Fina was too present in her life. She couldn't have gone without telling her. Ever since Julia had arrived in France, her life had been punctuated by Mama Fina's visits. She was her rock. Julia felt like she was falling from a cliff.

"Mom? Mom!"

Ulysses' voice woke her. It was morning and she was still sitting at the foot of the bed, her eyes swollen, her body convulsing.

"Mom, what's the matter?"

Julia flapped the letter she was still holding.

* Raúl Alfonsín became president of Argentina following the elections on October 30, 1983.

"It's Mama Fina," she said, choking back sobs. "She died last week."

The child looked at her, frightened.

"And Theo?" he asked.

Julia blinked helplessly. "Theo?"

"Yes, Theo!" Ulysses repeated. "Is he dead too?"

"But that's got nothing to do with it, my angel," Julia answered, standing up with an effort.

Ulysses looked her up and down, his eyes filling with tears.

"Yes it does! You always say Mama Fina's going to find him."

Julia sat down on the bed, closed her eyes, and hugged Ulysses tight.

"Oh, sweet angel! I'm so sorry." She stroked his hair. "We'll find him, you and me, I promise."

The family sent Anna on a special visit at the end of the summer. Paris was very hot. One afternoon Julia took her sister for a stroll through one of the old neighborhoods in the city. From the Marais they ended up by the river in search of slightly cooler air. They sat down in the shade of a chestnut tree on the banks of the Seine, admiring the view of the succession of bridges. Anna slipped off her shoes and dangled her feet above the water. Seated beside her, Julia seemed happy.

"Maybe it's time you found yourself a boyfriend," Anna said without thinking.

Julia burst out laughing. "Do I look like a spinster?"

"That's just it. You don't."

Julia shot Anna an enigmatic look. "I have male friends."

"I'm sure you do. But I'm talking about having a man in your life."

"Hmm. I still find it hard."

Anna slipped her hands under her thighs, her body tense.

"Julia, you know Theo's not coming back."

"I don't know, actually. You all lied to me for ten years."

"Stop it," Anna interrupted. "Dad and Mom thought they were doing the right thing. And you weren't fooled for long."

"I don't know about that. Maybe I'm still waiting for him."

"Listen, Julia. Mama Fina and I searched everywhere. We pursued every possible lead."

"But if he was dead Mama Fina would have sensed it, and she would have told me."

Anna heaved a sigh, took her sister's hand, and looked her straight in the eye.

"Julia . . ." She broke off, bit her lip, then added: "But I don't know if I should. I decided I would never tell you."

Julia pressed her to continue. "It's too late now, Anna. You've started, so you have to finish."

"It might hurt you, Julia."

Julia hugged her knees and turned to face Anna. "Right. Tell me whatever it is you need to tell me, Anna. I'm hurting anyway, and I've been hurting for too long."

She leaned in close to Anna and added gravely: "You don't have a right to hide this from me."

Anna blew a lock of hair off her forehead and threw her head back. "This was several years ago," she began. "Rosa was still in the psychiatric ward at Devoto. No one ever went to visit her except Mom and me."

She paused and then continued: "But the first time I went, there was someone else there."

Julia sat stock-still, hanging on Anna's every word.

"It was a young girl. I thought she must be a cousin, someone in her family. But when I got closer, I heard her asking Rosa if she recognized her. She said she'd been in Castelar too."

A shiver went through Julia.

"I acted straightaway. I thought she could tell me something. So I introduced myself. I said I was your sister. But as soon as I said your name, she got up to leave. She was like you are now: trembling, pale."

Julia seized her sister's arm. "Was it Adriana?"

"Wait, let me speak."

Julia made an effort to control herself.

"I told her that if she left, I would follow her. The guard came to see what was up. We both sat down again next to Rosa as if nothing was the matter. That was when she made me promise I wouldn't tell anyone I'd seen her, not even you."

"But . . . why? I don't understand. So it wasn't Adriana?"

"Yes, it was Adriana. But she was scared to death. She told me that if the military found her, they would kill her. I asked her what she was doing in Devoto in that case—she'd walked straight into the lion's den. She gave me to understand that she'd changed her identity and that Rosa was one of her alibis."

Julia jumped to her feet, twisting the belt of her dress in her hands.

"My God, didn't you ask her where Theo was?"

"Of course I did. That was my reason for being there!"

"And?"

"She didn't want to give me any details, but she pleaded with me to convince you not to think of him anymore. She said that you have to forget him. She was crying as she spoke, Julia."

Anna had stood up too. She tried to move closer to her sister, who stepped away.

"I don't know what happened to Theo, Julia. But I do know what happened to Gabriel. I found out from the Jesuits. Mama Fina told me you knew. You can imagine . . ."

"I don't want to imagine any longer! I've been imagining for the past ten years!" Julia shouted.

Anna tried to take Julia in her arms.

"Don't touch me, Anna. You don't understand. I have to know what happened to him."

"But . . . what happened to him is what happened to thousands of other young Argentines. He died in one of the secret camps during the dictatorship. That's all you need to know. As for the rest, the details . . ."

"But that's exactly it, Anna! I want the details. I want to know who killed him, how, where. Theo is not a statistic. He's

the father of my child, the man I love. I want to know everything! Everything!"

Anna just stood there, a crushed expression on her face.

"And Adriana? Why didn't you give me her address, her
new identity?"

Anna was fighting back tears so hard she could barely
speak. She managed to whisper: "Julia, I'm so sorry. She didn't
want me to know. I lost track of her."

32

BUENOS AIRES

Boreal Winter
2000

Ulysses was sitting at the dining room table chatting with Olivier. The air was just turning brisk. Julia got up to shut the door to the garden and adjusted her sweater. She finished clearing away the plates, tidied up the kitchen, and came back to sit down with them.

"Your grades are excellent," Olivier was telling Ulysses. "I shouldn't think you'll have any difficulties, whatever you decide to do."

"But I don't know what I want to do," Ulysses answered. "That's my whole problem."

"It's only to be expected. You've been studying for a long time."

"And I'm not sure I want to go any further."

"It's like I said: the hard part isn't getting into med school; it's sticking with it."

"You must be kidding, Olivier! It's all hard."

They exchanged a smile.

"But that doesn't change anything," Ulysses went on. "I like what I do. I probably wouldn't have studied medicine if it hadn't been for you, but . . ."

"I think it's in your blood," Olivier broke in. "I've watched you: you're very good, and it's not because of me." He added proudly: "Even if I did change your diapers."

"Yeah, you changed my diapers and then you vanished into thin air for one heck of a long time," Ulysses retorted.

Olivier pretended to give Ulysses a slap on the head. "You're feisty today!" he said, laughing.

"He's right," Julia intervened, putting her arms around Olivier's neck. "It's the truth, isn't it?"

Olivier and Ulysses rolled their eyes at each other, chuckling.

"Right, sure, that's exactly what happened, Mom. Let's just pretend you didn't say that!" said Ulysses, getting up to leave.

"Wait, we haven't finished," Julia said, trying to catch hold of his arm.

"I have to go. I promised my friends I'd meet them in half an hour."

"Your friends or your girlfriend?" Julia asked, standing up.

"My friends. I'll go see my girlfriend afterward."

Olivier headed for the door too. "Do you have your keys?"

Ulysses shook a bunch of keys in Olivier's face.

"Very funny. But your mother's not the one who gets up at midnight to let you in."

Julia gave Olivier a kiss on the cheek.

"Oh! I nearly forgot. I'm taking the car, okay?"

"The gas tank's almost empty," Olivier warned him.

"Be careful, angel," Julia added as she shut the door after him.

Olivier and Julia looked at each other, shaking their heads.

"It won't do him any harm to get a bit of fresh air. He works too hard," said Julia.

"True, but he'll have to stick with it if he wants to do a fellowship."

"Six years is a long time. Maybe he needs a break."

"Yes, I was thinking the same thing. I could take him with me over the holidays. He could help me out at the clinic."

"It wouldn't really be a break," Julia said, taking his hand. "I did think of getting him an internship at the institute. But on second thought . . ."

"Aha! I see you've got an idea in mind."

"No, not really. In any case, I'm not sure it's a good idea."

"Go on, tell me."

"I think that, in a way, Ulysses is spoiled. Maybe too spoiled. We live in this beautiful house, he has everything he wants. . . ."

"So?"

"I was thinking he should find out how people in other countries live."

"Africa?"

"No. Actually, I was thinking Argentina."

Olivier sank down onto the living room couch. Julia looked at him in silence, then went to make some coffee. She returned with two cups and a bar of dark chocolate. She placed everything on the side table and switched on the lamp. Olivier had his head between his hands and a serious expression on his face.

"Listen, I hope this isn't about your old ghosts coming back."

Julia stirred her coffee. "No. Not really. In fact, I just received a letter from the consulate. My visa application has finally been accepted. I can go to Argentina again."

"And you want to take Ulysses with you?"

"I think I'd like him to go first. Without me."

"Why is that?"

"Maybe so he can discover an Argentina that's free of the weight of the past. He has all his cousins who would love to meet him. I've talked to Anna about it. She'd be thrilled to have him stay."

"Correct me if I'm wrong, but it sounds like everything's already been decided."

"Absolutely not. First of all I wanted your approval. And then Ulysses has to want to go."

———

Olivier and Julia drove Ulysses to the airport. He left with nothing but a backpack, ignoring Julia's pleas to take some Christmas gifts with him. He had organized a trip to Patagonia with his cousins and would be celebrating Christmas at Mama Fina's house in Buenos Aires with Anna and Pablo, who had been living there for years, and the twins and their families, who would come to join them. It was the end of a millennium, after all, as well as his twenty-fourth birthday, and Ulysses wanted to experience it his own way.

Julia returned home feeling down.

"It was your idea, darling. You have only yourself to blame."

"I know. It's just that it's hard to watch him go."

"Don't make a big thing out of it. Two weeks is nothing. And besides, it'll give us a chance to ring in the year 2000 as a couple."

She gave a faint smile and crouched down in front of the fireplace to light a fire. She turned around at the sound of a cork popping. Olivier was pouring champagne with a practiced hand.

"Might as well start celebrating right now," he said as he approached, holding two flutes.

"Okay. Let's drink to our new life together."

"It's taken me long enough to convince you! If Ulysses hadn't helped me, I'd still be at it."

"I couldn't before. I had to make sure I'd exhausted every possibility."

"Was it the letter from Amnesty International?"

"That might have helped," Julia said thoughtfully, sitting down on the arm of Olivier's chair.

The organization had mobilized a network of volunteers to champion Theo's case, and they had proven to be very active. Scattered all over France, they took it upon themselves not only to request information from the Argentine authorities but also to demand answers from relevant international bodies. They had managed to bring the case to the attention of a number of journalists, thanks to whom the officials had taken an interest in Theo's file, which otherwise would have been forgotten entirely.

For her part Julia had written hundreds of letters and received an equal number of discouraging replies. She had traveled within Europe and to the United States to ask for help. Invited to participate in a number of international conferences to raise awareness of the fate of the *desaparecidos*, she had met high-ranking people such as Thorvald Stoltenberg, the UN high commissioner for refugees at the time, and Adolfo Pérez Esquivel. They had all tried to help her, but in vain.

Adriana's disappearance was extremely frustrating. Anna had never stopped trying to find her. But since she didn't know Adriana's alias, she had hit a brick wall. Each time she requested information she found herself at the bottom of an endless list, because there were thirty thousand other files like Adriana's, more than fifteen thousand cases of people executed by firing squad, and one and a half million exiles, and on top of that, the person she was looking for was not even a relative of hers.

The final letter from her Amnesty International contacts had eventually arrived. Julia put it away in her desk drawer without even opening it, locked the drawer, and went out for a walk.

The phone rang. Julia hurried across the living room to answer. She wasn't expecting Ulysses to call her this soon, but she'd been hoping he would.

"Mom, thank goodness you picked up! I've got something urgent to ask you."

Julia smiled. "Yes!"

"Mom? Are you there?"

"Of course I'm here, my angel. Now, I want to know how you're doing. How's it going with your cousins? Have you met the twins' kids yet?"

"Yes. I'm very happy. I love this country. But I'm calling about Theo."

Julia sat down.

"Mom?"

"I'm listening, angel."

"It's nothing bad, don't worry. But I had a visit from a young woman called Celeste Fierro. She works for a forensic anthropology team."

"A what?"

"Mom, forensic anthropology. There's a group of young researchers. They're a mixed bag—archaeologists, anthropologists, doctors, biologists, computer scientists. Well, anyway, they've started up a DNA collection program."

"What? What does that mean?"

"They investigate the bodies they find in mass graves. They use the DNA from the remains of the bodies they exhume to identify them and find their relatives. I don't know how they heard I was in Buenos Aires, but the young woman came to see me to ask me for a blood sample. They've already exhumed more than a thousand corpses from mass graves. More than half of them are still awaiting identification."

"I see. Yes, of course, you must do it."

"I'm going to, obviously, but Celeste, the young woman, asked if you're coming to Argentina. They want to see you too."

"But my DNA won't be of any use to them."

"They don't need your DNA, Mom. They need concrete information."

"What kind of information?"

"They only have bones to work from. So they try to find out things like the person's height, their medical record, whether they were ever in an accident or had an illness or an operation, that sort of thing."

Julia was silent.

"They also need to know about the torture, and Castelar. . . ."

"Is this the government's new pet project?"

"No, Mom. It's a private organization."

33.

THE FORENSIC
ANTHROPOLOGY TEAM

Austral Summer
2001

Almost a year to the day since Ulysses' first visit there, Julia found herself looking for the offices of the Argentine Forensic Anthropology Team. The meeting had been scheduled for 11:00 A.M. It was a hot day, and Julia was wearing her emerald green printed cotton dress and a round straw hat with an upturned brim, which gave her a retro look. The taxi dropped her off on a noisy shopping street in front of a dilapidated building covered with graffiti. It wasn't the modern tower block she'd been expecting; perhaps she'd imagined it would resemble the institute where she worked in Paris.

She was too early. She was tempted to get a coffee and do a bit of exploring. A swarm of stalls offering photocopying, printing, and binding services, stores selling electronics, and an invasive billboard gave the area the feel of a bazaar. Pedestrians and cars moved around amid the noise and the pollution. Julia pushed open the heavy wooden door and entered the building. Inside, the air was cool and the noise from the street was muffled. Light filtered into the lobby through etched glass panels. Facing her was an old-fashioned cage elevator with a folding metal door, which didn't look entirely reassuring. She was overcome by the desire to leave without going any farther.

The office was located on the second floor. It could also be reached by a steep, narrow staircase that was as run-down as the building's facade. The floor was partitioned off into a series of small offices, with the exception of two spacious rooms that had skeletons laid out on display tables. Farther along there was an archive room with stacks of numbered, color-coded boxes containing human remains that were in the course of being identified. The walls, marked and grubby through wear and tear, contrasted with the newly painted mauve doors. The grayish computer terminals visible through some of the office doors that had been left ajar suggested a careful allocation of resources. It took only a glance for Julia to locate Celeste Fierro's office.

According to her watch, it was exactly 11:00 A.M. She decided to wait for a few more seconds. Then she knocked on the door, struggling to keep her composure, which made her realize how nervous she was. She was immediately called in and greeted by a young woman with a pleasant smile who was wearing gray pants and a sky-blue lab coat.

She quickly realized she was dealing with a skilled professional whose youth belied her in-depth knowledge of the case. Celeste Fierro was in charge of the *desaparecidos* of Castelar. She knew all the details inside and out: the identity of every prisoner held in the police station, the cells they had occupied, and the duration of their detention. She could describe the layout of the place as if she'd been there herself and recite the names of the prisoners and the guards from memory.

When Julia sat down opposite Celeste, she felt as if her past were looking her in the eyes. Speaking in a calm voice, Celeste told her about each of her fellow prisoners. She had taken out a bulky file containing thousands of names and photographs, including faces Julia recognized. A digital matrix of names, places, and dates completed her database.

By comparing the accounts she gathered, Celeste Fierro had developed an information-verification system. She could accurately establish the names of the dead and of the survivors and thus, by a process of elimination, the names of the *desaparecidos*. This list served as a starting point for the fieldwork carried out by the anthropologists in mass graves and cemeteries.

Interviews with survivors were therefore just as important as the scientific work. They enabled the anthropologists to cross-check information and to broaden their range of conclusions. Celeste told Julia that it was through her sister Anna's evidence that Theo had been identified as the prisoner in cell number 4, whom none of the Castelar survivors could recall ever seeing. Julia was informed that Paola had died and that Rosa had committed suicide. She also learned of the death of Oswaldo, the young man in the cell across from hers, whom she used to talk to when Sosa was on guard duty.

"Do you remember a girl named Maria? She was detained in Castelar at the same time as you."

Julia struggled to concentrate on the young woman's question.

"Maria? No, there wasn't any Maria; I'm sure of it," she answered. "But I remember a young man called Augusto. I ran into him again in Villa Devoto before I was deported."

"Yes, in fact, I'm meeting with him next week," Celeste said, peering at her file.

"That's such good news! I'm glad he finally got out. I'd like to see him."

"Good, I can arrange that. It'll be very important. But this girl Maria," Celeste insisted, "she must have been with you. She was very young at the time; she must have been barely fourteen, curly auburn hair . . ."

Julia felt a chill run through her. She hesitated, instinctively afraid of flipping a coin that would decide her fate.

"There was a young girl and yes, she was fourteen, but she was blond," Julia began, turning very pale, her mouth suddenly dry.

Celeste faded into the background, pushing her chair into a gloomy corner of the room.

"I became very close to her. Her name was Adriana. I'd like to know . . . I believe my sister saw her once. Have you found her?"

The young woman studied Julia, gauging her ability to take in the information she was about to give her.

"No," she replied slowly. "We haven't found the remains of an Adriana. But a few years ago, Maria came to give evidence. She didn't seem to remember anyone. That can happen sometimes, after traumatic experiences such as yours. But she did tell us the date she was arrested, and so we were able to find out which group she was imprisoned with. Unfortunately, we haven't been able to tie in her evidence, because we have no Maria in our files. I'll have to ask Augusto if he remembers Maria. You seem to be the only two female survivors. It would be useful if you got in touch with her too. I have her contact details; she works for a human rights organization."

Julia stared for a long time at the telephone number Celeste jotted down on a sheet of paper.

34

THE CHOICES

Austral Winters
(*1976, 1987, 1997*)

A s soon as he heard the name Josefina d'Annunzio, Captain Torricelli allowed Adriana on board with no further
questions. He took her up onto the deserted bridge of the
transatlantic liner, where the flags flapped overhead in the
cold wind. Adriana watched as, down below, the boatswain
shouted orders and the passengers standing on the quayside
boarded the ship slowly, as per the precise instructions of
white-uniformed officers. There were separate lines for each
class of travel. The port was teeming with people and the sight
of it, with the city in the background, made Adriana anxious.

"Are you sure she isn't here yet? She hasn't tried to contact you?"

"I'm certain. My crew keeps me informed of every single
detail."

"What shall we do?"

"We're sailing in three hours. It's up to you to decide. Once your friend is on board, there'll be no going back."

The long wail of a ship's horn tore the silence.

The man held out his hand. Adriana jumped as if she'd been caught doing something wrong.

"Oh, sorry," she said nervously, taking the envelope Father Miguel had given her out of her pocket.

The captain tucked the envelope into the inside pocket of his jacket. He studied Adriana for a moment, then took her by the arm to show her the way down.

"I'll ask one of the crew to go with you to get your friend. I trust him completely; you've got nothing to fear."

He added: "If your friend is as weak as you say he is, we'll have to pass him off as a crew member who's had a bit too much to drink."

Adriana adjusted her head scarf and set off, shoulders hunched. The captain placed his hand on the top of the frame of the watertight door and ushered the young girl out, pointing to a metal staircase at the end of the bridge. She walked in the direction he'd indicated. The stairs were steep. A uniformed sailor stood by the guardrail, ready to hold out his hand to her. The captain waved him over and whispered a few words into his ear. Then he turned to the young girl. "Follow him," he instructed. "Don't waste any time. You have to be back here within three hours."

The sailor attempted to help Adriana down the steps. She pulled away nervously. The man looked surprised.

"Excuse me," she murmured, ill at ease.

She hurried down the ship's three decks, almost fell against a capstan, but chose to cling to the rail rather than accept the muscled arm offered to her.

When they reached the dock, it was all Adriana could do not to run away. Anxiety was making her clumsy. She felt as though she was being watched, which made her act even more awkwardly. Two men in black leather jackets brushed past them. The sailor took Adriana by the arm and growled at her in a loud voice.

"At least that way people will think you're mad at me," he said, eyeing her coldly. "You have to calm down."

Adriana wrested her arm away furiously and walked on at a brisk pace. When they reached San Ignacio church she turned to the sailor.

"Thank you," she told him, still on the alert.

The man smiled at her.

"I'm going to get my friend."

"I'll come with you."

"No. I prefer to go by myself.."

"Give him this uniform. He'll need it," the man said, handing her the small bundle he'd been carrying under his arm.

He watched her go and lit a cigarette, leaning against one of the columns in front of the church.

Adriana found Theo sitting where the sacristan had left him, on the balcony behind the organ. He'd been given something to eat and had washed his face. *We'll have to say he's been in a fight,* Adriana thought as she looked at him. Theo greeted her with a grimace, still racked with pain.

"Julia's disappeared," Adriana whispered, once she was within earshot. "The captain has given us three hours to get on the ship. He's sent one of the sailors to help you board."

"Let's go," Theo replied unhesitatingly.

"Theo, you don't understand," she said. "Julia isn't at the meeting place."

"I heard you. But we have no choice. She's still got three hours to show up, and we can't go looking for her."

"Listen, Theo, I've been thinking." Adriana moved a little closer to him. "We can't leave without her."

"If we stay, they'll kill us. And Julia's sacrifice will have been pointless."

"So she has to die so you and I can escape?"

"We can't save her. She knows that we have very little chance of success. If she was in our shoes, she would leave."

Visibly pained, Adriana knelt down beside him. "Theo, Julia saved your life. She went to get you in your cell. If it hadn't been for her, we'd have had no chance of getting away. Father Miguel, the money, the ship: it's all thanks to her."

Exhausted, she slid to the floor and hid her face in her

hands. After a moment she looked up again and added: "If she's not on the ship, we have to stay behind."

"Let's go to the ship. I'm sure she's already there. Let's not waste any more time," Theo decided.

Adriana held out the sailor's uniform.

"Here, put this on. I'll go and find the sailor."

They boarded the *Donizetti* in time. Captain Torricelli's plan had worked. Theo had walked the whole way leaning heavily on the sailor, who stopped at every street corner to make sure no one was following them and to catch his breath.

They boarded the ship through an open cargo door. A group of sailors dressed in the same uniform as Theo were busy loading the last of the supplies. Their escort led them through a maze of stairways and corridors to the far end of a section near the engine room. He opened a heavy water-tight door that led into a small windowless cabin with a triple bunk bed.

"I'm going to lock you in until we sail. Captain's orders. We don't want any nasty surprises."

"But I need to know if Julia's on board," Adriana said in an anguished voice.

The sailor looked straight at her. "I'm sorry. If your friend was on board, she would already be here."

"Give me ten minutes, please," Adriana pleaded. "If she doesn't come, we'll have to stay behind."

Theo sat down on the bottom bunk. "That doesn't make any sense. Even if Julia isn't here, we need to leave."

"I can't leave without her."

The sailor announced he was going to inform the captain.

"I'll be back in twenty minutes. I don't know if he'll give you permission to get off."

He locked the door and went away.

Adriana shook her head slowly.

"How can you even think of leaving without Julia? She would have given her life for you."

"I would have given my life for her too," Theo murmured. "If she's been captured, nothing will save her. They'll kill her, they'll kill me too, and they will have won."

"You can't admit defeat. Not now!"

"Look at me! I'm a wreck, a piece of human garbage. I can't even walk. You want me to go and play the hero in this state?"

There was a heavy silence. Then Adriana ventured to continue: "You're not the only one who's suffered. We're all recovering. We can look for her together, help her."

"I don't want to stay. I can't avenge the deaths of those who have died if I'm dead too."

"Theo . . . Julia's carrying your child."

Theo shook his head.

"She's not carrying my child anymore; you know that as well as I do. They killed everything I loved, everything I had, everything I was."

"Theo, wake up! You are more than the person they tried to turn you into."

"Would you like me to go and turn myself in to make their job easier?"

Theo clutched his stomach, racked with a searing pain. He choked as his body jerked.

"I'll tell you what I'm going to do," he whispered, his breath coming in gasps. His dark eyes glittered in their sockets. "I'm going to find my brother's killer. That's the only thing I want."

Adriana shut her eyes and threw back her head. "Revenge, hatred. You're thinking just like them."

The door opened. "We set sail in ten minutes. If you want to get off the ship, it's now or never."

Adriana stared at Theo. He turned his face away.

She stood up, arranged her scarf on her head, and stepped out the cabin door.

Maria looked at herself in the mirror. It had been more than ten years since she'd chosen to stay in Argentina. Now she could resurface. She liked her new identity. She had a straight black bob that contrasted with her milky skin and bangs covering her eyes, making her look older than she was. These changes were accompanied by a new attitude. She was a charming woman.

She buttoned up her floral dress with the round neck,

threw a white sweater over her shoulders, and made sure she
had enough money in her wallet to pay for the bus ticket
downtown. These days she was working as an assistant ac-
countant in a busy office. She had taken up her new job as a
challenge after spending almost seven years as a bookkeeper
in the secluded confines of San Ignacio church, for fear of
being recognized by a police informant. But now she had
nothing to be afraid of. The military were no longer in power,
and she no longer needed to stay hidden.

She was about to leave, then changed her mind. She fished
the lipstick she had just bought out of her bag and went to the
mirror to apply it. The result took her aback. She would have
to get used to it, she told herself as she shut the door of her
apartment.

It was a mild day that felt just like early spring. The women
seemed somehow prettier dressed in cooler clothing. A small
cluster of people had already gathered at the bus stop. Maria
went to the street corner to buy a newspaper and returned to
stand in line. The bus was approaching.

"Adriana!" cried a voice behind her.

She turned around automatically. Two schoolgirls were
running toward her, shouting to a third girl to get on the bus,
which had just pulled up. The girls arrived, out of breath, and
pushed their way past the other passengers, jostling each
other. Maria was annoyed with herself. After all this time she
should have been able to control herself.

The bus was full, but she found an empty seat in the back.

She sat next to the window and gathered up her purse to let an overweight woman with a bag full of groceries sit down next to her. Maria watched unseeingly as the streets unfolded.

If Papá were alive, I'd go back to my real name. But I prefer Maria. Her face was reflected in the bus window. She had another hour before she would arrive at her destination. *Maria is strong. She can speak out; she's comfortable around men. Maria. Maria Cruz.* The woman sitting next to her had dozed off with her mouth open and her bag of groceries jammed between her legs. *He couldn't have found a better name. Maria Cruz. It's a name that doesn't attract attention. It's short. Practical when you have to forge papers.* She smiled to herself. *But my Jesuit wasn't the most imaginative. Maria Cruz, for heaven's sake!* The bus turned onto a main road and accelerated.

Maria folded her newspaper into quarters so she could read it without bothering her neighbor. There was a short article in it about a forthcoming Sting concert at La Plata Stadium on December 11, 1987. The journalist mentioned the singer's visit to the Mothers of the Plaza de Mayo at the square. Maria admired the women. They'd been braver than she had; she hadn't dared to show her face. She leafed through the pages. Thankfully Julia had left Argentina. *I wouldn't have been able to carry on living if anything had happened to her.* She rested the newspaper on her knees. At least she'd stayed, out of solidarity; she would never have gotten over her remorse if she'd left. The bus drove past some tall trees in a park that cast a refreshing shadow. She would have liked to go to the concert. But the

Adriana in her didn't yet feel ready to venture out on her own. The bus emerged from the shade back into the sun.

The woman next to her stood up to get off. Maria let out a sigh of relief. She was happy. She was free; she had a job, a new life. There were things she wanted to do: wear perfume, go to the cinema, eat ice cream. A young girl took the fat woman's place. *I wonder what her life is like. Her son must be eleven years old now.* The sun had become overbearing. It was starting to get hot inside the bus. She fanned herself with the newspaper and the girl next to her looked grateful. They passed the dome of the Church of the Immaculate Conception. Maria was only a couple of minutes away from her stop. She was about to get up and ring the bell when she went white as a sheet.

His hair was longer and he had put on weight, but she would have recognized him anywhere. She had felt his eyes burning into her before she had seen him. The man in a gray suit and tie standing behind some other passengers and looking straight at her was El Cabo Pavor.

She forced herself to look away so she could get her emotions under control, but she couldn't contain the flood of adrenaline or stop her mouth from grimacing. Beads of sweat trickled down the nape of her neck. *He can't have recognized me. I'm Maria. He can't do anything.* The bus came to a stop. She watched him out of the corner of her eye. Just as the doors were about to close, she got up, smiled at her neighbor, who quickly made space for her to get past, and jumped off the bus.

She walked straight ahead at a rapid pace. The bus drove off, and Maria could see El Cabo Pavor's face glued to the window. He was staring at her.

Maria waited until the bus had disappeared from view before turning down the first street on her right and running until she was out of breath. *He'll never be able to find me.* She went into a café and called her office from a phone booth. She told them she was sick and wouldn't be coming in that day. Then she placed a second call.

"Father Fabian? It's me. I have to see you right away."

She didn't want to keep them waiting. She ran her fingers through her curly hair, arranged the files neatly on her desk, put on her sneakers, and ran downstairs. The girls on her team were waiting for her on the first floor of the building. They had completed their preparations for the following day's protest march and printed banners with the words JUSTICE AND TRUTH, the letters formed with the names of some of the thirty thousand "disappeared." In the street, workers were hanging Christmas decorations on electricity poles. Bystanders looked on approvingly. She steered her young colleagues away for a drink before they went home to rest in preparation for the march the next day: December 8, 1997.

"Good work. We won't go unnoticed," Maria told them. "There could be a lot of people."

"How many, do you think?" the youngest girl asked her.

"We never know. Sometimes there'll be a hundred of us, sometimes a thousand. It's very hard to tell exactly how many. We take a look at the crowd and make a rough guess."

"Have you been on a lot of protest marches like this one?"

"A few."

The waiter brought their drinks and left the bill on the table.

"What did you do before you started working for the foundation?"

"This and that. I worked for a church, I was an accounting assistant at a big company, and I did some tutoring. I even worked in a factory. But my dream was always to do what I'm doing now."

The girls looked at one another, slightly intimidated. One of them got up the courage to ask: "Did you know any people who were captured by the military?"

Maria looked around for the waiter.

"No, not really," she replied, standing up. "Sorry, I'm very tired. I'm going home. See you tomorrow."

She picked up the bill, slipped a banknote into the waiter's hand, and left. The bus station wasn't far—a ten-minute walk at most. But at this time of day there were fewer buses. She would have to wait awhile. She fished around in her bag for coins. She opened her wallet and stared at her ID card. When Father Fabian had gotten her the card, she had had black hair and bangs. This new incarnation of herself, with curly red hair, still took her by surprise.

The bus stopped right in front of her. Three other passengers got on. Ignoring them, she went to sit in the back. The fluorescent lighting in the vehicle gave her the unpleasant feeling of being in a moving window display. A few minutes later a man sitting in the middle of the bus stood up, ready to get off. While waiting for the bus to stop, he looked over in her direction and smiled. Maria blushed and then felt even more embarrassed. She could still feel her cheeks burning once the stranger had gotten off. *I'm like a little girl.* She ruffled her auburn curls automatically to try to drive away her thoughts—*I must get better at this*—and got off well before her stop so she would have to walk.

The Buenos Aires she longed for was within arm's reach: bustling streets, laughter at sidewalk tables, charming men. And yet she still refused herself any contact with this animated, noisy world. It wasn't because of them. Not entirely. Soon she would be brave enough.

The sound of organ music caught her attention. She tried to work out where it was coming from. For the first time she noticed a small Baroque church squashed between two chipped buildings from the 1950s. She pushed open the heavy door out of curiosity. Inside, a haze of incense hung in the air. Maria dipped her fingers in the font and slipped inside in search of cool air. Sitting with her back against a white pillar, she contemplated the Madonna paintings in lavish frames decorated with gold-leaf arabesques and allowed herself to be carried away by the deep, sustained notes of the organ.

There were quite a few people in the church, mainly women

praying, and a short line in front of the confessional, which was tucked away in one of the side aisles. This ritual always intrigued her. She had made up a few sins the one time she had gone to confession and had never returned because she felt she would only make things worse by not knowing what to say.

The door to the confessional opened and a penitent came out. The man blinked. She recognized him before he saw her and stood transfixed. He was wearing the same gray suit and had the same haircut he'd had ten years previously. She watched him make the sign of the cross and turn around, too stunned to think of ducking behind the woman sitting in front of her. The man's gaze met hers. She lowered her eyes and picked up her purse. Her hands were trembling. *He's still looking at me. He's recognized me.* She stood up, made her way out of the pew, apologizing, and walked rapidly down the nave. El Cabo Pavor stared at her as he emerged from the embrace of a priest clad in a soutane and a clerical collar who had greeted him effusively. He hurried to reach the doorway before her.

Maria sped up, panic-stricken. She pushed open the door and the noise from the street burst in as if to save her. He caught hold of her arm and pulled her back into a dark corner of the entrance hall. He pressed his body against hers to stop her from moving and clamped a hand over her mouth. He looked at her with the same mad stare, the same bulbous eyes, as before. She could feel his breath fogging up her eyes.

"If you talk," he said slowly, "I'll kill you."

He pinned her to the wall with his full body weight.

The door rattled and two elderly women came out. The man let go and stepped back just far enough for Maria to free herself. She fled into the street, the women staring after her disapprovingly.

Maria ran, frightened by the echo of her footsteps on the asphalt, certain he was following her. She spent half the night crouching in the doorway of a building, watching the street. Day was breaking by the time she got home, having made a thousand detours. She collapsed onto her bed, shivering with fever, and felt herself spiraling back down into hell, lost in the insanity of Castelar. Hands were roaming over her body and she was sweating as she tried to break free, her sheets giving off the bitter smell of fear. She fell from the bed as she struggled in her nightmare and came to gasping for breath. She remained lying on the floor for a long time, her eyes motionless. *He will never touch me again.*

When she stepped outside, she felt she had finally left behind what remained of Adriana.

In the street, men hurried past her blindly. Maria took her time walking to the bus stop and watched undismayed as she saw the bus pulling away. She hailed the first taxi she saw, climbed in confidently, and gave the driver the address. *It's taken me twenty-two years, but now I'm ready.*

Father Fabian was waiting for her at the corner, dressed in jeans and a gray T-shirt, a bulky file under his arm.

35.

MARIA

Austral Summer

2001

Julia left the building without the least desire to go back home. The piece of paper with Maria's telephone number was in the pocket of her printed cotton dress. She walked down the avenue, staring straight ahead. Several taxis went by, but she made no attempt to flag one down.

When she got to Mama Fina's house, she found there was a family meeting in progress in the dining room. She tossed her straw hat on the table in the entryway, threw her shoes under a chair, and went to join the others. A lively discussion was under way. Olivier was sitting next to her father, answering a slew of questions from the twins. Ulysses was laughing along with his cousins: Anna and Pablo's three sons and the twins' children. The laughter grew louder as Julia entered.

She hugged Ulysses and Olivier, blew the others a kiss, then sat down next to her father and took his hand.

"They're serious," she explained. "The woman who saw me, Celeste Fierro, knows all the names and arrest dates and the secret detention center where we were sent. It's a simple and efficient system."

"But it still took me a year to convince you to come here, Mom," Ulysses broke in.

Julia was silent, her good humor momentarily fading.

"Are they getting results?" Julia's father asked.

"They've already managed to identify about four hundred bodies. It may not seem like much, but it's a huge achievement."

"Is that right? Do you think there could be more bodies, darling?"

"They say there are thirty thousand *desaparecidos*."

"I can't believe it," her father said. "How do they go about finding them?"

"First they have to locate the mass graves," Ulysses explained. "Then they carry out a proper archaeological dig: clearing away each layer of soil, registering locations, that kind of thing. Previously the government used to open up the mass graves with a mechanical shovel, so obviously there wasn't much left to recover."

"I read somewhere that they found a hundred bodies without hands in Avellaneda Cemetery," said one of the twins.

"*Tío*, you're making that up!" Anna's youngest son interjected.

"It's true, I assure you. They used to cut off people's hands in the morgue in the cemetery so they wouldn't be identifiable by their fingerprints."

"Celeste told me about that too," Julia confirmed.

"But how can they identify anyone in those conditions?"

"They compile information," Ulysses answered carefully, watching for his mother's reaction. "DNA from family members is very important. But they also try to match up all kinds of data: diseases, dental characteristics, what have you. They reconstruct each person's history."

"Celeste is amazing," Anna commented. "She keeps all that information stored in her head, like a computer."

"That's true," Julia said. "She spoke about some of my fellow prisoners as if she'd known them personally—she even knew details I'd forgotten: she asked me if I could remember three corpses being brought to Castelar for the inmates to wash. Paola was the one who'd told me about it; it had happened a few days before I arrived at Castelar. I just know the story because Paola said she felt mortified at the thought of someone handling her dead body to wash it."

Her voice wavered as she added: "Celeste told me Paola's remains have been identified."

"Can we be sure the DNA testing is reliable, Olivier?" her father asked, to divert attention away from Julia.

"If a body has been burned or the bones have been underwater for a while—if the person drowned, say—then the DNA is affected," Olivier explained. "But the technology is constantly improving. These days it's possible to reconstruct a person's DNA sequence if we have DNA samples from their wife and child, for example. By subtraction, if you like."

"Did they ask you for a DNA sample?" Julia's mother asked.

Olivier stood up from the table and began clearing away the last remaining glasses.

"Yes," Julia said. "I promised I'd go back to the lab before I leave."

The next morning Julia received a phone call from Celeste. The Mothers of the Plaza de Mayo were organizing a rally. Supporters were to meet in front of the Casa Rosada the following Wednesday for their annual march.

"They've been organizing these marches for years now. This year they're demanding nonpayment of the foreign debt."

"Really? What does that have to do with anything?" Julia asked.

Celeste laughed softly on the other end of the line. "They're making a stand. They're speaking on behalf of people who have no say."

There was a silence, then she continued, "As a rule I steer clear of these protests, but I'm mentioning it because Maria was the one who told me about it. She just called me."

"Did you tell her about me?" Julia asked.

"Yes, I let her know we'd met."

Celeste paused again, then added: "Maria will be at the Manuel Belgrano monument at six in the evening. She seemed quite overwhelmed at the prospect of seeing you."

"Could you give me the details again?"

"Tuesday, December 11, Plaza de Mayo, 6:00 P.M."

Celeste hung up. For a moment Julia felt as if she were standing on the edge of a precipice. She stared at the telephone in her hand. She had a choice. She could still decide not to go.

The fact that she'd even considered it appalled her. She had spent twenty-four years waiting for this moment: why run away now?

"Everything okay, darling?"

Julia felt Olivier's arms around her. She buried her face against him and stood motionless, breathing slowly. He took her face in his hands and made her look at him.

"Don't be too hard on yourself," he said.

She'd made up her mind: she wouldn't go. What could she learn that she didn't already know from the thousands of hours she'd spent looking for Theo? This rationale gave her a strong sense of peace over the next few days. But when the day came, at the last moment, and for the same reasons that had convinced her otherwise before, she grabbed her straw hat and left the house without her purse, as if she were just getting some air.

She was swallowed up by the crowd long before she reached Plaza de Mayo. The closer she got to the monument to Belgrano, the more she needed to elbow her way through the crush of people. In her mind she was back at the rally when Perón had openly attacked the Montoneros. How many of the people who had been in the Plaza de Mayo that day were still alive? From what Celeste had told her, only a handful.

She looked up and realized she had nearly reached the monument. A large banner concealed the faces of some young people who had climbed on top of it and were hoisting others up. She looked around for a familiar face. A young couple, hand in hand, forced their way through the gathering, heads down. Julia caught hold of the young girl's arm and followed in her wake; others did the same behind Julia. They came to a stop right under the banners in front of the Casa Rosada.

About a hundred feet away, in the thick of the crowd, a woman with curly red hair was giving orders. Julia recognized her instantly: it was Adriana. The woman began to shout out her instructions in a rousing voice. There could be no mistake. Julia let out a cry before she had even made up her mind to approach the woman. Maria turned and their eyes met. They rushed unthinkingly toward each other. They hugged for a long time as if in shock, not smiling or crying.

There was no way they could stay among the crowd. Holding hands tightly, they searched for a way out. Once outside the square, they walked slowly, arm in arm, gradually starting to speak.

"And Theo?" Julia murmured, her hand tightening in Adriana's.

"I don't know, sweetheart," Adriana answered after a long silence. "I mean, I don't know if he's dead or alive. It's a long story and a sad one, because it's taken us so long to meet again. Do you remember the evening we last saw each other?"

"I could describe it by the second."

"After you left, I had a tough time of it with Theo. We walked for two days before reaching Father Miguel's."

"How come I never heard about it?"

"Father Miguel was arrested soon after we saw him, then killed at ESMA."

Julia was no longer sure she wanted to hear the rest.

"He was very helpful. He gave us the envelope with the money. He hid us in the sacristy of a church near the port."

"Did you go to the *Donizetti*?"

"Yes, I spoke with Captain Torricelli while Theo waited for me in the church. He was in terrible shape. A sailor had to practically carry him on board."

"And then? Did you leave?"

"We got on secretly an hour before departure. We were hoping you would already be on board."

"But I never made it."

Adriana and Julia walked until they reached a public square, then went to sit on one of the benches. Julia hugged her knees to her chest. The air was still muggy, despite the breeze rustling the treetops. Children were playing soccer along the paths. The ball flew into the air after a kick and landed between the two women's legs. They laughed as they tried to send it back. The tussle for the ball moved closer, at one point encircling their bench. Julia and Adriana swung their feet out of the way and waited for the tornado of children to pass.

"Theo stayed on the ship."

"Theo stayed on the ship," Julia repeated in a hoarse voice. "What about you?"

Adriana sighed, propping her chin up with her hands.

"What about you?" Julia asked again.

"I couldn't."

"You couldn't what?"

"I couldn't leave without you."

Julia shook her head slowly, tears filling her eyes.

"No, don't tell me. . . ."

"Yes. I got off a few minutes before the ship sailed." She ran her hands over her face. "I was scared to death. I didn't know where to go, and every time I saw a uniform I panicked. . . ."

Julia's eyes were dull and unseeing. "And . . . ?"

"I don't know. That was the last time I saw him."

"You got off and he stayed on the ship."

"Yes, that's it. He was very sick, Julia."

"Yes."

"Not just physically. He was devastated by the death of his brother."

"What? But he couldn't have known that Gabriel was dead!"

"He knew everything. Who had tortured Gabriel, where, how, every single detail. He had become obsessed with it."

Adriana's knuckles were white where she gripped the edge of the bench.

"He also thought your baby was dead."

"He had no way of knowing."

"I'd told him . . . how you . . . how they . . ."

The boys went past again carrying the ball, taking turns spinning it on one finger.

"But still!"

"It was what I thought too. It was impossible for the baby to have survived, Julia." Her face was twisted with sadness.

They reached for each other's hands, refraining from saying any more, and watched the children leaving.

"When did you change your name?"

"Very soon after Theo's departure. I was terrified. You can imagine. And when I finally got up the courage to go outside, I came face-to-face with El Cabo Pavor on a bus!"

"Oh, no! God, what a nightmare. That must have been horrible. During the dictatorship?"

"No, thankfully. I ran away, moved house, changed my job, everything."

"I think I'd die if I saw any of them again," Julia murmured.

"Did you know we managed to get him sentenced? He's in prison, and he won't be coming out for a long time. Celeste helped me. They identified Paola's body and I testified. We have an excellent set of lawyers. My friend Father Fabian introduced me to them. I want you to meet him. He could help you too. He saved me in more than one way. I'm looking for the rest of them now."

"That's good," said Julia, staring into space. "But sometimes I think prison's too good for them."

Maria took Julia's hands in hers and kissed them. "Yes. But we're not like that, remember?"

36.

UNCLE MAYOL

Austral Summer/Boreal Winter
2001–2002

He opened the door before she'd even put her key in the lock. Olivier had waited up for her until dawn. They didn't exchange a single word. In the days that followed, it was as if they were living on borrowed time. They skirted around each other, unsure what to do or say. He finally left for France because of unexpected work, while Julia stayed on for Christmas with Ulysses as planned.

After Olivier's departure, Julia became more methodical, almost cold.

"I think we need to start over from scratch," she told Anna one evening, when the young people had gone dancing at one of the *boliches* in Buenos Aires.

"I don't agree. We know now that he didn't die. And he didn't search for the two of you either."

"What if he came back after the World Cup?"

"I followed up on that too. A hundred-odd Montoneros came back between 1979 and 1980 to launch a counter-offensive. Many of them were discovered by the intelligence agencies. Theo's name doesn't appear anywhere. He's not on the official lists or the lists of the disappeared."

"But the fact is he completely disappeared."

"Maybe we should check out his old place again. I often go past it. The house is completely abandoned; it's sad to see. But you never know."

Julia had already decided to extend her stay in Buenos Aires when Celeste had called and asked her to come to her office with Ulysses. Julia had thought it had to do with new DNA results and promised to stop by the next morning before Ulysses' flight.

They had found Celeste perched on a stepladder, taking down one of the numbered boxes in the archive room. She had caught sight of the expression on Julia's face and apologized profusely. "I called you about something totally different," she had added as she led them down the hall.

The piles of documents on Celeste's desk seemed to have multiplied since Julia's last visit.

"Is this about the DNA results?" Ulysses had asked. "Did you manage to match up the data?"

"I haven't finished yet. It'll take time. We still have more than five hundred bodies left to identify, and unfortunately most of them will never resurface."

"Well?" Julia had asked.

"Well," Celeste had continued, hunting through her stacks of files, "one of our researchers went to San Francisco to attend a conference of leading scientists, and . . ."

She had pulled out a file triumphantly.

"And he was introduced to a professor who's been working at NASA for the past few years. It turns out he's Argentine. He works with microorganisms or something like that."

"And what . . . ?" Ulysses had asked, glancing discreetly at his watch.

"The fact is he wanted to know absolutely everything about our work, because he too has family members who disappeared."

Celeste had held out a photocopy of the conference program with a photo of the professor in question.

"The reason I wanted to talk to you is that his name is Mayol. Ernesto Mayol."

"Wait," Julia had said. "Ernesto Mayol? Isn't that one of Theo's uncles? Anna spoke to him once, if my memory serves me right."

"I think this is him."

After Ulysses had left, Julia had spent the entire afternoon dialing the phone numbers Celeste had given her. Each time she had reached an automated menu with a selection of options, none of which had connected her to the person she was trying to contact. Finally she had decided to send an e-mail. Professor Mayol's reply had arrived soon after. He would be willing to meet with her, but only if she could travel to San Francisco. Julia hadn't thought twice. She had replied that she could make the trip at the end of the month.

As she fastened her seat belt, Julia realized she was wearing a red dress, just like the first time she had flown out of Buenos Aires in 1977. She peered out the window. Olivier still wasn't answering her calls.

She arrived in San Francisco the day before her meeting. She left the hotel, choosing to lose herself in the grid of streets in order to stay out of the wind. The cold chilled her to the bone. She turned left onto Leavenworth Street. This trip was absolute madness. If Theo was alive, he would have a family, a job, a home of his own. Looking up, she found herself at the bottom of an impossibly steep street, which zigzagged its way uphill. She began to scale it. *I'll go to the meeting anyway.* She climbed on, past the houses and the fallow flowerbeds with their frozen hydrangea stalks. When she reached the top, she opened her arms wide as if she could fill herself with space.

The next day Julia got to the meeting early. In the hotel lounge, a man of indeterminate age, wearing casually elegant clothing, got up from the maroon velvet armchair next to the fireplace. He slipped his horn-rimmed glasses into the inside pocket of his tweed jacket and looked expressionlessly at Julia.

"*Buenos días*," he said coolly. "I'm Ernesto Mayol. I suppose you are Julia."

Julia looked him over and took her time going forward to shake his hand. He suggested they go for a walk, despite the fog and cold. They turned into a street heading toward the pier. They walked in silence, their hands in their pockets, collars turned up, and shoulders hunched. In the end they pushed open the door of a diner with misted-up windows and sat down facing each other, stirring the coffee a waitress in a miniskirt had been in no hurry to serve them.

"I have waited for years to have this conversation." Julia's hands gripped her coffee cup tightly. "Why didn't you try to get in touch with me before?"

"It wasn't up to me to contact you."

The conversation couldn't have started on worse grounds and sharply came to a halt. Julia didn't want to ask any questions and the man didn't want to give any answers. They made small talk, sidestepping the subject that had caused them to meet.

The waitress came up to them, a pencil behind her ear.

"Will that be all? I have customers waiting for the table."

"Two more coffees, and some water," Mayol said without taking his eyes off Julia.

The waitress pursed her lips and stalked off. Julia plucked up courage.

"Are you in touch with him?"

"I can't answer that."

Julia stood up slowly, placed a bill on the table, and murmured, "You just did."

She left without looking back.

She was already in the corridor with her suitcase in her hand when the telephone in her hotel room started ringing. *Ulysses again. He'll want me to get him something else.* She hesitated for a moment, then retraced her steps. Ulysses could reach her on her cell phone. She opened the door, threw her coat onto a chair, and sat down unsteadily on the edge of the bed.

Before picking up the receiver, she already knew.

"Theo?"

37.

EL DIABLO

Boreal Summer
2006

Theo?"

Mia walked toward him, eyes half-closed, not quite awake. Still standing in the hallway, Theo was looking at the photo he had just taken with his cell phone. He quickly slipped the phone into his pocket and stood motionless, sweating despite the coolness of the morning. Mia drew up to him and tried to get him to put his arms around her. Theo wriggled free. She took hold of his hand and, surprised to find it damp, let go of it almost immediately.

"Come on, let's not keep standing here."

Theo took a step back, uncomfortable.

"I'm going to leave, Mia."

He was breathing heavily. There were dark circles under

his eyes, and in this first light of day he seemed worn out. Mia
tried to pull him close and kiss him, but the hard look in his
eyes took her aback.

"We've still got time," she murmured.

He avoided her gaze and fiddled with his cell phone for a
moment.

"I have to leave."

Through the large bay window Mia noticed that the streetlights had gone out. The garden was still sleeping under a sil-
very glow.

"But we'd talked about it," she ventured to say.

Mia stood there, draped in morning glow, totally nude, her
long hair snaking down her body. Theo stepped back.

"No, we've never talked about it."

Light filtered through the drizzle as he rode back. The motor-
bike skidded at every turn, forcing him to focus on the road. In
vain. His temples were pounding. Adrenaline ran through his
veins like poison. It was still the same face, despite the effects
of time. He couldn't get the image of his torturer out of his
head. Even dressed up for his daughter's wedding, he remained
the same cold-blooded murderer. *There he is, so close to me after all
these years. Within arm's reach, to take from him what he took from me.*

The engine roared beneath him. He put his foot down on
the straight stretch. El Diablo loomed in front of him, his

expression locked in fixed surprise, his right eyebrow puck-
ered. *I would have recognized him with or without that scar.* Theo's
nostrils flared as he passed the cars on the Merritt Parkway.
Why Mia? Why her of all people?

The mouth of the tunnel yawned up ahead, closer to swallowing him up with each passing second. He accelerated and
leaned forward, bursting with rage.

He screams as he enters the darkness. The man is standing
there, legs apart, in his spotless navy-blue uniform. Theo is
watching him from the depths of his agony. He can feel urine
trickling down his leg like acid. The man is inventing new
forms of torture to drive him insane. Theo has lost all sense of
time; his only sun is the beam from the projector. The voice of
the Führer thunders, drowning out his screams. His nose is a
pulp; oxygen enters through his wounds, gill-like. His body is
reduced to orifices: the existing ones and the ones El Diablo
has created.

"Do you understand, you filthy pig?"

He can barely hear the voice. His brain is throbbing with
pain, glutted with fluids. A bucket of sewage is thrown into
his face. Everything stings. But still he licks his lips, out of
dehydration.

"Nothing more to tell me, you filthy pig?"

The projector is going to start up. The nightmare too.
Theo's teeth are chattering. Is there some detail he's forgot-

ten? A crumb to appease the monster? His hanging body convulses. Theo knows he is going to die. He wants to die quickly.

The man laughs. Theo sees his mouth: the fleshy red lips, the perfect teeth. Others join in the laughter.

"So where's your sister? You haven't told me anything about your sister."

A sound emerges from Theo's throat, deformed, incomprehensible.

"No, you do have a sister. A sweet little homo face she has."

The projector comes on.

"Yes, they look so much alike it's striking; watch."

Theo receives a blow in the stomach.

"Even like this, transformed into a piece of shit," says a new voice.

"We gave it to her good, your sister. Want to see? We have the photos. We archive everything, just in case memories need refreshing."

El Diablo dangles a Polaroid in front of Theo's eyes.

"Look, you filthy pig. See how much fun I had with your sister."

At first, Theo sees nothing. Then he makes out some red and black shapes. He understands. He is shown around twenty photos in quick succession. They are images of his brother Gabriel being tortured. Close-up shots, taken at the height of his suffering. Theo sees all the details. He pisses himself again. He doesn't want to see, but he can't shut his eyes and he howls and cries and chokes. The scenes remain seared in his brain,

with the smell, the voices, the torment. Indelible images, unbearable ones. They secrete their never-ending venom.

"Identical, these two Trots. The same chromosomes. I
knew from the start that you were going to squeal. Just like
your brother. I rewarded him, though. I made him my mascot.
Look, rat."

Suspended like a piece of meat, Theo looks. He shouldn't
have. Writhing at the end of the rope, he screams with a fury
that makes him vomit.

Laughter, always their laughter around him, everywhere.

"But him, I let him go. I freed him. Yes, I did. I'm not saying it just to please you."

The sound of footsteps, and the projector begins to whir.

"I'll let you go, too. But not yet. After all my efforts I'm
entitled to a little party."

The reel starts spinning, but this time it is neither the voice
of the Führer nor the black-and-white images of the concentration camps. Unmistakable, the eyes of his brother Gabriel fill
the screen. His face in close-up, disfigured. He is on his knees,
begging, crying. Then a wide-open mouth, a silent scream as
Gabriel is pushed out from the plane into the void. The fall,
and their laughter, and the fall over and over again, and the
reel running idle. And their laughter.

Theo exits the tunnel screaming, blinded by a steely sun. He
slips between two cars and vanishes onto the exit ramp.

He had stopped trying to see her. Theo came back every evening to an empty house and paced from the kitchen to the living room like a caged animal. *She doesn't exist. She is his. She is nothing to me.* He didn't want to take Julia's long-distance calls either. He couldn't stand her carefree attitude. He needed silence. *I only think about her because I think about him, and I think about him all the time. I'll have him on his knees. I want to be the only thing he sees before he dies.*

Theo began to work out twice as hard. Luckily Mia had stopped coming to the gym. He never wanted to see her again. Her car had disappeared from the parking lot. She was avoiding him too, probably.

One day, feeling self-destructive, he walked by Mia's office, just to check.

"She's on vacation," a coworker of hers informed him, with a look Theo found irritating.

"I'd loaned her a file. Too bad . . ."

"All the files she's working on are on her desk. Would you like me to take a look?"

"Yes, please. I'll give you a hand."

He'd found some photos, addresses. But Theo wasn't satisfied.

"So she's gone to visit some friends?"

"Yes, lucky her! I'd love to go to Argentina. But it's expensive. Having a husband helps, that's for sure."

Argentina! There was no way she could have figured it out. Theo rubbed the back of his neck and went to the water fountain, his throat dry. *Nobody has ever known, not even Julia.*

The sheets were damp and acrid with sweat. Theo woke from a restless sleep, his mind racing. He went downstairs to the kitchen. A ray of moonlight fell across the living room. He wished Julia were there so he could forget Mia. Mia: the monster's daughter. Mia: between him and me. Theo was shivering. He sat down on the stairs, a bottle of water in his hands, unable to slake his thirst. He finished the rest of the bottle in one long gulp. *I want him to know that he has lost.*

The first light of dawn drove back the shadows. He got up, got dressed, and set off for the beach. The vast orange sky awaited him like a promise of oblivion. *But I can't turn back anymore. I will be forever haunted. Even my own death won't grant me any peace.* Theo picked up a few pebbles and sent them skimming over the water.

Mia was back, paler than before, he'd been told. He was extra-careful. He moved his car to a different spot in the parking lot several times a day. He steered clear of the gym, preferring instead to run on the beach in the early morning. But one evening when he got back from work, she was waiting for him in her car outside his house. Intrigued and wary, he parked and walked over to her.

"I hope you don't mind me coming to see you at home."

She had become very thin, which made her eyes look even more striking. He went around her car and got into the passenger seat.

"Theo . . . you never explained."

"There was nothing to explain."

She bit her lip.

". . . I went to Argentina."

"I know."

"Aren't you going to ask me why?"

"I don't want to know."

"I'll tell you anyway. I went because of you."

He muttered something incomprehensible and opened the car door to get out.

"Theo. Listen to me. You owe me that much. Let's go for a drive."

She added by way of explanation: "I'll feel more comfortable telling you about it with the noise of the engine."

Theo reluctantly shut the car door. She started the car and searched for his hand.

"I wouldn't have gone to Argentina if you weren't important to me."

"That doesn't change anything."

"For you, maybe. But for me, everything's changed."

"Mia, you don't understand."

"Yes, that's true. There are far too many things I don't understand. You left with no explanation. . . ."

"I don't owe you an explanation. I don't owe you anything."

On the outskirts of town, Mia turned into a narrow road skirting a small forest of evergreens. It was growing dark. Here and there a few houses had lights on, their windows like eyes.

"Yes, you do, precisely. You owe me an explanation. But there's something else. I need your help. What I'm carrying inside is too heavy for me. And you're the only one who . . ."

"Mia, we shouldn't see each other again."

"I'm not talking about that. Even if I wanted to! No. I've come to you because I think you know things about me that I don't know about myself."

The car came to a stop at the edge of the forest. Mia switched off the lights.

"What do you think I know, Mia? I don't know anything."

"Yes. You do. You have a lot of information. It's your job. I think you know something about my mother's death. I think you can help me find the person who killed her."

"What are you talking about? Your mother committed suicide. Isn't that what you told me?"

"Yes. That's what I was led to believe. But that's not how it happened. I checked the archives, I talked to people. My mother was murdered. The police found her mutilated body. They also found photos the killer left behind."

Mia's voice began to shake.

"She was at home when she was killed."

"How do you know you really are her daughter? There were so many crimes during that war. . . ."

Mia pushed her car seat back and hugged her knees.

"I got in touch with the Mapuche."

"The Mapuche?"

"Yes. With my mother's family."

"But how?"

"There are lots of Mapuche Web sites. That's how I contacted them, before even thinking to make the trip. Things went quickly after that. My mother's brother sent me a reply. He asked me to go and see the family in Argentina. They wanted to make sure it was really me. In fact, they thought I was dead."

"Make sure how? They couldn't recognize you."

"No, of course not. But we went to a center that researches the disappeared. They do DNA testing."

"That's crazy! How could you do all that in such a short time?"

Theo was thinking hard, his head in his hands.

"Did they ask you where your father was?"

"My mother's husband? No. He was an Argentine army captain named Ignacio Castro."

"And?"

"And so it turns out that my biological father . . . isn't my father. Not the one I call my father, in any case."

"Did you get your DNA tested against his too? Did you see photos of your biological father?"

"Yes, a few. Of their wedding day. My mother's husband looked very different: tall, slim, blond. Quite a handsome man, actually. It's obviously not the same person. I would recognize my father anywhere. I have to admit he's not very good-looking. In fact, he's rather ugly."

Her childlike laugh rang through the car.

There was nothing of El Diablo in her. Her Asian eyes, her high cheekbones, her pale skin. Theo moved back to get a better look at Mia. And yet. El Diablo had pulled it off brilliantly. With her Asian features, Korean name, and perfect English, the girl would be untraceable. It would be impossible to establish a connection between Mia and Argentina unless Mia revealed the secret of her Mapuche origins, and her father had warned her against this. The feeling of shame he had instilled in Mia because of her mother's suicide was an additional safeguard. Finally, El Diablo had hidden his treasure at Swirbul and Collier: where better than a CIA contractor to keep enemies at bay? All the employees were CIA protégés in one way or another, bound by a secret related to their own personal story that went beyond the scope of professional confidentiality. It was the reason he himself was working for Swirbul. In exchange for the information Theo had passed on to the American intelligence agencies, he lived a sheltered life, protected by a structure that made him invisible. That same structure had thwarted all of Julia's attempts to track him down. It had also enabled him to pick up the trail of his torturer. Or so he had thought until now. Through the company's archives, Theo had found out that El Diablo had come to the United States before the end of the dictatorship, but he hadn't expected his torturer to benefit from the same protection as he had. Which, he now realized, explained the lack of accessible information on El Diablo, and Theo's own fruitless search.

Her rounded forehead, her silky black hair. There is nothing of him in her. And yet. The red lips, the perfect teeth, that distant smile.

"He's fat," Mia went on, "and short, with a big nose and black hair. And anyway, his name isn't Ignacio Castro!"

"So who is he?"

The young woman was taken aback by his aggressive tone. Her brow furrowed in concentration.

"I don't know. They say lots of children were given up for adoption back then. My mother's brother thinks maybe that's what happened to me. I looked, but there doesn't seem to be a record of adoptions. I don't even have a birth certificate in Argentina."

"But your real father can't have vanished into thin air. He didn't leave you on the doorstep of a church!"

"My biological father committed suicide shortly after my mother was killed. He drove his car off a cliff. The car blew up—"

Theo interrupted: "And no one ever found his remains." He put his hands on his knees and said bitterly, "Take me back home, Mia. I can't help you."

It was pitch-black. A glimmer of light somewhere in the distance accentuated the contrast of Mia's profile. Theo watched as she hid her face in her hands. He refused to be moved. She turned the key and the engine purred obediently. A couple of deer caught in the headlights froze for an instant, their eyes red, then bounded away into the trees.

Nothing should derail me. Not even Mia. Squatting in the garden holding a hand rake, Theo admired the hydrangeas. Julia's return would give him a break. He thought he saw his neighbor looking enviously at his well-kept flowerbeds. He gave the old lady a wave and smiled. *It's impossible not to make the connection. It's written in black and white. Or else she's her father's accomplice.* Theo wiped away the large beads of sweat rolling down his face. A bumblebee hovered a little too long at the corner of his eye. He flicked it away in irritation. *After this I can live my life again. I'll go away with Julia. Far away.* He pushed the spade into the ground and turned the soil over. The bumblebee returned, stupid and stubborn, and began buzzing in concentric circles around Theo's head. Disheartened, Theo threw the spade and the rake to the ground and walked back into the house.

The parking lot was full. Swirbul was always a hive of activity on Mondays. He found a spot at the far end, next to a shiny new white SUV with oversize tires. Driven by an involuntary curiosity, he walked around the car to inspect it. When he came out late that evening the huge lot was empty, but the Chevy Crossover was still there. Theo hovered for a moment to give it another once-over before getting into his car.

He was just about to pull out when a car raced across the parking lot, tires screeching, and came to a stop right in front of him. Mia got out wearing an emerald green suit. She was furious. Eyes brimming with tears, she yanked open Theo's door and shouted, "I hate you. Do you hear me? I hate you!"

A man emerged from the complex at that moment and came striding in their direction, fiddling with his keychain in one hand and holding a black crocodile briefcase in the other. Theo recognized him immediately. It was one of the company directors.

"Get in," he ordered.

Mia did as she was told. The car reversed, pulled away, and drove out of the parking lot. Theo accelerated, hurtled down the avenue, turned right, and braked in front of an imposing mansion surrounded by a large park. He turned to Mia, grabbed her forcefully, and kissed her.

"I hate you," she said again, beating at his chest with her fists.

Theo wiped her tears away with the back of his hand.

"I hate you too. I can't tell the difference anymore between my love for you and my hatred, Mia."

"But why? Why me?" She had a sudden thought. "It's because of my wedding photo, isn't it?"

He caressed her face. "No. But I think I know who killed your mother."

Mia's breathing quickened. "Yes, I could sense it. That's why I went to Argentina. To understand, Theo."

"You really don't understand?"

Theo grasped her face to force her to look into his eyes.

"But I'm telling you I don't understand! You're hurting me, Theo. And you're really scaring me. What happened to my mother?"

Theo remained silent for a moment. He stroked her lips with a finger, then leaned back against the door.

"You grew up with your mother's killer, Mia. Your father's name is not Samuel Matamoros, and he's not Spanish."

"What are you saying?"

"He's Argentine, and he's also your biological father."

"That's crazy! He isn't . . . he can't be . . ."

"His name is Ignacio Castro Matamoros and he was a captain in the Argentine air force. He was also known as El Diablo."

Mia stared at him in horror.

"He was in charge of one of the torture centers during the Dirty War, Mansión Seré. Mia, your father is a murderer."

Her tears left glistening streaks down her face. She couldn't draw enough breath to speak.

"It's not true. You're wrong. You're mixing him up with someone else. Ignacio Castro committed suicide."

"Your father lied to you. From the start, about everything. Except one thing: your mother's identity."

Theo's voice changed. "And I don't know why."

"It's not possible. . . . How do you know all of this?"

"I've been searching for your father for thirty years, Mia. I recognized him in your photo."

"You must have made a mistake. Maybe they look alike. You don't know my father. He's a wonderful man, he . . ."

"Stop it, Mia. You wanted to know. Now you know. I had no intention of revealing any of this to you. And I have no idea why I'm doing it now. But I think you have a right to know who this man is."

The first-floor lights of the mansion went on. Someone looked out the window.

"I'd lost all trace of your father for years."

"And you want me to believe you found him again by accident?"

"Yes. I think about it all the time. It's very strange. Either it's destiny or . . ."

"Destiny? There's no such thing, Theo."

A police car with tinted windows cruised past. Theo started the car, then drove to the junction and under the railway bridge. He decided to take the old road that wound from one town to the next. They were no longer pressed for time.

"You must have known it was me, Theo! You have access to all that company information."

Mia's emotion turned into nausea. She opened the window to get some air, her mouth drawn into a grimace.

"So you used me, Theo? That's it. You knew . . ."

The car jolted as it crossed a narrow bridge overlooking a marina. The lamps along the landing stage were reflected on the rippled surface of the water like a scattering of stars. Theo stopped the car on the side of the road, pulled up the parking brake, and switched off the engine.

"No, Mia. You know perfectly well that's not true." And he added, as if to chase away his own doubts: "You didn't know either."

A painful silence followed, each of them weighing up the other, uncomfortable.

"Are you looking for him on the company's behalf? Do you have to . . . ?"

Theo cut her off. "No, the company's got nothing to do with it."

"What am I supposed to think, Theo? You're looking for him just like that, for no reason!"

The blood had drained from Mia's face. Her lips had turned bluish, emphasizing the pearly sheen of her skin. Her mouth trembled, hesitating.

"Where do you know him from?"

A muted violence struggled to surface, like lava rising.

Theo's voice shook, his skin blotched and red as he tried to control it.

"El Diablo . . . tortured my brother," he said in a strangled voice. "Then he killed him."

Mia could hardly recognize the man looking at her—the blue-tinted veins protruding from his temples, the dry lips edged with white saliva, the flared nostrils, the bloodshot eyes.

"He took photos, he filmed it. . . . He showed me everything."

The young woman shrank into her seat.

"He also tortured my wife . . . who was expecting our child."

All at once, Mia was gripped by spasms that shook her body violently until they reached her throat. She opened her door and vomited.

38.

OF LOVE AND HATE

Boreal Summer

2006

It would soon be dawn. They walked barefoot down the stairs and out of the house across the damp grass to the beach. They stayed close to each other, the cool sand giving way under their feet, their bodies still seeking each other, unsated. Around them the dark expanse was filled with the reddish glow of a dying campfire. The gentle lapping of the waves reminded them of the presence of the sea. But they sat down with their backs to the water, fascinated by the embers of the fire that they were set on rekindling.

"I've been having nightmares for days."

"I've been having them for years."

Theo turned the logs over. Timid flames began to lick at them.

"I don't think I will ever be able to free myself from all this."

"Knowing comes with a price, my love. Ignorance is bliss," Theo said, kissing her neck.

"But I love him, Theo. Before you, I thought I could never love any man more than my father."

"Don't talk about him, please."

"But I have to. You're the only one who can understand."

The crackling of the fire distracted them for a moment.

"I dreamed that my mother was talking to me. I never knew my mother; it feels strange to have heard her voice."

"Maybe you stored it in your memory from when you were first born." Then, changing tones, he added, "Julia's grandmother would've said your mother was contacting you. People used to say she was some kind of psychic—it exasperated my parents."

"That's odd. My uncle told me my mother was a *machi*. I'd always thought that was a princess. But actually it's her name— Mailen—that means 'princess.' Do you know what a *machi* is?"

"Yes, they communicate with spirits, have premonitory dreams. . . . It's a form of shamanism, right?"

Theo went to get some dry branches from a pile that had been placed not far from the fire.

"My uncle said that was the reason she was killed."

"What do you mean?"

"Her husband didn't want . . ."

"Your father?"

"He would have forbidden her to practice, but I think she kept on doing it without his knowledge."

"Have you gotten back in touch with your uncle?"

"No. I don't know if I will. I wouldn't know what to say to him."

The heat was becoming almost unbearable. Mia shielded her cheeks with her hands.

"The thing I'm dreading most is talking to my father again."

The fire suddenly leaped up. Amid a shower of sparks, they got up and rolled the dried-out tree trunk they had been sitting on farther away.

"What are you going to say to him?"

"I don't know." Mia continued, "You see, I think I could have even forgiven him for killing my mother. . . ." Her voice broke. "But I can never forgive him for what he did to you."

Dawn was breaking. They stood up, holding each other tight, and threw sand on the fire to put it out. A stray dog trotted toward them with its tail between its legs. It sniffed at the ashes before scampering off. The tide was retreating slowly, leaving a froth of green algae in its wake. In the distance they could see the silhouette of a runner approaching. He sprinted across the sand with a feline grace. Mia watched with envy as he ran past.

Theo dropped Mia off at her place and went to the airport to pick up Julia. He parked near the arrivals gate and got out of the car. The summer was drawing to a close; a delightful breeze softened the heat rising from the asphalt.

He saw her come out wheeling her suitcase. She was wearing the white dress they had bought together in the spring. She got into the car, blithe and sunny, radiating a happiness that immediately caused him to tense up. He sped toward the Bronx to get on the Connecticut Turnpike. Julia read his impatience as a mark of affection. She forgot to be tired.

"Let's go out for lunch, Theo. We've got lots of good news to celebrate."

"The sushi bar in Westport?" he answered, inserting a CD into the car stereo.

The shrill sound of a guitar burst out of the speakers. Julia leaned toward him, lowered the volume, and slipped her arms around his neck.

"The first bit of great news . . ."

She leaned back to better assess the effect her announcement might have on him. Theo smiled at her, seemingly focused on the road, while his thoughts were elsewhere. Maybe Mia would be at the sushi bar with Kwan. Then they would have to say hello, make introductions. Or maybe Julia and he would sit down at the next table and he and Mia would pretend to be strangers.

"Are you listening, my love?"

"Yes. I don't want to miss the exit. This is where I always get it wrong."

A sea of cars was stopped at the toll booth. Theo switched off the engine and opened the windows.

"Okay, go on. Tell me. What's the good news?"

"Theo, you're going to be a grandfather!"

Theo opened his eyes wide as if surprised. He turned the engine on again. The vehicles in front of him had moved. Maybe he would be jealous seeing her with Kwan. When he wasn't with her . . . This was absurd.

". . . a name for a little boy. I'd be very happy if it was a little Josefina. Can you imagine? What do you think?"

"Me?"

"Yes. What would you prefer?"

"Doesn't matter. Both."

"Stop being silly! If it's a boy, what name would you like? You can't call a baby both names: Ignace-Josefina!"

"Ignacio? Why Ignacio?"

"Ignace, not Ignacio! You haven't listened to a word I've been saying. It's her father's name!"

"Whose father's name?"

"Ulysses' wife's father, of course! They've decided that if it's a boy she gets to choose the name and if it's a girl, Ulysses will."

"Oh, I see. Right. I didn't know."

They would name their child however they saw fit, Theo thought. It was no longer his problem.

He turned up the volume. A frenzied drum solo made further conversation impossible. In any case, all his solutions were bad. The worst was to do nothing. No way. El Diablo would pay one way or another, even if death was too good for him. Theo would almost rather see him live as he himself had lived all these years: in the shadows, and in shame.

". . . a house overlooking the water, on the rocks. You'll love it. We'll have to book our tickets right away. It can be hard to find tickets at Christmastime. Is that okay?"

"Is what okay?"

"Going to visit them in December."

"We'll see. We've got plenty of time."

Theo took the exit ramp and stopped at the red light. It was stupid being this head over heels in love, like a teenager. He had only just left Mia and all he could think of was seeing her again. He drove slowly down the avenue, looking for a place to park; the sun was blinding. He passed the restaurant, holding up a hand to shield his eyes, and spotted her immediately. Mia was sitting at a small table on the sidewalk. She looked up. And smiled.

They had gotten into the habit of meeting at the hotel in Fairfield, which was halfway between the office and their respective homes. It had been a sultry afternoon. Large black clouds announced an imminent storm. They gazed at each other in the darkness. To him it felt like Mia's body was made of ether, almost like the result of a vision. The low hum of the air-conditioning did little to cover the noise from the highway. The world rumbled in the distance. He held her tighter.

"You never told me the details of that dream about your mother."

"It was more of a nightmare."

"Tell me about it."

"I was in a forest, surrounded by trees. All of a sudden, I lost all notion of who I was; I blended into the universe. I was the sky, the grass, the trees. I was breathing through them. I was just beginning to become myself again and to recognize that I had a body when I heard a voice speaking to me, coming from outside. So I tried to remember who I was."

"And . . . ?"

"That voice was my mother's voice. It seeped into me like the sap of a tree. Her words went round inside me and I didn't understand. I breathed. I breathed out her love, her suffering, her life."

"What a strange dream."

"I think about it all the time. That voice keeps haunting me, Theo."

"What did she say?"

"She told me a story about a girl who had lost her mother and then found her again one day. I don't know if I was the girl, the mother, or the daughter of the girl. I only knew I was one of those three women. When I felt like I was the girl, I saw her searching for her mother behind every tree in a dark, humid forest. In the end, the voice said the mother was coming back, and I felt a bright light spreading through me, but I didn't experience a feeling of release. I kept feeling the mother's fear and suffering, like poison in my veins."

"A real nightmare."

"Her voice was telling me things that I can't really make

any sense of. To get out, to leave, I think. But I can't shake off this suffering. I wake up tired, as if I was mourning something bigger than me."

Mia placed a hand on her forehead and followed the line of a first wrinkle, running like a pencil stroke from one temple to the other.

"I can't go on living knowing what he's done. I don't want to carry the genes of a monster. I'm scared of being who I am." A bead of sweat glistened above her mouth. "But I won't let you kill him."

"Don't say that, Mia."

"Bring him to justice. He'll pay for it in prison."

"That would be rewarding him."

"I don't want you to become a monster in turn because of him."

"That's what I'm sentenced to as long as your father is alive."

Mia turned over in the bed, overcome by the heat.

"But you're not a killer, Theo."

"Mia, you know I'm the only one who can make him pay."

"Don't you understand? Death would be a release for him!"

"You're saying that because you love him."

"Of course I'm saying it because I love him." She turned and looked at Theo with frantic eyes. "But I'm also saying it because I hate him. I hate him because of what he did to you and your family. I hate him because of what he did to my mother. And because of what he did to me: for keeping me for himself, for calling me 'Mia.' Mine. His thing. A reward for his depravity." She moved back to get a better look at Theo. "But yes, also because I love him."

"You have to choose, Mia."

"I know what I don't want to be."

A cell phone on the floor buzzed insistently. Theo didn't even bother turning it off.

"I don't want to be like him, Theo, I don't want blood on my hands. I'd rather die in his place. Avenge your brother's death by killing me. I'm the most precious thing he has."

"You're crazy."

"You're the crazy one. What kind of life would we lead if you killed my father? Could you go on, knowing that I could only hate you?"

"I prefer your hatred to your death."

"Theo, the two go together. Love alone can give life."

Tenderly, he brushed back the strands of hair sticking to Mia's face. He looked at her in contemplation.

"I'd rather die than live without you, Mia."

The sailboats rocked gently on the mirrorlike surface of the water, a forest of masts reaching skyward. Mia and Theo were sitting at one of the round tables outside, overlooking the marina. Inside the restaurant, waiters wearing frock coats and white gloves swarmed around the customers, holding their trays aloft without looking at one another.

The chiffon of her ecru dress rippled in the breeze like a second skin. Mia gathered up her hair and twisted it into a bun, securing it with a pencil. She slipped off her high-heeled sandals and irreverently wriggled her bare toes on the wooden slats. The maître d' pretended not to notice and served them crystal-clear water in glasses filled with clinking ice cubes. The man took a step back. Waiting for Mia to deign to notice him. She turned confidently to Theo.

"What shall we order, darling?"

Theo answered hurriedly, hoping to be left alone, but the waiter returned almost immediately to pour the champagne with a flourish. Theo watched him, smiling. He wouldn't have changed a single thing. As soon as the waiter left, he kissed Mia's hand. She gave him an amused look.

"Well?"

"Well, Julia's leaving me."

"Julia's leaving you! What do you mean?"

"She knows about you."

Mia traced a design on the tablecloth with her fingers. "How did she possibly find out?"

"I think she ran into Ben and his wife."

"But what could they have told her?"

"They asked her to dinner and mentioned they would invite you too."

"And so?"

"I suppose it was the way they said it. Ben was with me at the gym when you called off our first date, remember?"

"I see. Fat Betty also made a snide remark at work when I got back from Argentina."

"None of it matters anymore, my darling."

"It might. My father called me."

Theo remained stone-faced.

"Don't you want to know what he said to me?"

"No, I don't want to know. I really don't."

"Well, we'll see."

She took her glass of champagne and held it up, moving closer to Theo.

"To our love."

"To an eternity together," he answered.

They interlaced their fingers. For the first time Theo experienced a sense of release. The sea was a precious jewel and the sky was worthy of his gaze.

Mia was his.

The waiters marched solemnly up to their table, presenting the dishes and uncovering them in unison. The sun was beating down on everything except their table, which basked in welcome shade. But Theo and Mia were oblivious to their surroundings; they carried on laughing and enjoying themselves under the envious gaze of a couple at the next table who hadn't exchanged a single word.

Once they had finished their meal, Mia pushed back her chair to face the sea and stared into the distance. She followed a flock of seagulls returning from the open sea. The sky was an expanse of smooth blue separated from the sea by a long mauve line. A slight breeze sprang up, rippling the plate-glass stretch of water. Mia arranged a shawl over her shoulders.

"I don't think I've ever been this happy."

As she said these words, he took the blue velvet box out of his pocket, placed it gently on the white tablecloth, and opened it. He removed the solitaire, reached for Mia's hand, and slipped the ring onto her finger.

"So that nothing will ever separate us."

The young woman sat on the side of the bed, her head heavy. She had had nightmares all night long. Theo caught her by the waist before she could get up, wanting to kiss her, but she freed herself. She went into the bathroom and took a long shower. When she came out, a cloud of steam billowed into the bedroom as if following her. She shut the bathroom door. Theo was standing by the window, about to draw the curtains. She made him stop. She had been avoiding sunlight for days.

He watched her slip on her black dress and knelt beside her to help her slide her feet into her heels. He couldn't bear it when she returned to her apartment. Ever since Julia had said she was leaving him, Theo had become needier, almost possessive.

Mia left him and returned to the bathroom. She emptied out her purse into the sink and stood in front of the mirror, pushing away the damp towels still lying on the floor with her foot. She pulled her hair back and expertly twisted it into a bun that shone like onyx. Then she leaned close to the mirror and rummaged through her makeup. She went through her daily routine, but with extra care.

When she had finished, she examined herself with satisfaction. *I look like my mother.* For the first time, the thought of resembling her mother wasn't left to the realm of abstract concepts. She turned around instinctively and she saw that Theo was staring at her. There was a strange intensity in his look. Unsettled, she glanced around the room, as if someone else was looking at her.

She finally shrugged, laughing.

"I keep feeling like he's going to jump out at us."

She extended her arm to caress Theo, who grabbed it with fervor. She broke free, nervously picked up her handbag, and left, shooting him an "I'll be back soon" look before pulling the door closed behind her.

When the elevator doors opened on the lobby floor, Mia saw a swarm of men in blue uniforms going up and down the corridors and stationed at all the exits. Police cars were parked at the entrance, lights flashing.

She intuitively backed away, feeling guilty without knowing why. The police? What were they doing here? *What if they're looking for Theo?* The thought hit her like a sledgehammer. She went pale, seized with panic. *What if Theo killed my father and didn't tell me?* An officer stared at her from the other side of the lobby. She looked for the nearest exit. *No, that's impossible. We haven't been apart for days.* The policeman bent to whisper something into the ear of another officer, who nodded without turning around. *He's not a killer. Not yet.* The policeman crossed the lobby with a firm step, heading toward her. Mia could feel her knees about to give way. *Maybe my father's just killed Theo. They've found Theo's body in the room. They're coming to question me.* She met the policeman's eyes. *That's ridiculous. I'm losing my mind.* The officer approached Mia cautiously. He introduced himself politely, one hand resting on his gun.

"Good morning, ma'am. We're evacuating the hotel, and we need your full cooperation."

She could feel the sweat pearling on her forehead. She half listened to the questions the officer was asking, heart pounding. The man became aware of her distress and asked in an authoritative voice: "Ma'am, are you all right?"

"Yes, yes, I'll be fine," she stammered.

"I repeat: was there anyone else with you in the room?"

"No, no, I was alone."

Checking his files, he continued: "You say you were in room 410. But according to the hotel register, the room was booked in the name of a Mr. Theo d'Uccello."

"It's . . . Maybe Reception made a mistake," Mia replied, still in the grip of her imagination.

"That's okay, ma'am. Don't worry," the man said in a protective tone. "We still have time to get everyone out. Go see my colleague by the entrance; she'll tell you how to proceed. It's important to get all the cars out of the parking lot as soon as possible. We think the plane will manage to land at a nearby airport, but we have to take protective measures."

"Yes, yes, of course," Mia replied, wild-eyed.

A hotel employee was holding the main door wide open to make way for a dozen guests, who couldn't get out fast enough. As Mia began walking, she glanced to the left and saw the officer posted by the staircase moving toward the emergency exit at the end of the corridor. She followed him, pushed open the door to the stairs, and disappeared.

She reached the fourth floor out of breath. Holding her shoes in her hand, she raced down the empty corridor and slipped into the room. Theo was still lying naked on the bed waiting for her with the radio switched on. The strident wails of sirens filled the room.

"I knew you'd be back."

39

THE PLANE

Boreal Winter
2006

Julia rushes outside. She wants to call for help, to run as fast as she can. She turns back in a panic, takes the stairs two at a time, hunts for her car keys in her handbag, and tears back downstairs.

The movers' truck is blocking the driveway. She bears down on the driver. The guys in the back heaving furniture and cardboard boxes grumble, but the driver obeys.

Julia is at the steering wheel. She calls Theo from her cell phone while the truck is backing out: once, twice, twenty times. He has switched off his phone.

She sends him a text message. Three words: "Danger. Death. Leave."

If there's no traffic and she drives flat-out, she can get to the hotel in twenty minutes. She accelerates, heading for the Connecticut Turnpike. It'll be too late. She has to make it there in fifteen minutes. She'll have to run all the red lights. Too bad!

She presses the hands-free button on the steering wheel to call Diane. No answer.

"This is insane!" Julia shouts, banging the steering wheel.

She gets on the ramp and steps hard on the gas. The other cars are traveling at moderate speed. The left lane is empty; without hesitation, she pulls into the fast lane. Julia has never driven so fast in her entire life. Her phone starts ringing. She sees Diane's number flash on the screen. She pushes the button on the steering wheel to answer.

"Diane, Theo's in danger. I can't reach him. His phone is off. He's at one of the hotels in Fairfield. I can't remember the exact name!"

"Is this a fit of jealousy by any chance, darling?" Diane answers, laughing.

"I'm talking about the plane, Diane! We have to get him out of there!"

"Calm down, Julia. I can't understand a word you're saying. What are you talking about?"

"The plane, Diane! The plane's going to crash. We have to find the phone number of the hotel!"

"Oh, I see! The plane that's making a crash landing. I've just been following it on the radio. It's okay, darling. It's going to land on a runway in Stratford. You don't have to worry."

"Diane!" Julia screamed. "Listen to me, please! I saved your life; the least you can do is believe me! You have to warn the hotel: the plane is going to crash into it. Do you understand?"

"Okay, okay, don't freak out. I've got you. I'll call. Don't panic, honey."

"Of course I'm panicking! Hurry, please."

She has just passed Bridgeport's red-and-white-striped smokestack. Julia hangs up. *I'm fifteen minutes away. No, ten!* She floors the gas pedal. A warning sign over the highway announces a mandatory detour. Julia is forced to slow down. The highway is closed at exit 23. A police officer is directing traffic.

"We have an aircraft in distress over the area," he explains to the drivers who lower their windows as they pass him. "Keep going, keep going!"

All the surrounding streets have been closed off. A security cordon is blocking access to the neighborhood. *I've got to make them understand.* Julia talks to a policeman, but she manages only to annoy him.

"Get out of here, or I'll have to arrest you!" he bellows.

I absolutely have to get through. She gets back in the car and drives slowly along the barricade but finds no way in. On the radio a young reporter is announcing that the plane has suddenly dropped in altitude.

Julia lowers the windows and pokes her head out. She can't see the plane or hear its engines. It must be farther away than she thought; she might still have a chance. She parks the car in the residential area and walks with her hands in her pockets toward a house just outside the police cordon. The officers are busy informing the residents. They all have their backs turned to her. Julia slips between two houses, crosses a garden, skirts the garages, and enters the neighboring garden.

She's done it. She's inside the cordoned-off area. Julia starts running as fast as she can, heading straight ahead. She jumps over hedges, crosses streets, squeezes through bushes. The neighborhood is deserted. In the distance she can see a mall and the sign of a Stop & Shop. The railroad tracks can't be far. Julia keeps running.

The bicycle in front of the house with the pretty white picket fence seems to be calling out to her. Julia jumps on it and pedals away, letting her instinct guide her through the maze of streets. *Please let me get there in time; please don't let the police stop me.*

Before crossing a large avenue, Julia brakes abruptly and straddles the bicycle on the sidewalk. She takes out her phone and checks her messages. Theo hasn't replied. She copies the text message and sends it to the various e-mail addresses Theo uses.

She starts cycling again, back hunched, pedaling even faster. The roar of jet engines suddenly fills the air. She looks up. The plane is there, hovering in front of her, flying ever closer to the ground. It looks poised, unshakable. Julia recognizes the hotel building to the right. The plane is losing altitude too quickly. It won't manage to avoid it. Julia is paralyzed with fear. Her telephone rings once, twice, thrice, then goes silent.

"Theo!" Julia screams at the moment of impact.

The force of the explosion throws her to the ground. Thick black smoke begins coiling up into the sky. Julia teeters away from the bicycle, stunned. She's sifting through images of Theo in her memory. She sees him now, exactly as he was when they first met at Anna's birthday party. There he is again, a broken man standing on her doorstep when they met in New York.

Before her the flames, the spirals of black smoke, the police, the firemen. There are ambulances too. Julia keeps walking forward. The carcass of the plane is smoking, its nose crushed against the concrete and the steel bars. She reaches the parking lot of the hotel without anyone paying attention to her.

Theo's car is there, intact.

Julia feels her cell phone vibrate in her pocket. She pulls it out mechanically. There's a message from Theo in her in-box. She looks around, mad with hope. She reads it: "Thank you, my love."

Julia looks anxiously at the picture he has attached. It is a wedding photograph. She doesn't recognize any of the people. She enlarges the image impatiently and looks more closely. A fat, almost obese man reminds her vaguely of someone. She sifts intently through her memory. The image comes back to her in a second, neatly. She looks away, astounded. Mama Fina's newspaper clipping! Julia collapses to the ground in tears. El Diablo! Standing next to him, wearing a lace wedding dress, she recognizes Mia Moon.

Such a beautiful day. The leaves on the hundred-year-old trees along the avenue flutter, playful, trying to catch the wind. Julia looks out the window. A smooth blue sky. The mauve line between the sky and the sea. Another beautiful day. Another day without him.

Julia goes to sit on the bed. A plane flies over the house. Strangely, she doesn't think about the accident. Instead she is brought back to their last night together, when, soothed by the engine hum of another plane, she prayed to remain by his side forever.

She moves to the mirror on the landing, fixes her hat with its black veil, and slowly goes downstairs. Ulysses is standing next to the front door waiting for her. *What a handsome man he is.* He holds his hand out to her as she comes down the last few steps. When she is close enough, he strokes her cheek.

"Sweet Mom."

"Let's go, my angel. I'm anxious to get there."

Ulysses silently follows each of her movements. He hastens to open the door for her. Julia walks down the front steps and lingers for a few moments to ruffle the fluffy blue blossoms of the hydrangeas.

"It's that easy. Look."

She does it again, as if she were caressing a child's head.

"There's no secret to it. Love, Ulysses: nothing but love."

Ulysses continues to watch her in silence. Ever since he's been back, he finds there is something endlessly moving about his mother.

"Do you want me to drive, Mom?"

"No. I know the route. And I want to stop thinking. Driving will force me to focus on the road."

"Mom . . . Are you sure you're okay?"

She raises herself on tiptoe and kisses his cheek.

"I'll feel much better afterward."

Julia rummages in her handbag, checks to make sure she has her phone and black gloves, takes out her sunglasses, and climbs into the car holding a tube of lipstick.

As she is touching up her makeup in the rearview mirror, Ulysses sees the neighbor pulling open her curtains to watch them. The door opens and the elderly lady comes hastily forward, a bouquet of mauve flowers in one hand. Julia lowers her window.

"That's so kind. Thank you. I'm very touched."

The old lady hands the bouquet to Ulysses. Her blue eyes are filled with tears.

"I can't believe she is the one offering me her condolences," Julia says, reversing out of the driveway.

She emerges from the tangle of streets around the house, crosses the large avenue running through the town, and speeds onto the highway entrance ramp.

"Is it far?" Ulysses asks.

"Half an hour or so. It's a pretty little cemetery in Westport. Not far from their office, with old trees and plenty of birds. I went to visit it with Kwan."

"Kwan?"

"Yes, Kwan. Mia's husband."

She turns on the radio. Theo's CD automatically starts playing. Julia leans over the steering wheel and hurriedly switches it off.

"It's so stupid," she says, drying her tears.

She checks her side mirror to make sure the route is clear and adds, having calmed down, "At least this way I'll really look like a widow."

Ulysses takes her hand.

"Oh, Mom."

They leave the Bridgeport factory smokestack with its wisp of white smoke behind and, shortly afterward, pass the small town of Fairfield. From the highway they can see that the partially destroyed hotel is already rising from its ashes. A team of workers in high-visibility jackets have taken over the site with construction vehicles and dump trucks. Ulysses moves forward in his seat and stares at the place.

"I'm so glad you're with me. I wouldn't have wanted to be alone . . . in front of all those people. The coworkers . . ."

"Olivier called me. . . ."

Ulysses observes her profile: the head held high, the soft-ened features.

"You look so young, Mom!"

"You're just saying that to flatter me."

"No. I'm saying it because I think Theo is stupid."

"Don't ever say that, Ulysses. No one can judge."

"He was incapable of loving."

"Hate and love are the two sides of the same coin, Ulysses."

The road turns seaward and away again to plunge through a forest of majestic trees. Everything seems immense: the as-phalt spooling into the horizon, the infinite sky full of motion-less clouds, all suspended in the swath of blue.

"Mama Fina used to say the dead see through their loved ones' eyes."

"Mom, you don't really believe that!"

Her eyes glow like burning coals.

"Oh, yes, darling, I believe it more than ever!"

Embarrassed, Ulysses avoids her gaze as the car forks right. They drive up a small road skirting some beeches, a scattering of white houses visible through the curtain of trees. Closer to the road, they pass a kneeling woman placing flowers on a tombstone in the middle of a garden of maple and willow trees.

"Is this it?"

"No. That was the colonial cemetery. Ours is a little farther on. See how beautiful the light is, filtering through the trees."

Ulysses does his best to take an interest in the landscape.

But something he can't quite put his finger on is making him feel uneasy.

"Who's going to be here, Mom?"

"Not many people, I suppose. A few colleagues from the office, Mia's family, and the two of us."

But when Julia drives up the path leading to the cemetery gates, Ulysses realizes it's not going to be an intimate funeral. A dozen black limousines are jammed into an overflowing parking lot. Julia maneuvers onto the shoulder near the main entrance and leaves the keys in the ignition. She throws a quick glance around her. A few people dressed in black are starting to make their way slowly up the path. Behind them, next to the entrance, a group of men wearing black sunglasses are leaning against the trunks of some tall evergreens, smoking.

"I have to speak to them for a minute. Would you wait for me here, darling?"

Without giving Ulysses time to answer, Julia hastens toward the men. Ulysses sees them throw away their cigarettes as she approaches and formally shake her hand. Julia talks to them for a while, turning frequently to glance at Ulysses, takes her cell phone from her bag, and holds it out to show them the screen.

She comes back to Ulysses and takes him by the arm.

"It's time. Let's go."

Julia takes her black gloves out of her bag, lowers the veil over her face, and walks up the path to the group of people waiting. The crowd parts at their approach, making way for them to join the priest standing between the two graves. Julia nods her thanks. She finds her sister, Anna, among those present and hugs her, overcome with emotion.

"When did you arrive? You never told me . . ."

"Pablo and I landed in New York this morning. We weren't sure we would get here in time."

Julia puts a hand on her sister's arm and begins to pull her along, but Anna holds back for a moment to introduce her to a white-haired man Julia doesn't recognize.

"Soy Augusto," he says.

Julia identifies his voice immediately. He sweeps her up, smothering her. She feels she could surrender herself to this man's arms. She would like to tell him so but holds back.

Diane is there too, and Ben and his wife, Pat. Julia takes Diane's hand in hers as she passes and kisses it. In the sea of faces she recognizes Conchita, who makes her way through the crowd to come and hug her, red-eyed. Julia swallows back tears as best as she can. Alice is there too, impeccable with her stewardess poise. Olivier is the only one absent.

In the first row Julia recognizes Swirbul's top executives with their wives. Kwan and his family are standing stiffly next to the priest. Julia says hello and goes to stand on the other side with Ulysses and Anna. Ernesto Mayol, Theo's uncle, is already there waiting for them.

A woman facing her on the other side of the coffins smiles sadly and gives her a little nod. Julia is sure she knows her. But it takes her several minutes to figure out it is Nicole, Mia's stepmother. Julia clutches Ulysses' arm. She takes a step back. Anna catches hold of her and helps her stay upright. She sees the shoes of the man standing next to Nicole. Huge shiny black shoes.

The coffins are lowered simultaneously using a system of pulleys. Kwan breaks down for a brief instant, then pulls himself together. The flowers, the soil, the words, later the silence and the wind.

People crowd around Julia. Hands are held out, kisses are offered. Julia is elsewhere, she is alone.

As the crowd scatters, a vast flock of birds flies, trilling, across the sky. Julia dares to raise her eyes to look at them, and in the movement her gaze stops at the man.

She is no longer afraid. She wants to observe him carefully now. She begins to coldly dissect the human being facing her from head to toe, incapable of any feeling. A scar above his eye keeps his face frozen in a single expression. Strands of unnaturally black hair barely conceal his severe baldness. The thick lips have the texture of overripe fruit. The sagging face is perched atop an enormous, flabby body. Only his balled-up fists with their protruding knuckles betray a muted violence.

Kwan and his family are already heading for their cars. Julia stands up straight and allows her friends and family to embrace her. She takes a deep breath, drops Ulysses' arm, and walks forward serenely. Ulysses and Anna stand aside. The men in black sunglasses walk rapidly up the path and quietly encircle the elderly couple.

The man she is staring at remains absent, incapable of moving. His wife pulls gently at his sleeve, obtaining no reaction.

Julia plants herself squarely in front of him.

"Captain Ignacio Castro."

The man lifts his head and stares at her with empty eyes.

"I am Theo's wife," Julia says. "I met you at the Mansión Seré."

EPILOGUE

It is a winter morning at dawn. Julia brings her suitcases downstairs and places them by the front steps. It has snowed during the night. This odd encounter between sand and snow fascinates her. She is moved by the appeal of touching, as if by doing so she could put an end to her own incongruities. She's out.

In front of her a red sun emerges from the water like a ball of fire into the cold yellow winter sky. Julia steps forward, stretching out her hands as if to grasp it. Her footsteps crunch on the immaculate surface.

All of a sudden, out of nowhere, a pair of deer emerge and spring over the red sun and over Julia. They bound down the avenue, hesitate, then disappear into a backyard. All that remains is the imprint of their steps in the thick snow on the beach.

Julia no longer doubts.

The young uniformed woman sweeps the pages with a light beam, as Julia holds out her passport. She stares at Julia and back at the photo on her ID, then returns it to her.

The line seems endless. Julia waits her turn patiently, holding her shoes in one hand and her bag in the other. She places all her things in the screening bin and walks forward with her arms at her sides. Her cell phone starts ringing just as she is about to pass through the metal detector. A security officer orders her to switch it off. She takes it out of the bin, glancing at the screen before obeying. It is a call from Ulysses. The officer glares at her, spiteful. *Now I'll be here for hours.* Her bag is indeed selected to be searched. Ulysses will have to wait.

The other security staff has been tipped off. Every single item of her makeup is inspected. Julia has to wait even longer. When she reaches the private lounge, the flight attendant informs her she has only a few minutes before boarding. She pours herself a glass of wine and dials Ulysses' number. She gets his voice mail. Disappointed, she refuses to leave a message. The phone vibrates again. A series of text messages start pouring in. She reads Adriana's first: "Hello, Julia. Good news. El Diablo's trial is scheduled for early next year. Some new witnesses have come forward. I've also found Sosa. Augusto has confirmed he'll testify. Well done, Julia, and Merry Christmas!"

Merry Christmas? Probably not. Julia will spend it on an airplane; by the time she reaches New Zealand the celebrations will be over. Her thoughts drift back to Olivier. He will be joining them in New Zealand toward the end of her stay. Ulysses insisted on it. Julia can't help but smile. The two of them have always plotted behind her back.

A flight attendant approaches discreetly.

"Ma'am, you have to go to the gate now."

"Fine. Thank you."

She doesn't want to take off before talking to her son. Sighing, she gets up. She begins walking down the interminable corridor leading to the boarding gate. Her phone vibrates endlessly. She checks it as she walks. Dozens of messages keep pouring in.

When Julia is finally ready to dial her son's number, seat belt buckled, coat and bag stowed away, her cell phone rings again: Ulysses calling. The flight attendant bends over her.

"Please hurry, ma'am. We'll be taking off soon."

She grabs her phone and answers in haste. "Angel, I saw you'd called me. I was going through security and I had all these problems with the staff because they went through all my things and your . . ."

Ulysses breaks in gently.

"Mom. Mom, please, listen to me."

"That's what I'm doing, angel. I'm all ears."

"Mom, I've just sent you lots of photos."

"Okay. I'll look at them."

"Mom, I have to tell you . . . Are you listening?"

"Of course I am. I only have ears for you!"

"Are you sitting down?"

"I'm on the plane; we're about to take off. Tell me quickly. I have to hang up."

"Mom . . . I became a dad an hour ago!"

"Oh, my God! Ulysses. And on Christmas day! I can't believe it!"

"Me neither!"

"The baby came early. How wonderful! I wish I were there, I can't wait. . . . Is it a girl or a boy?"

"Mom, you're the grandmother of two little girls!"

Julia holds a glass of champagne, studying all the while the photo she has in front of her.

Mama Fina is sitting next to her, amused by the expression on Julia's face.

"I was waiting for you," Julia states without raising her eyes.

Mama Fina smiles.

"Now, tell me, which one of these two children has inherited the gift?"

It is Julia's turn to smile. She leans toward the window.

The sea and the sky have turned into one.